COLD
COMFORT

Carol Ervin

Cold Comfort
Copyright © 2013 by Carol L. Ervin

ISBN (Paperback): 978-1-4929215-0-9

Original Cover design by Valentina Migliore

Learn more about author Carol Ervin at http://www.carolervin.com

CHAPTER 1

The first shriek startled Wanda like a sudden blast of wind. Since noon, she'd heard nothing but the squeak of leather, the horse's breath and footfall, the rush of water. Only broken weeds suggested there might be another traveler on the grassy road. She twisted in the saddle but saw no one behind, no sign of anyone on the slope of charred trees or across the rocky river.

The howls repeated, high blasts of fury, a woman somewhere at the end of her wits. Maybe hurting a child, or being hurt herself in a terrible way.

Wanda's horse, a red mare, stopped under a young tree at the roadside. She kicked the animal's fat sides and jerked on the reins to pull up its head, but it did as it had all day—exactly as it pleased. When it stretched its neck to graze, she stood in the stirrups, pulled her knife from its sheath and cut a switch from the tree. Before she could slap the switch against its rump, the horse took off at a trot. Her butt bounced and her hands gripped the saddle horn. It was too late to wonder if she was better off alone.

She'd welcomed the loneliness and hardship of travel from North Dakota to West Virginia, choked by engine smoke, bone-rattled and sleepless for three days and nights. Pacing depot platforms, waiting for the next train. Sitting near family groups, bouncing other mothers' children on her lap, avoiding men, lying about herself.

In Elkins she'd bought the horse for the last leg of her journey. After a full meal and a night's rest in the Delmonico Hotel, she had no fear of following an unknown road on horseback. Everything ahead should be familiar, though she'd left the mountains way back in 1900, fifteen years younger. She told the stableman she'd ridden before. He'd given her a skeptical look.

By midafternoon, she liked everything but the horse. The road wound through narrow, shady valleys beside a fast-flowing creek. The oldest trees were dead and black with char, but mountain air brought memories of finding her way in the woods. Little by little she replaced bad thoughts with wonder at shades of green, the grays of boulders and rocks, the glimpses of white in a blue sky, the sense of justice to come. With few people on the road, none she knew and no one near, there was no need to guard herself or pretend she was fine. Her goals felt right—get back at Granny, take something away, cure her own craziness or put it to good use.

The shrieks grew louder. Around a curve, the horse came to a sudden halt behind a mule-drawn wagon. A man sprawled on the wagon cover like he'd fallen backwards from the bench, while a young woman knelt over him, screaming and slapping his head. The man lay still enough to be dead.

In one smooth motion, the woman looked up, grabbed a shotgun from a sheath alongside the wagon and aimed it at Wanda's chest.

"Hey, no need for that," Wanda called.

The woman lowered the gun and thumped her chest like she was trying to slow her heart. "I'm sorry... sorry to greet you like this. There's robbers..." She gasped. "I'm afraid..."

Wanda tightened the reins and wrapped them over her hand to keep the horse from wandering, like they'd shown her at the stable. "If you don't want to be noticed, you shouldn't make so much noise."

The woman pushed away dark curls and brushed a sleeve over her eyes. She waved the gun toward the man. "He give out on me. Fell dead while we was driving along." She had a new widow's stare of disbelief.

Wanda rode a few steps closer. "Maybe he's in a faint."

"I've had my ear to his chest! There's no air in him."

His eyes were open and his mouth gaped. He didn't look like he'd be slapping back.

The woman glanced at the sky, then up and down the road. Her shoulders heaved. "We can't do nothing for him. I've been here a while, and I need this load off my hands. Can you drive my wagon?"

"I doubt it," Wanda said. "Can't you?"

"My hands is delicate, and John never showed me how." She had round dark eyes, plump cheeks and a bow mouth. Maybe the type to make a man do everything for her.

"Now would be a good time to learn," Wanda said.

The woman sucked in air like she was building to another sob. "The wagon has to be braked and all. I could never do it."

Wanda's rear felt numb in the saddle, but on this road the wagon bench would be a harder seat. "Maybe you should stay here awhile. Till you're more yourself."

"I guess I'll go on. I feel relieved to have your company. I'm Virgie White. This here's John, my husband."

"Wanda Wyatt." She and Virgie had a lot in common—dead husbands, screaming fits, and this near-abandoned road.

Virgie slid the shotgun into its sheath. "Do you live close to here?"

"A long way off."

"You're not traveling by yourself?"

"I do all right."

"Good for you," Virgie said. She laid her fingers on her

3

husband's eyes and closed his lids. Then she eased his feet from the bench and sat in their place.

"I'm sorry about your man," Wanda said.

Virgie straightened like she was gathering herself. "This is no good time to grieve, but when is? Have we seen each other before?"

"It's possible." Sooner or later people in thinly-settled places met, saw or heard of everyone else, but Wanda had been away most half her life. "Will this road get me to Winkler?"

"It will, about a day from now. Is that where you're riding to?"

"It's on my way. I've come to see my granny, Lucie Bosell. She called me home."

"Did she now? Lucie Bosell, and you come. That's sweet." Virgie smiled, a sign she'd set her mourning aside, or was rattled.

Wanda hated to ask, but anything she could learn about Granny might help. "Are you acquainted with Lucie?"

"I've heard of her. I think we's in the same business."

"What business is that?"

Virgie glanced at her wagon. "Corn business."

"I see." Most likely corn liquor. "Do you know where she lives?"

"Don't you?"

"I ain't seen her since I was little."

"I believe the Bosells was burned out, same as John and me." When she said his name, Virgie's chest began to heave. Soon she was crying and blowing her nose.

Wanda waited for her to settle. "Mrs. White, I can't drive your wagon. I can barely drive this horse. You'll have to wait for somebody else."

"I guess I can try." Virgie picked up the reins.

"I'll follow along. Use the brake if the wagon starts to go faster than your husband drove it."

"I never paid much attention." Virgie held out a rope. "Maybe you could ride ahead and encourage my mule. Put this lead on him."

"Is your load heavy?"

Virgie puckered her brow. "Why you want to know?"

"I don't want to be ahead if we go down a grade and you can't figure out how to brake."

"It's somewhat heavy. It's corn."

Since the month was June, either the wagon carried a load of grain from last year, or Virgie's corn liquor was under the tarp.

Wanda leaned from the saddle and fastened the lead rope. The mule nuzzled her horse.

Virgie sniffed. "A mule loves a mare, because its ma was a mare."

The mare kicked out with its hind leg. Virgie giggled. "A little slap, there's a good Ma."

Wanda supposed the giggle could be crazy grief, unless Virgie hadn't cared that much for the man who'd dropped dead.

Virgie pushed down on a lever at the side of the wagon. "I think I got it. Let's go. It'll be dark before we get there."

"To Winkler?"

"To Jennie Town, up a-ways. There's a place we can stay over."

Fifteen years ago, she'd boarded the train at Jennie Town, headed west to Fargo.

With the mule eager to get close, the mare stepped ahead at a better pace.

"Look to the brake," Wanda said. "We're starting downhill."

A waning moon dimly lit the building where Virgie halted her mule. "Here we are. Jennie Town, what's left."

Another settlement that had come and gone with its sawmill. By train, Winkler had been only a few hours farther up the grade.

"I think this was the depot," Wanda said. A strip of light showed around a door.

"The depot, so it was. Roy's made it into a public house." Virgie called from her wagon seat. "Roy, you there?"

Wanda swung down from her horse, stiff as an old woman. She smoothed her skirt over her trousers. A scent of boiling potatoes set her mouth to watering.

A straggly-bearded man with a lantern came around the side of the building and limped to the wagon. "Virgie. I been wondering where you got to. I see you brung somebody." He peered at Wanda, then at the body on the tarp. "Is John sick or drunk?"

Virgie sniffed. "He ain't neither. He fell over dead."

"What?" Roy lifted the lantern over John's body. "You sure?"

"Feel of him."

Wanda stood beside her horse, un-greeted, ignored, and hungry.

Roy touched John's arm. "Holy horseshit, you're right. He's getting stiff. Virgie, I'm sorry. What we gonna do now?"

"Bury him," Virgie said.

Riding had beaten Wanda down and left her prickly. "I'd like to eat and stay the night," she said.

Roy leaned to Virgie and lowered his voice. "I mean what we gonna do about our business."

"You're gonna pay me and we'll bury John and then we'll see. If you're wondering who this is, it's Lucie Bosell's granddaughter. Wanda's her name."

Roy lifted his hat. "I've spoke to Lucie once or twice, but I didn't know there was no young Bosells. You're welcome to Roy's, ma'am. Welcome anytime."

"Thank you," Wanda said.

The depot door slammed against the wall and a shaft of light flowed out. Against it stood the dark, bulky shape of another man, who bellowed, "I got you this time!"

Wanda flinched as his boots thundered across the platform, and she took a step back when he jumped off near the mule. The mule startled, jerking the wagon.

Virgie leaped from the wagon and grabbed the mule's bridle strap.

The man wrenched it away. "Roy, this is my product! Her and John stole it from me."

"Hargis Boone, you liar!" Virgie latched onto the harness, slapped at the man's arms and kicked like a kid in a tantrum. The mule reared and Roy shouted.

Wanda held onto her horse, which was now shaking its head and backing away from the fracas.

The man named Hargis appeared to be winning. He shoved, and Virgie fell against the mule. It sprinted forward, rattling the wagon and nearly throwing John's body to the ground.

Virgie and the men ran after the wagon. When the mule slowed, Hargis latched onto the harness and pulled his way to the mule's head. Catching up, Virgie took the shotgun from its sheath.

Roy shouted, "Now, now…"

Wanda cupped her hands at her mouth to carry her voice. "Virgie! Hargis! Why not talk this out while we eat?"

Virgie kept the gun pointed. Wanda sheltered her horse at the shadowed side of the depot and watched from the corner, ready to leave if the argument got worse. If there were other houses left in Jennie Town, they showed no lights. The safest thing might be to get back on her horse and bed down later, somewhere along the road.

Hargis ignored the gun and stepped close to the wagon. "What's the matter with John? He looks dead drunk."

"Just dead," Roy said.

"You don't mean it." Hargis's voice broke.

Virgie swung the gun toward her dead husband and back to Hargis. "Dropped over from the strain of life. You threatening with the law didn't help."

"He stole my corn."

Since Hargis had gone from bluster to whine, Wanda figured the fight could be winding down.

Roy stood off to the side, holding the lantern. "Virgie, Hargis, let's talk."

"We don't need to talk," Virgie said. "Roy, get my money."

"I ain't sure I should buy," Roy said. "Not till you two settle."

Virgie sweetened her tone. "Hargis and John had a deal about the corn."

"He never paid," Hargis said.

"I didn't say he paid, I said you had a deal. Wanda, come and hold my gun while I take Roy inside to get my money."

"I'll stay outa your quarrel for the time being," Wanda said.

Virgie aimed the shotgun at Hargis's lower parts. "Roy, do what I said or I'm gonna shoot. Right about there."

Hargis hurried to the other side of the mule. "Go ahead, Roy, get her money. She'll pay me later. Ain't that so, Virgie?"

"I don't know," Virgie said. "My man just dropped over and I can't think straight. You sure John never paid?"

"Did you see the money?"

"John didn't always tell me everything."

"A skinflint. You never should of married him."

"You've said it often enough. He's dead, so you can stop now."

"I'll have to count the jugs," Roy said.

"There's twenty-six." Virgie bawled like a lost calf. "How am I gonna get along?"

Weary of them all, Wanda rested her head against the building.

Virgie sniffed. "I got to think of my future. Hargis, let's make a deal."

"I had a deal with John."

"Shut up, I'm gonna keep your deal. I mean let's help each other. How's that sound?"

"It don't sound good with you holding a gun. I ain't sure I trust you."

"It's time you tried," Roy said. "Virgie's your sister, and she's got nobody else I know of. That right, Virgie?"

Virgie sniffed. "Stepsister, but family all the same."

Hargis pointed to Wanda. "How about her? Can we trust her, hearing this and all?"

Roy held the lantern over Wanda and beamed like he was offering a gift. "This is Lucie Bosell's grandgirl."

Hargis stepped close, straightening his shoulders. "Well blow me over. Miss Bosell, how you do? I'm a friend of your family."

She wasn't surprised. Hargis Boone seemed the type her granny might tolerate. "My name's Wyatt."

Virgie lowered the gun.

"Let's find a place for John," Roy said.

Roy, Hargis and Virgie buried John that night, then generously sampled his corn liquor and cried over his hardscrabble life. Wanda sat with them, with one hand on the knife hidden deep in her skirt pocket, and the other brushing Hargis away each time his arm draped over her shoulders. He had a strange-shaped head, the bottom small and the top squared like a box. He also had arms like a blacksmith.

The tavern had no other patrons. Dim light did not hide the grit on the floor. Roy served potatoes and onion stewed in goat's milk and gave them a choice of hard cider or corn liquor. Wanda sipped water from her canteen and wished Virgie would stop whining.

When Hargis wasn't shifting his arm to her shoulder, he was leaning close to whisper, roughing her cheek with his prickly beard. "You're lucky to find me, Miss Bosell, because Lucie and me is close. Not many people know where she is, but I can take you to her doorstep."

She watched their shadows on the walls and made no new attempt to correct her name. With Granny well-known, Bosell was the one that would stick.

Her lack of comment didn't stop Hargis. "How is it again that Lucie's your granny? Do you belong to Ruth or Piney?"

Lucie's letter had said nothing about Wanda's aunts, and this was the first she'd heard their names in a long time. She wanted to hear more, but did not want to talk about family with this man. "My folks are dead. Nobody you'd know." She feared he might.

"They say Lucie's distillery blowed up and started one of the big burns," Roy said. "Hargis, did Lucie ever say if that's true?"

Hargis shrugged. "Lucie don't like questions. She don't say and I don't ask. Miss Bosell, do you know something on that score?"

She tightened her lips.

"Never mind." He winked.

She knew the most important thing. The one time she'd met Granny Bosell, she'd been about twelve, old enough to see the old woman was deaf and dumb to anyone but her own self.

Lucie had written a year ago. "Come and bring your man if you got one. I'll make it worth your while." At the time, Wanda had laughed at the notion of obliging her in any way. Then Homer died, and his space in her life filled with anger for an old wrong.

Hargis might know the way to Lucie's door, but having him along would be as comfortable as a rope around her neck.

When Hargis and Virgie commenced to mourn life's sorrows, Wanda slipped away to one of the depot's stuffy bedrooms. Talk about Lucie had revived bad thoughts. The old woman wouldn't be offering charity, and even if she did, Wanda wouldn't like taking it.

She'd never doubted herself until Homer was gone, then she'd labored through her days pretending she wasn't crazy. Work should have let her sleep, for she spent long hours ironing bachelors' shirts and scrubbing their union suits. Her child should have brought some comfort.

The first fit had struck after she sold Homer's Model T. No one then saw her scream and pull her hair. The fit left her cold and weak, but brought relief, like waking from sickness. Other outbursts followed, often with men who tried to take advantage. She didn't scare herself until the day she wrenched Evie from her chair, threw her platter of beans against the wall and a cup through a window. Evie, eight years old and too quiet, had covered her ears and run into the yard. Still in a fury, she'd ordered her to come inside, but Evie had run away to May Rose, Wanda's stepma.

When Wanda reached the cottage, Evie was playing with other children on the hard orphanage grounds, where grass had no fair chance to grow.

May Rose offered a cup of tea, which she drank, standing, watching her child. Evie stretched her arms and held tight to girls in her line, all facing a line of boys. The girls chanted. "Red Rover, Red Rover, send Henry right over." A knock-kneed boy ran to break through their linked arms. The girls held fast, and they circled the boy and added him to their line of defense.

"It was like I changed into someone else," Wanda said. She was afraid to say *crazy, demon-possessed.*

May Rose stood close with her arm around Wanda's waist. "Children try us in every way. Evie's lost her pa. You've lost your husband."

"Almost a year ago. I don't know why I wanted to hurt her. You know Evie. She's no trouble."

May Rose, who burdened her life with other people's heartaches, tried to find hope in everything. "You have a lot of worries."

"I never worry." She couldn't afford their house. Could barely put food on the table.

"This will get better. I'll help."

"Ma, I've got nothing."

"You can stay with me." A two-room cottage that belonged to the orphanage.

At the curb, children gathered behind a wagon where a man flaked chips from a crystal block of ice. She and May Rose watched them run back to the playground, sucking on slivers. Evie, a red-haired freckled remake of Homer, looked happy as any.

"It's an awful feeling," Wanda said.

"Let Evie stay with me for a while. Till you're better."

She didn't expect May Rose to suggest she work at the orphanage. The children looked fine, but they had troubles enough. The tea calmed her. "I might make a trip."

"Travel can be good," May Rose said. "New places help us see different."

"I've thought about Granny's letter. Maybe this is a good time to see what she wants." She smiled so May Rose would think she wanted a healing trip, not a chance to turn her fits on someone who deserved them. Granny had offered, hadn't she, something worth her while? It might go a long way toward easing her worries, if worries was what she had.

"West Virginia is so far away. And you've said you don't like your granny."

She'd never said "don't like." She'd said "hate."

"A trip like that will not be restful," May Rose said.

"Ma, I know. We traveled from there to here."

"I was young. I had no idea."

"You're still young."

"I'm thirty-six."

Her stepma had a glowing smile and crown of golden hair. Beside her, Wanda felt large and plain and often older. She was twenty-eight.

"You had to come," Wanda said. "I need to go."

On the playground, children taunted: *"Red Rover, Red Rover!"*

Wanda lay awake long after Virgie stumbled into the tiny bedroom and fell on the bed. Without Homer, she hated herself. She also hated Homer for not being here to straighten her out.

Chirping birds woke her before first light. She tip-toed to the public room, where a lantern burned among jugs and dirty plates. She carried the lantern to Roy's horse shed. With a lot of grunting and error, she threw the blanket over the horse's back, then the saddle, then pulled the bridle over its head, the first time all by herself.

The air felt frosty for June. She left the lantern by the trough and led the horse to a rock for an easier mount. When they turned onto the road, she looked back. The depot was shadowy and quiet. She hoped Hargis had drunk enough to sleep until noon.

CHAPTER 2

The horse plodded along without need of a switch, freshened by a night's rest, maybe leery as Wanda of the dark road. The slap of fast water eased her mind about going the right way. They were following the river upstream.

Dawn grayed the sky not long after they left Jennie Town but was slow to reach the hollows and valleys. As light grew, she saw how the road rose and the river fell. Every view repeated itself—burned trees rooted to the slopes or piled at the roadside, living brush and mountain laurel, giant boulders in the river.

The horse stopped and stretched its neck to drink from a stream that crossed the road. Wanda chewed on jerky, wondering if Hargis ever told the truth. He wanted something. He'd been too strong about showing her the way, more interested in her and Lucie Bosell than in the prospect of sharing Virgie's still or the load of corn liquor. And he stood too close.

Mid-afternoon, the road that snaked between mountain and river opened to a valley. At the roadside, a rough board displaying the word 'Winkler' lay in the fork of a spindly tree.

Wanda inhaled sharply. She hadn't expected every contour to look wrong, even the curve of the river. No railroad tracks, no high stacks of lumber, no terraces of company houses on the eastern slope. In their place, piles of brush, scattered buildings. On the mountains across the river, a tract of burned timber stood like a black wall.

Two herd dogs and two hounds ran barking to meet her. Wanda raised her knees as the dogs circled the horse and nosed her boots. On the other side of the river, a man waved his hat and walked toward a footbridge.

She hoped he was Will Herff, who wrote now and then to May Rose. They hadn't heard anything from him in the year since he'd forwarded Lucie's letter. In that time, anything could happen.

She kept trying to puzzle the town back. On the weedy street ahead, the company store building and church stuck out like orphans.

The man flung a mattock at a stump. When he got to the road, he shoved his hands in his pockets and waited. The dogs ran back and forth between them.

Wanda nudged the horse closer. She spoke first. "I know you." Like his brother, he had black hair and eyes and a sharp chin.

He tilted his head. "You got me."

She'd seen him last as a thin, scruffy boy. "You're Will Herff. You look like your brother, Charlie."

"Charlie." He studied her a moment. "Then you might be Wanda."

"Bull's-eye." Will Herff's likeness to his brother made her feel like grabbing him in a hug. When they'd traveled to Fargo, she'd been fourteen, Charlie nine. May Rose had made them a family.

Will squinted. "Is everything all right at home? May Rose?"

"All fine."

"I was sorry to hear about Homer."

"Blood poisoning." Talk about Homer's passing came easier, like cuss words said so often a person lost track of what they meant. Still, she could not dwell on him for long. "May Rose talks about you so much I feel we been friends all these years."

"It's the truth. She's writes about your family and all, but I'm shocked to see you're a grown up woman." He looked down, like men did when they didn't want their thoughts to show. "Ready to get off that horse?"

"More'n ready. I think I'm glued here."

He held the horse's bridle. "I guess living in the West hasn't made you a cowgirl."

She slid to the ground. "I never cared to ride. Your brother's the one crazy about horses. I wasn't surprised when he went off to be a cowboy."

Will's black eyebrows arched, like his brother might be a painful topic. "If it wasn't for May Rose, we'd of gone on thinking he was dead. Pa took it hard when she wrote how Charlie run off to Fargo with you-all. I always thought he'd come back when he grew up."

"You know how it is. The longer you stay away, the harder it is to go home."

"Charlie never wrote, not one time. Or came to see us. But here you are. My best visitor in a long while."

"Your best? You didn't know me."

"Now I do. I remember your hair."

It was thick and springy as a bush, the color of rust, and strong enough to push off a hat that wasn't tied down.

He tried to correct himself. "It's not bad, just different."

"I know." It was bad. She'd never let herself care.

With so much gone, the valley looked smaller. The Winkler Company sawmill had clogged the space between road and river. The mill's foundation stones now peeked from weeds like unattended grave markers, and white goats grazed where there'd been a maze of tracks.

"I've come to see Granny."

He smiled. "Not me, then."

"Her letter brought me. The one she gave you to send on."

He wiped his brow with a kerchief. "That was a while ago. I've known of Lucie since she moved over this way, but didn't know she was your granny till she came asking after you. Someone told her my brother and you were in the same place."

He paused. "There's stories about her, none good. Some might be true."

"Not a surprise." She liked the gentle caution in his voice and how his face relaxed when she showed she knew about Lucie.

He led her horse. "I've got cool spring water and coffee. I hope you won't ride farther today."

"Not till I know where to go. Lucie's letter didn't say she'd moved. Maybe you can tell me where."

"I know the general direction. Stay here a few days—someone will come to trade and we'll ask." He was thin and wiry-looking, with a sweet, lazy smile. "You're safe with me. Worst I'll do is talk your head off."

"I'm not worried about my head, though you could steal my heart, the way you look like Charlie."

His tanned face turned deep red. She laughed. "I always could make Charlie blush." Homer too.

She counted six houses scattered on the hillside above the main street. "Not much left of the town."

"Population one. I'm fixing up places for new settlers. Take your pick."

"Maybe someday." She and Homer had talked about coming back.

The dogs raced ahead. Will paused and picked up the mattock he'd left by the road. "Does your girl look like you?"

"Like Homer, and sweet like him. When you write to May Rose, tell her if she wants to know how you've grown up, she should think of Charlie. 'Course we ain't seen him for five or six years. She misses him, misses you too."

"I guess not enough to come back."

"Your brother never did try to figure out what's right, but May Rose does. She won't leave the orphanage to visit the next town."

"And she has cousins to keep her there," Will said.

"We don't see them much. They got families of their own."

"I'm glad you've made the trip."

"I needed to do something."

17

Will was quiet, maybe answering his own questions. She had questions too, about the brother who couldn't stay and the one who wouldn't leave.

He pointed to a mound covered with blooming honeysuckle vine. "Right there was the boardinghouse where you and May Rose lived. First it burned—nothing living there at the time but rats. Then most of it washed away in floods."

Left to themselves, all proud things fell to ruin. Bad things too, like the whorehouse where her ma had worked.

She waved toward the slope. "Do you live in one of these houses?" The logging company had owned most of the valley. She knew he'd bought everything at a bankruptcy auction.

"I live in the store. It's handy."

He led the mare into a field where a bay horse waited behind a split-rail fence. While he put her saddle and bridle in a shed, she carried her saddlebags to the store's concrete steps. They looked the same, steep and wide with an iron railing in the center, but their edges had chipped. Shading her eyes, she studied the way she'd come. No Hargis. Yet.

Will came up beside her, bringing the smell of new-cut grass. "Just looking, or looking for somebody?"

"Wondering where the dogs have got to."

"Nosing around somewhere. They're good company, and they let me know when anyone's coming."

"Does that happen a lot?"

"Every day or two someone comes to buy or trade."

The doors of the company store fit her memory, side by side, one to go in and one to go out, with window glass at the top. She'd thought the store so fine. He opened the right-side door and a bell dinged. Inside, she was pleased to see the same oiled floors, high windows, and stamped metal ceiling, but there were only a few shelves of store goods. He'd added a cook stove and tin sink, a hand-cranked washing tub, and a table covered in red checked oilcloth.

She hung her saddlebags over a chair. "Do you know if Lucie's in the whiskey business?"

"I've heard she used to be."

In the mountains, stills were ordinary as guns. She had no ready-made objection to liquor, only to people like Lucie who made drunks of their children. "You know somebody named Hargis Boone?"

Will shoved aside the table's stack of thick books. "Hargis stops around, time to time. Have a seat, I'll heat the coffee."

She wandered to a shelf with tinned sardines, Prince Albert tobacco, sleeves of cigarette papers. "I thought the store was bigger."

He poked the cook-stove fire and hung the poker on a wall hook. "I built that wall across the middle, made sleeping rooms and a big storeroom in the back. It makes this part easier to heat. How do you know of Hargis?"

"He claims to be a friend to Lucie."

"Hargis claims a lot, wants to be the one who knows the most about everyone and everything."

"I met him last night, where I stayed at Jennie Town."

"Roy's Place."

"That's it."

She and Will stopped a few paces apart in the center of the room. A nice-looking man. She wondered how he got along without a woman, or if he did.

"I'll just go splash off some of this dirt," he said. "There's a washroom in the back. Toilet's old and cranky but it works most of the time. I keep a bucket of water there for extra encourage-ment. You want to wash or anything?"

"I smell like my horse."

"You first, then." He pointed to a door in the dividing wall. "Go through there to a hallway. The washroom is all the way to the end."

She opened every door behind the divider wall—first, the storeroom, shadowy and full of junk. Next a room with one bed and another room by the washroom with two. The washroom had a toilet with a high tank and chain and, most appealing, a long, claw-footed bathtub. There was a sliver of lye soap, but no towel.

The dogs barked. If they were greeting Hargis, he'd left Jennie Town soon after her, or had raced to get here.

At the washbasin she rubbed the soap between her hands and spread the sparse suds on her face, rinsed, then washed her arms to her elbows and patted herself dry with her dress hem. When she came from the washroom, sure enough, there was Hargis, jabbering away beside Will's barrel of salt fish, playing his eyes and voice like a snake-oil salesman. She stopped at a shelf of hammer and ax heads, wondering if Will sold knives. She liked having a spare.

Hargis broke off mid-sentence. "Why darlin', there you are. You rode off terrible early. I was just telling Doc, here."

"Doc?"

Will nodded toward the table of books. The one on top was *Haydn's Dictionary of Popular Medicine and Hygiene.* "I read medicine. There's no doctor in a long ways."

Hargis slapped Will's back. "The hill folks was used to coming to Winkler for doctoring. These days they put their trust in Doc. He knows everything in them books."

"Never enough," Will said. "Wanda, your coffee's on the table. Sit down to it while I wash up."

Alone with Hargis, she preferred to stay in motion. She carried her cup along Will's shelves and touched boxes of nails, chains, a stack of windows with traces of paint and putty on the frames, sheets of rumpled tin. The coffee was gritty.

Hargis trailed behind, his voice bouncing off the bare walls. "You hasn't said hello and that's my fault. I'm sorry I called you darlin'—that was overstepping. I was just relieved to see you. I feel like we got close last night, don't you?"

Will's store didn't seem to have knives or guns, but maybe he had them locked in a case somewhere. "I don't warm up to people," she said.

Hargis's smile showed small teeth and wide pink gums. "That's good, you're cautious. By the by, I paid for your food and bed at Roy's." He threw out his arms, like he was inviting a hug.

Wanda pulled a quarter from her skirt pocket and tossed it to the floor. "I planned to pay Roy on my way home. I hope you didn't give more than that, 'cause it wasn't worth it."

Hargis picked up the coin. "I won't tell Roy. His feelings would be hurt."

Will returned in a clean shirt. His hair was wet and slicked back. "Hargis, have you come to trade?"

"Not today. I followed after this lady, troubled she'd get lost searching for her granny. Our mountain roads is confusing."

"I'm good at finding my way," Wanda said.

"You won't find Lucie Bosell by yourself. Ain't that right, Doc?"

"Can't say." Will brought two cups of coffee to the table. "You-all have been resting in the saddle, but I been working, so I'm going to sit down. Hargis, if you want to help, why not fetch Lucie here?"

Hargis took a seat across from Will. Wanda strolled to a spot where she didn't have to see Hargis's eager grin.

"She might come," Hargis said, "if we give her a week or so. You never know how Lucie's gonna be. Maybe drunk, maybe sobering up, maybe sick with something else. She's old, you know."

When people got drunk or old, everything but their true natures wore off, which would make Lucie meaner than ever. "How far away is Granny's new place?"

Hargis twisted in his chair. "Two-three hours. I'll take you there first thing in the morning."

"No thanks," Wanda said.

"Why ever not?"

"For one, I don't like you. You don't want to hear number two."

Hargis laughed. "Sharp and direct, just like Granny."

"I'll show Wanda the way," Will said.

Hargis moved to another chair and leaned back with his hands behind his neck. "Now, I can see better, keep my eyes on the both of you. Are you old friends or new acquaintances?"

"Some of both," Will said.

"Ah, a story there." Hargis dug a finger in his ear. "Even so, Miss Wanda, I'm betting Doc don't exactly know how to get to the Bosell place. By the by, Doc, do you know when the preacher's coming next?"

"Supposed to be in July," Will said. "You wanting to get baptized or married, or will someone be needing a burial?"

Hargis answered with a girlish laugh. "Could be all three, we never know. But first I'm gonna settle down to one woman." He winked at Wanda. "I ain't handsome like Doc, but I got my charms. Don't ask who, it's best to let the lady tell first." He straightened in his chair like he'd forgotten something urgent. "Has Miss Wanda told you about John?"

"Which John?"

"Virgie's John. Dropped over dead. Miss Wanda was there when we put him in the ground. Pretty thing like Virgie'll not be alone too long. You might want to take her some comfort, since you once was so friendly."

Will's face reddened again.

Hargis stood and dug in his pocket. "Now, Doc, I'd like to carry some gifts to Lucie. She treats me good as anybody, you understand, but all women likes a present, don't they?" He brought out a quarter. "What have you got in the way of hard tack?"

Will set a candy jar beside a scale. "All that in candy?"

"I'll take half in coffee beans if you got 'em. Miss Wanda, if you're looking for a present for Lucie, I suggest a tin of petroleum jelly or a pair of ladies' gloves. She complains of rough hands."

"I won't be taking a gift."

"Well, sure, you're a gift in yourself for a granny that hasn't seen you—since when?"

"Mr. Boone, if you know Lucie, you know she's not like other grannies. How long since you've seen her?"

"Just before corn planting."

"And you visit often?"

"I carry trade goods here and there."

Wanda took two palm-sized tins of Resinol ointment to the counter.

"Very nice," Hargis said. "She'll like that."

Wanda smiled at Will. "For my aunts."

Will slid Hargis's coffee beans into a paper poke and wrapped it with twine. "Hargis is right. I don't exactly know how to get to Lucie's."

"Then I guess we'll all have to go," she said.

Will agreed.

Hargis took his packages and grinned from her to Will. "So, how we gonna entertain ourselves till tomorrow?"

Anything without him sounded good.

"I need to dig coal for my stove," Will said. "Hargis, I'll not charge you for supper if you'll ride over to Watsons and ask Ebert to come tomorrow and mind the store."

"There's a deal," Hargis said. "Would Miss Wanda care to go along?"

Her patience wilted. "Don't you know when to quit?"

Hargis tipped his hat. "Quitters never win." He paused at the door. "Doc's a handsome feller. Can I trust you two alone?"

His words hit close. These days she never knew what she might do, and Will was an attractive man. She unscrewed the ointment's tin cap and sniffed the strong, familiar odor. "Mr. Boone, don't worry yourself over me. I'm not your business."

CHAPTER 3

W hile Will dug coal, Wanda walked the valley past burn circles and piles of old lumber. Uphill, white-washed houses peered from brush that grew faster than his goats could eat it. She admired and pitied his efforts. He wasn't the only one who wanted to make something right.

Across the river, thick trunks of burned trees rose above what was left of the town. What happened to infant birds and rabbits when their forest raged with fire?

Half a lifetime ago, she and her real ma, Evalena, had left another sawmill town when their cabin burned. They'd hunched in their nightshifts near the warmth of its ashes until dawn, then Evalena had stood and told her to follow. Wanda didn't question, though her ma's ideas never seemed helpful. Her pa had already moved on to a new woman, and they had no friends but the men who kept them in squirrels and whiskey.

Evalena's pretty feet weren't hardened, like Wanda's, from running barefoot. The prickly road soon bruised her toes and slashed her soles, yet she pushed ahead like fire was at their backs. When the sun stood overhead, she turned uphill to an unpainted house. Granny's place. Wanda knew better than to ask why they'd never come before. Evalena sometimes told a happy story about her sisters, but uttered Granny's name only when drink took her near to passing out, and she never spoke of her pa.

Their first day was good. The aunts were sorrowful about the fire and that they'd come so far in their shifts. Granny looked Wanda up and down, grim-faced. The aunts carried water for baths, gave them clean dresses, and doctored their feet with Resinol ointment.

The fight started the next morning. Wanda ran out of the privy, certain from the screams that her ma was on fire. Aunt Piney stopped her on the porch and turned her toward a shed. "Let them have it out. There's something over here you'll like."

Wanda had four soft kittens tucked to her chest when Evalena ran to the shed and jerked her arm. "We have to go." No mention why. The kittens had fallen to the ground. She and her ma had walked another day and come to Winkler.

She wasn't sorry this town had burned and washed away. But there'd been singing, and she'd found May Rose, her pa's wife, abandoned by him the same as he'd done her ma.

At the upper end of the valley, she found the school on its knoll. Up close, she saw the broken windows, the missing front doors. One teacher had been kind.

The late afternoon air cooled, and she lay on a stone slab near the river. Trapped between sun and rock, her body warmed. She'd brought no heavy clothes, not expecting cool days, not planning to stay, not thinking at all. The next thing she knew a dog's wet nose was in her face, and she sat up and saw Will, waist-high in the river, washing off coal dust.

She laughed at the black streaks on his face. He dunked his head and lathered with a bar of soap. He wore no shirt. She couldn't see what else he'd stripped off.

"I'm coming out. Any ladies who don't want to be scandalized should turn their backs."

She covered her eyes with her fingers, then parted them for a peep.

Will laughed. His feet and chest were bare, but wet trousers clung to his legs. "You peeked. Bad girl."

"Don'cha know, I always was."

He jogged off to the store for dry clothes, and she lay back on the rock. May Rose would be pleased to hear how fine he looked and how peaceful she felt with him. Not crazy.

When he came from the store, he took her upriver to the old pond. Here lumbermen with pikes had pushed logs from flat cars into the water and poked them toward the gangway to the saws.

"This is a good spot for a grist mill," he said. "It'll get more people coming this way. Then I'll fix up the old school, be the teacher myself if I have to. Folks with kids will want to live here."

She didn't know why he wanted the town to grow back. The sawmill had made a constant whine and clatter. Smoke had hung over the valley, and there'd been a steady whoosh and chug of trains. Only at night had they heard the river and the wind in the trees.

"I've started Trading Days, a market every full moon while the weather lasts," he said. "And in a couple of weeks I'm going to have a stock sale. Word's getting around. Am I talking too much?"

"No, it's all good." He was good.

They sat on a stone slab and watched the fast-flowing river. He tossed in a stick. "This is my favorite view. I like how water carries things along. There's a lot of questions in moving things."

"You like moving things but you stay here."

"I don't move place to place, but I don't sit still. I change things where I am."

He'd been alone here for years, yet he wanted a town. "How old were you when all this burned?"

"First time, sixteen. I was working as a lumber stacker. Thought I was big stuff, danced with girls every Saturday night."

At sixteen, she'd married Homer.

"A sawdust pile caught fire. We always figured we had a fire bug, 'cause later on, empty houses burned too. The Company rebuilt the mill. At the time, there was still timber to cut. Then the logged-out places commenced to catch fire, and everything went from bad to worse, logging camps destroyed, trestles scorched and weakened. The mill shut down and the trains stopped running. That was in nineteen-eight. There was no work without the mill, no electric without the boilers, no school or doctor or store without the company payroll. I worked for a while on a crew for the C & O, pulling up rails."

"That's when the town emptied out."

"That was when. I might have moved on, but Pa didn't want to leave. I helped him make furniture—we hauled it to Elkins and Staunton, and sometimes folks came here to get it. But you know, when things get real bad, they get worse before they get better."

"I remember your pa's carvings." His carved birds and squirrels had gone missing, and Will's stepbrothers had accused her. She had nightmares about his stepbrothers. Donnellys.

"Pa started making mandolins and fiddles. Then squatters moved in and before we knew it, they were tearing down houses and hauling off parts to sell. Maybe that was okay, I mean we were squatters too, though Pa figured our house belonged to us because when the mill was here we paid rent. And we'd torn wood off a few ramshackle houses to make furniture. But he was a hot-head, do you recall?"

She remembered. A hot head who'd whipped his sons.

"Yeah, well, Pa shot at some of them squatters."

"Did that run them off?"

"They shot him dead."

She gripped the edge of her stone seat. "You told May Rose your pa passed on. We didn't know he was shot."

"I didn't like putting that in a letter. I found another town with a sawmill, made furniture on the side. I'm not as good as him, but I still got his tools."

And he was still trying to make things right.

He changed their talk to May Rose and Russell, her pa's brother. "Way back, us little kids run from Russell Long. He had those crazy, shifty eyes, like a wild man."

CAROL ERVIN

"He helps at the orphanage. My Evie likes him."

"May Rose didn't marry him, did she? She's never said, but she writes of him now and again, and I don't like to pry."

"She's too busy to take care of a man."

Will nodded. "I loved her. When I try to picture my ma, I see May Rose."

"Your brother called her 'Ma.'"

"I'd like to see her."

"She'd like to see you, too. People should live close to the ones they love."

"And keep their distance from those they hate," he said.

If this was a warning about Lucie, she didn't need it. "If you grow this town back, staying away from folks you hate might not be easy."

He kept his gaze on the river. "Everything has its good and bad."

And everyone. She'd heard her ma in a crazy fit just one time. Shortly after, Evalena had lost herself in drink at Suzie's whorehouse. For that, she'd never forgive Lucie Bosell.

Hargis returned, and they spoke no more of feelings.

CHAPTER 4

At the head of the valley, they took a road east through land that had escaped the burn, Hargis riding ahead on a pony, then Wanda on her contrary mare and Will on his pretty bay. The road twisted up and down, past cleared fields and hollows of young timber. Wanda ignored Hargis's chatter, counted turnoffs they took and those they didn't, and tried to fix landmarks. A shack set back from the road with the roof fallen in. A boulder like a shadow of a giant bear, a tumbled-down stone fence. The horses splashed through streams flowing across the road, or maybe the same stream twisting back and forth.

She yelled and pulled on the reins when Hargis passed a turnoff where a lettered board stood against a tree. "Hargis! This way!"

He waved a hand. "Pay no mind. That road will take you back the way you come, if it don't lose you forever."

"The sign says Bosell."

"It's one of your granny's tricks to stay hid. If you go up that road you'll ride all day and come right back down to Winkler."

"Surely there's folks who know."

Hargis rode back. "Them who know don't blab to strangers. And they stay apart theirselves."

"But Lucie lets you visit."

He grinned. "She admires me. Let's get on, we ain't far now." He rode ahead.

Tired of having him in her view, she studied the hillside patches of moss and fern. When she looked ahead again, he'd disappeared.

His voice echoed. "This way."

Will pointed to a dark gap in the trees on the low side of the road. "Down there."

Not until she took the mare to the road's edge did she see the backside of Hargis and his pony.

Going down, her horse's hooves slid in leaves and loam, and she straightened her legs in the stirrups and leaned back in fear of tumbling over its head. Below, dogs barked, and she glimpsed sparkling water. They rode into a valley shaped like the bottom of a green bowl.

Sunlight glinted on the tin roof of a stone cottage and on a pond half-full of lily pads. Three shaggy black and white dogs ran back and forth, and geese honked and scattered. By the pond, a man scything weeds turned around.

Hargis's face spread in a wide grin. "That there's your Aunt Ruth."

If her aunts had ever written to their sister or tried to help, Wanda didn't know about it. But she remembered the warmth in her ma's voice when she spoke their names. Seeing Ruth, Wanda felt Evalena holding her hand.

Ruth wore trousers held up by wide suspenders. A man's undershirt clung to heavy breasts. She let the scythe fall to the ground and untied a shirt from her waist, jabbed her arms into the sleeves and turned her back while she buttoned up. The dogs stopped yapping and followed her long strides toward Wanda and the men on their horses.

Ruth glanced at her and Will, then spoke to Hargis. "Ma ain't expecting you."

"Well, how would she? Pigeon-message? I didn't know myself till yesterday."

Wanda slipped off the mare. "I'm Wanda. Evalena's girl."

Ruth gaped. "I guess you are, though you don't look a bit like her. But for that bush of ginger hair and turned-up nose, you could be me."

"Hundred year ago," Hargis said.

Will lifted his hat. "Miss Bosell, I apologize for Hargis."

Her aunt shrugged. "I take no offense from a fool."

Wanda and her aunt were of even height, both with ample bosoms, long arms and large hands, but she didn't think they looked alike. Ruth's high cheekbones, darkened skin, and straight hair gave her the look of an Apache chief.

Hargis and Will got off their horses. "Doc and Miss Wanda wouldn't of made it without me," Hargis said. "How's Lucie today?"

"Her usual. Wanda, you come along." Ruth walked away toward the cottage.

Wanda dropped the reins and pointed to the mare. "Hargis, take care of this horse." She followed Ruth on a path of flat stepping stones, giving herself silent orders to mind her words and be careful with her aunts. She could pretend to submit to Lucie as long as the old woman didn't make her crazy.

Blue Morning Glories grew up the front of the cottage, and yellow curtains flapped in open windows. At the door, Ruth said, "Ma don't see good, but she thinks nobody knows. And she talks loud to hear herself."

Handcraft filled the room: stacks of baskets along a wall, a crock of long-stemmed grass heads, rag rugs. On a window ledge, plant cuttings rooted in jars of water. The house smelled of dried sage. Only the rifle and shotgun leaning together in a corner reminded Wanda of the old place.

By a sunny window, an old woman with knobby fingers bent over the start of a grapevine basket. A smudged cobbler apron covered a faded dress, and a gray braid curled on her shoulder like the shed skin of a snake. The woman looked up. "Ruth, who you brought in here?" Her voice was gritty.

This was the woman who'd started Evalena on corn liquor, who'd thrown her out and ignored her ruin.

Ruth raised her voice. "This is Wanda. Evalena's girl."

Granny Lucie's face and hands were dark and withered as old apples. She bent over her basket and worked a vine through upright spokes. "You're too late. I made other plans."

Not a welcome, but none expected. Even better, her dismissal left Wanda free to lie. "I don't give a fig for your plans. I come to meet my family."

Lucie pulled a vine like she hadn't heard.

"Ma," Ruth said, "Hargis is here. And Doc Herff. You want me to ask them in?"

There was no way to tell from Lucie's face if the men were welcome or not. She set her basketwork on the floor. "I'll tell you when. Go fetch Piney. Make her take her shoes off outside, you too. First, get this girl a chair."

Nasty as ever. "I'll stand. I been in the saddle all morning."

"I said, a chair, and put it here beside me so I can see what I'm talking to."

Ruth flashed Wanda a sideways grin and moved a chair with a braided pad.

"Get going," Lucie said.

The door closed. The old woman angled her head from side to side and peered from the corners of red-rimmed eyes. "You had any kids?"

"Two boys, stillborn. One girl. She's eight." Speaking of her children felt disrespectful, like she'd brought them to a bad place.

"Where's your man?"

"Dead."

Lucie sat back in her chair. "Dead? How old are you?"

"Twenty and eight."

"You might marry again."

"I got no such intention." Wanda stared at the yellow curtains, so pretty.

"Then you're no use to me," Lucie said.

"I didn't come to be useful to you."

Lucie lifted the basket to her lap. "You'll get nothing from me."

"I don't want anything you got." Want and need were not the same. She had need, and Lucie had want. She doubted Lucie had a tender spot for babies. More likely, she wanted descendants, a stronghold of young Bosells and her granddaughter as breeder.

They stared at each other until the old woman dropped her gaze and jerked a basket vine the length of her arm.

Wanda pressed her lips to hide her satisfaction. Lucie was bold and rotten as a skunk. In her ears, back-talk likely had the ring of truth.

The door opened and Ruth came in with a woman who startled Wanda to her feet. Aunt Piney looked like her ma in the happy time, when her round dark eyes were clear, her cheeks full, and her arms plump and pinched to tiny wrists and hands.

Piney wrapped her in a hug. "Oh, sweet girl." Her voice was soft as petals. Wanda's chest heaved. When she'd seen her last, Piney had been almost too timid to speak.

Lucie clicked her tongue. "Evalena's Girl, sit back down here."

Piney let her loose, and Wanda sat again at Lucie's side. Piney and Ruth waited by the door, shoeless, their feet broad and their stockings leather-stained at the edges of soles and toes. Wanda felt Ruth's interest. Piney, only a few years older than Wanda, smiled like a child who could not be held back.

Lucie tapped a cane on the floor. "Piney, once for all, are you gonna marry Hargis?"

Pleasure fell away from Piney's face.

"Ma, not that again," Ruth said. "Hargis Boone is a miserable excuse for a man."

Wanda imagined her ma standing between Ruth and Piney. She liked how Ruth took up for her sister.

"Hargis grows a big cornfield," Lucie said, "plus he's got a genuine interest in the business. The time has come to decide."

Piney lifted sad eyes to Ruth. "I laid down with him, like Ma said to do, but I didn't care for it. And I got no baby from it, neither."

"Ma, she don't like him," Ruth said. "If you want another slave, marry Hargis yourself, neither of you is beyond such foolishness. If you do, go live at his place. Piney and me built up this here, and we don't want him in it."

The vine shook in Lucie's hand. She turned her restless eyes to Wanda. "These girls has been a drag on me a long while. Never had the gumption to go their way."

"We'd so sorely miss our life of leisure," Ruth said.

Lucie acted like she hadn't heard. "Ruth, you go now and fix a cot or bedroll in your room for Evalena's Girl. She wants to get to know us."

Ruth smirked. "You don't say."

Wanda stood, and Piney hugged her shoulders.

Lucie waved like she was swatting flies. "Get out, all of you. Piney, get Hargis and Doc in here."

From the tiny bedroom's window, Wanda watched Hargis and Will stride to the cottage on the stone path, Hargis in the lead, looking sure of himself, Will carrying his doctor bag.

Ruth spoke behind her. "I don't believe you come to get to know us, after the way things was left the last time. But in case you did, have you learned enough?"

Wanda turned from the window. "Seems I stepped in the middle of a fight. I'm curious how it will come out."

"You staying that long? It won't end until the old woman's gone." She moved stacks of quilts from a long bench. "This is the closest thing we got to a cot. We also got a rope hammock outside."

Wanda glanced at the narrow bench. "I'll try the hammock."

"Fine." Ruth replaced the quilts. "It'll do no good to pretend you care about us. Only Piney would believe that."

"Do I sound like I'm pretending?"

"I ain't heard you say much."

"I'm not a big talker."

"That's a relief. But I'm glad you come. I'm sorry I didn't fight on your ma's side. I must of been drunk."

"Ma said you were sick. She had the same trouble."

"It's a sickness of the heart," Ruth said, "when you love what makes you that bad off." She measured the space with her arms. "I guess we can hang the hammock inside. Be better than sleeping in the rain."

"Anywhere is fine."

"When you're ready to go home, I'll guide you back to Doc's."

"Kind thanks, but when I'm ready, I'll find my way."

Ruth's face broke in a smile. "You do remind me of myself. Ma won't care for that."

Wanda turned back to the window. "It don't matter."

"We'll see. She'll make you earn your keep, but if you are like me, work won't bother you. There goes Doc. Find out what Ma said to him and let me know. She don't tell us much. And by the by, be careful what you say to Piney. For one thing, she gets hurt easy, and for the other, she spills everything to Ma, even if she don't mean to."

Wanda brought the Resinol tins from her pocket and set them on the bed. "For you and Piney."

"Well," Ruth said, blinking. "Piney will be tickled."

Wanda followed her into a center hall where they stopped for a moment and listened to a murmur of voices in the front room.

"Me and Piney have to shout," Ruth said, "but she hears a whisper from Hargis."

Ruth led through a kitchen and outside to a roofed porch connected to a stone cellar house. "I still don't know why you come."

"Granny invited me. And I needed something to do." A small change in those words fell closer to the truth. *Something needed to be done.*

The air on the porch was heavy with the odor of fermenting fruit. Two five-gallon crocks, their tops wrapped in cheesecloth, stood against the cellar house wall.

Ruth lifted her head like she was sampling the aroma. "Serviceberry wine. It takes a heap of sugar. Now that Ma don't drink like the old days, she's stingy about sugar. I don't suppose you brought any?"

"Hargis brought a few things."

"Not for nothing. Ma holds the little cash we got, and I got nothing he'll trade for. This fall we'll dig seng, pay the taxes and have a few dollars left over, if the price don't take a tumble. Ginseng. You know of it?"

"Where we first lived, Ma found a spot for senging. I helped."

"Them oriental fellers thinks the ginseng root puts power in their loins, if you catch my meaning. It brings seven dollars a pound or more if we can take it all the way to Elkins or Staunton. Otherwise, we have to trust snakes like Hargis and end up with half."

They left the porch and walked with even strides through the grass toward Will. Near the pond, Ruth picked up her scythe.

Will pointed beyond the pond to a field of young corn. "I been talking to Simpson Wainwright about building a grist mill in Winkler. You interested in grinding your corn there? I told him I'd stir up some customers."

"I'm interested in grinding anywhere," Ruth said. "We got two years' harvest stored here, and I'm awful tired of potatoes and fish. Ma's living in the past, won't let us sell or grind it. Rats are chewing it up."

Pleased with herself, Wanda let Ruth and Will do the talking. Piney was lovable, Ruth might be a friend, Lucie hadn't turned her away, and she couldn't remember the last time she'd eaten fresh fish.

"Ever since West Virginia went dry, too much corn has gone to make liquor," Will said. "It's drove up the price and made things hard for folks who don't have enough ground to grow their own. Better lock up your corn. If prices get real high, some will look to steal it."

"Ha," Ruth said. "I'd like to see a man try to steal from Ma. Her hand might be shaky but she don't care what she shoots at." She took a whetstone from a pocket and swiped it over the blade.

Wanda stood with Will in somber silence and watched Ruth move away, swinging the scythe. A frog plopped into the pond, and bubbles rose around the lily pads. The air was sweet with drying grass, so different from the old place with its smell of mold, thick pines, and tall board house with peeling paint.

She remembered Ruth's request. "What did Granny have to say for herself?"

"Very little. She wanted to know why I come. I said I wasn't going to trust an old friend to Hargis. She bought a bottle of iodine and told me to go, said she and Hargis had business. Did she give you a good welcome?"

"About the same. You said there's bad stories about her. Like what?"

"Huh. Nothing proved, or she'd be hanged. There was a revenue man went missing, his body found a couple of years later near the old Bosell place, a bullet in him. Money in his pocket."

"Lucie was thought to of done it?"

"The revenuer was known to be looking for her distillery, but there was no evidence to arrest her. Then there was her husband, another one missing, found dumped in a sink hole, bullet in him, too. But she and her man had enemies, and the law don't waste much time on the death of a rascal."

Pappy Bosell, another one her ma wouldn't name. Wanda remembered him sitting on a porch, shooting crows.

"And folks think Granny killed him?"

"She's said to have been quick to raise a gun. Even today, nobody cares to mess with her."

"Except Hargis."

"Hargis has too much confidence in himself, and he thinks Lucie will make him rich."

"What about Ruth and Piney? Would they still be with her if they thought she'd killed their pa? Or anybody?"

"Ruth might be no better; I don't know if she's had a chance to show her colors. Maybe you should find out what Lucie wants and ride on home with me. Learn more of her from a safe distance. The way Hargis horned in yesterday, we didn't catch up on much."

She liked the invitation. "You'd be better company, but I need to stick here for a while, see what she wants." And learn what she could take away.

"Well, then, I'll come back next week."

"That'll be good. Bring sugar for Ruth. I'll pay."

Seeing Hargis come from the cottage, she put her hands to Will's shoulders. He flinched at her touch and widened his eyes. She went up on tiptoe, brushed her lips across his cheek, and whispered. "On your way home, see if you can get Hargis to talk about what's going on between him and Lucie."

Will commenced to breathe like he'd been running. He gripped her waist. "You sure are a different kind of girl. I don't like leaving you here. Come home with me."

She liked the feel of his hands. "For strangers, we got a lot between us, don't we? Go ahead and pass me a kiss, it'll give Hargis plenty to gossip over. Unless you don't like to be talked about that way."

"Talk never bothers me." He bent and touched her lips.

Hargis called out. "Now, now, you two. What about poor little Virgie?"

Will dropped his hands and stepped aside. "Hargis, you ready to go?"

Hargis's grin showed his pink gums. "Lucie's invited me to stay a few days. Things here may of changed."

Wanda had meant the kiss for show, a message to Hargis and

Lucie that someone they knew cared for her. But for a moment, the press of his lips made her forget her purpose.

Hargis shoved his head forward, like he was waiting to be asked what had changed and why Lucie was allowing him to stay. They left him and walked toward Will's horse.

Will cleared his throat. "So I guess you'll learn for yourself what's brewing between Hargis and Lucie."

"I guess I will. I'm sorry it's him staying and not you."

He leaned close, whispering. "I don't know what's going on here."

"I'll find out what Lucie wants."

"Not that."

She shifted her gaze to the cottage. "We just met. I don't intend to change your life."

"I could do with a change."

"Virgie is free now."

He put a foot in the stirrup and swung into the saddle. "That was over and done long ago."

She touched his horse's neck. "Thanks for the kiss. It helps."

"You're a puzzle."

"I puzzle myself."

Piney came running, shouting and waving her arms. "Doc, Doc, I'm sorry we had no dinner ready. It's unfriendly, letting you go away without a meal. Wanda, you can't be going too. Ma wants to see you now."

Will leaned down to Piney. "Don't worry yourself about feeding me. I didn't give you notice, and I have to get home to my dogs and goats. You take care of Wanda."

Piney put her arm around Wanda's waist. "All of us will."

He snapped the reins and his horse trotted toward the hillside path. When he turned and waved, Wanda mouthed, "Sugar."

He tipped his hat.

CHAPTER 5

Wanda watched Will ride out of sight, a strong and generous man, and tempting, even with Homer wounding her every thought. She needed to rein in her urges.

"Now let's find out what Granny wants."

"You go," Piney said. "She didn't ask for me."

"Come anyway. We'll see what happens."

Piney shifted her eyes. "She'll be mean."

Wanda urged her along the stone path. "A little meanness won't bother us. Do you remember when Ma brought me to see you at the old place?"

"I remember the fighting. You were like my little sister. I wanted you to stay."

"It worked out all right."

"I miss Evalena so bad. I don't like to think of her dead. Ruth and me should of clobbered Ma. We was big girls, women. We could of been the boss of her."

Wanda's exact thought. At the cottage, she stepped ahead and opened the door.

Lucie squinted. "Evalena's Girl, you can sit. Piney, you can get back to work."

"You should say her name," Piney said.

Lucie sat forward in her chair. "What's that you say?"

Piney's voice fell to a whisper. "Her name's Wanda."

"Thank you, Aunt Piney. It's all right if she calls me 'Evalena's Girl.' Makes me recall how she was with Ma, last time."

Lucie's lips opened and shut. She flapped her fingers. "Piney, go. We got private talk."

Only the thought of stealing something from the old woman kept Wanda in the room. She put her arm through Piney's. "It's all right with me if she stays. I've nothing to hide."

Lucie tapped her cane. "Piney, get to the pond and cut down them lilies. Evalena's Girl will come to help by and by."

Going out, Piney said again, "Her name's Wanda."

Lucie made no show she'd heard. "Evalena's Girl, sit here. I have a couple of needs, and some offers. You want to hear them?"

Wanda sat and stretched her legs like a man, good at hiding herself only if she pretended to be someone else. "Might as well. Needs and offers, fire away."

"Them coal men's buying up burned-over land, getting it at tax auctions. They bought my place. I want it back."

"Your old place."

"That's right. The law lets me redeem it afore the end of the year, what they paid for it plus some extra. The time to do that is near up, and I ain't got the money."

No money, so nothing to steal. But Lucie needed her for something that was supposed to be worth her while.

"Why do you care about the old place? It's nicer here."

"For one thing," Lucie snapped, "it's been in my family three generations. And for another, the coal men want it, and that means there's money to be had."

Money, but not soon. "I guess Hargis Boone comes into this some way."

Lucie brushed her sleeve across her yellowed forehead. "Well, Lord, I can't do a thing with just those girls of mine. Piney's got no gumption, and Ruth drinks too much."

"They've made a pretty place here," Wanda said.

"Pretty is as pretty does. Long as she can make wine for herself, Ruth don't care about getting back in the business. Hargis wants in, but he wants more than a cut—he wants to own everything."

"Meaning after you're gone."

"Meaning that, which ain't gonna be for a long time. You don't object to distilling, do you?"

"Not the distilling, just the drinking."

"Good both ways. Hargis will marry into this family some-how. He'll even give his kids the Bosell name, but I don't know about Piney. She'd like to have babies. I think it might be all she's good for, but she should've been doing that fifteen-twenty year ago. You, now. You're of a better age to breed."

Wanda matched Lucie's scowl. "I see what you're about. I don't like that man."

"I'm not ordering you to like him, just give him a legal tie to us." Lucie narrowed her eyes. "I'm giving you a chance to learn the business. Most of what Hargis knows about it is wrong, but he'll help us set up the still and get the product out to sell. Since the government is shutting down legal distillers, moonshine is on the way to being big business. I don't want to be left out just when the money gets good."

"Last I heard, Hargis was going into business with Virgie White."

"That don't mean nothing. Virgie and John was never more than small-time. I ain't met her, but I suspicion she's useless for all but having babies, too. She might have them now with Doc—there was talk about them before she married."

"You do have things laid out," Wanda said.

Lucie picked at the space between her front teeth. "I know what to do, but time's short before I lose my land."

"You might have started sooner."

"You don't say. Year ago, I wrote for you and your man to come."

"He wouldn't have been one for your business. I don't know that I am, neither."

"You can manage Hargis, and that's what I need. Piney can't, Ruth won't, and you see how I am, not seeing good, not hearing half of what goes on. You're like me, Evalena's Girl. God has sent you to me."

Wanda nearly laughed, but she saw the light of advantage. "I guess you have a plan to get the old place back."

"I have the most of one, but we won't talk of it now. I think you can make Hargis your puppy dog. If you don't want to do that, you can go back where you come from. You understand?"

Wanda stood and walked to the door. "I guess I do."

"I ain't said you should leave yet."

"If you want my help, you won't tell me when to come and go."

Lucie wiggled her hand like she was trying to find her words. "Then ... go help Piney."

"That I'll do." But make Hargis her puppy dog? Nothing from Lucie would come easy. Maybe instead she'd steal Piney away, something Evalena would approve. With that thought, she closed the door.

Sunlight fell across the pond. Piney stood in the water among green lily pads and yellow flowers, slicing at stems below the water. Her cheeks were pink, her pale hair shone, and from a distance she looked young.

At the pond's edge, Wanda sat on a rock and pulled off boots, stockings, and the trousers under her dress. She waded carefully into the pond.

"You don't have to come in here," Piney said. "You'll get your dress dirty."

"I got another in my saddlebags." Unaccustomed to walking in waist-high water, she took a step to widen her stance. Her toes sank in mud. Her skirt floated and she pressed it down. "I'd like to help."

"Oh. Well, you need a knife."

Piney had a heavy knife with a long blade. Wanda's hunting knife was shorter, but its blade was broad and thick.

"We cut lilies back every summer to keep them from filling the whole pond. A little is pretty, a lot is bad."

"Ain't it the way."

"They grow back. Sometimes I cook a few, just for something different, but none of us cares for the taste. I like being in the water, don't you?"

"It's colder than I expected."

"It's spring-fed, takes near to August to warm up." Piney paused and watched a brown mother duck and two fuzzy babies paddling near. "The poor thing hatched ten ducklings. Every night, something takes a few more."

"Foxes? Owls?"

Piney bent and pushed her arms into the water. "There's all kinds of varmints waiting to take advantage. Every time I love something, it disappears."

Wanda could understand a varmint killing to feed her young, but not a mother who ruined her daughters for the pleasure of getting rich. Lucie took advantage of Piney's softness. It frightened her to think she herself might do the same, not just with Piney, but Evie too.

Something moved at the edge of her vision. Smiling wide, Hargis leaned against the rock beside her shoes and trousers. He reached down, picked a blade of grass, chewed.

She reached underwater, grasped a stem with her left hand, cut it with the knife and tossed the severed lily to the bank.

Hargis leaned back on his elbows. "I sure like what I see."

She cut another stem. "We're not here for your entertainment."

"Pay him no mind," Piney said. But her bright cheeks drooped.

Wanda bent, cut, and tossed lilies to the bank.

Hargis made a show of eye-popping and licking his lips. "How's that water feel on your legs? Cold? Come here, I'll warm you up. One or both of you, I'm good for it."

She caught Piney's eye. "Is he always like this?"

"I'm sorry. Try not to see him."

He hung her trousers around his neck and put one of her stockings between his teeth. Something had made him bold. Permission from Lucie?

"Come on! Come on!"

She'd never been able to stay away from a fight. Her feet were in cool mud and half her body in cold water, but heat rushed from her toes to her scalp. Homer had likened her anger to an ax head flung from its handle, useless for getting the job done. She cupped her hands and splashed water on her face. The water might as well have been hot.

"That's it," Hargis called. "Wet yourself down!" He fanned his face with his hat. "Hoo! What a wet dress does to a man!"

She sloshed out of the water, swinging her knife. Her skirt slapped against her legs, and she pulled the cloth away to walk without stumbling.

Hargis wiggled on the rock. "Hoo-hoo, honey!" He hollered until she brought up the knife and touched it to his throat.

He leaned back. "Careful, now."

"Hoo-hoo," she said. "Stay clear of us."

He flung out his arms. "What am I doing? Sitting here."

Piney came running. "Wanda. Give the knife to me."

She tossed it in the grass.

"There now," he said. "Play fair."

His laugh was deep with satisfaction, like the boy who'd swung her cat by its tail. Like the one who'd jumped on her back and taken her knife. Like the boys who'd held her down in the woods.

She unfastened her belt and grasped the buckle. Her fingers trembled. "Fair?" She whipped the strip of leather at his head.

"Hoo!" He scooted backwards over the rock, giggling and shivering like she was tickling his skin.

She slapped the belt on the rock. "What's fair?" Hit his legs, arms.

He crossed his arms over his face. "Hey! I said be careful!"

Someone else was calling. Piney.

Hargis rolled off the rock, got to his feet and danced around. "Hoo-hoo! Come on, Sweetheart!" He grabbed at her skirt.

She swung the belt in circles, stinging herself.

Piney caught her around the waist and dragged her away. Wanda dropped to her knees.

Hargis whooped. "Oh, Ma, ain't she hot!"

"Hargis," Piney said. "Take yourself off."

Wanda knelt on the ground, aware of him jogging toward the cottage, turning, walking backwards, hooting. "Oh, Ma!"

Piney stooped and stroked her back. "Honey, don't worry. We'll take care of you."

Her nose dripped. Somewhere, Hargis was still laughing. Not at the cottage. Lucie stood there, her face darkened by a wide-brimmed hat.

Piney tucked her in bed and laid a wet cloth on her forehead. "I'm sorry Hargis was rude."

Ruth came in and sat at her feet. "Your ma had her rages. And Hargis and Ma together can be too much for any sane person."

But they'd won, because she'd hardly been sane. She'd have to do better.

CHAPTER 6

She lay awake on Ruth and Piney's bed, arms and legs like water, images of her ma and Evie flashing behind closed eyelids until her heartbeat slowed and her head no longer felt squeezed in a vise.

The odor and sizzle of frying fat drew her as far as the kitchen doorway. A table for four crowded the kitchen alcove, Lucie and Ruth at the ends and Hargis on a bench against the wall. He winked. She'd get nothing to eat without a measure of trouble.

Lucie rapped her cane on the bench where Hargis sat. "Evalena's Girl, there's your place." Piney set a platter of crisp potatoes on the table and flashed a timid smile. Ruth's shrug urged her to forget everything.

Those at the table sat close enough to eat from each other's spoons. Hargis shifted on the bench, grinned his gummy smile and patted the space beside him.

She frowned at Lucie. "I'd just as leave take my meals outside."

Lucie passed a platter of small fish, headless, gutted and fried. "What's put on the table is ate here. If you find food outside, you can eat it there."

Piney's forehead wrinkled. "It's bluegill, bony and not many bites, but sweet and good."

The aromas undid her. She side-stepped in the space between Lucie's chair and the wall, hating that she was hungry enough to sit beside Hargis.

They ate without conversation. Piney sat across from Hargis and Wanda, smiling each time Wanda looked up from her plate. Lucie pried away the skin and thin fish skeleton with her fingers. Ruth attended to her pint of deep red wine.

Until his plate was empty, Hargis got his elbows in her way and chewed with his mouth open, spraying bits with every turn of his head. When he'd asked in vain for more, he pressed his leg against hers. She pulled her skirt away and set her coffee mug on the bench so the hot liquid slopped on his trousers.

Ruth smiled when he flinched. Lucie wiggled her arm across the table. "Ruth, don't hog that wine, get up and pour a glass for the girl, there."

Wanda motioned Ruth to keep her seat.

Lucie waved her fork. "It's time we got ourselves a still. So tomorrow, Hargis and me and Evalena's Girl is gonna go get Virgie White's boiler and such."

Neither Ruth nor Piney said anything. Hargis poked Wanda with his elbow, and she scooted farther away, so she was only half-sitting on the bench. What kind of man liked a woman in a fit? Maybe he figured to make her his puppy dog.

Lucie frowned. "Hargis says it's only a little turnip still, but Virgie's place is not much more'n a day away, and the turnip's a handy size to carry. It'll give us a start toward building something bigger, maybe here, maybe at the old home place." Lucie passed her empty plate to Piney. "We'll leave for Virgie's tomorrow. Early."

Wanda pushed her last bit of potato around on her plate. "I'll pass on your kind offer. I been on a horse the best part of three days, so I'm not inclined to get back on right away."

Ruth grinned.

Lucie might not have heard. "We need to teach Evalena's Girl the business. There's future generations to be thought of."

Wanda had spoken true—she didn't want to get back on that horse, especially not for a trip with Hargis and Lucie. She also liked the idea of a day or two with nobody but Ruth and Piney. "I said, I'll stay put."

Lucie pointed a crooked finger. "Right here and now, Evalena's Girl, is where you decide if you're in this family or not. I'm the one says who stays and who goes. If you don't want to go with me and Hargis to Virgie's, fine and dandy. You can light out tomorrow and keep on going."

It was like being the young bull, going head to head with the old one, gaining ground, losing. "If that's what you want. I guess it's time to go."

Murmuring, Piney grabbed up dirty plates and carried them to the sink.

Ruth poured more wine into her glass.

"Lucie," Hargis said. "Don't be hasty."

"She's made her choice." Lucie set her lips.

Ruth lifted her glass to Wanda. "Good for you. But I'm sorry for it."

She'd had no time to decide how to deal with Lucie, and now she'd trapped herself into giving up her prospects. She brightened her face for Ruth. "Our time has been too short. I hope we'll meet again."

Lucie got up, grunting, and left the kitchen. Hargis whispered, "I'll talk with her."

"Don't bother yourself," Wanda said. Hargis and Ruth followed Lucie. Wanda helped Piney clear the table.

Piney brushed away a tear. "You've just come."

"I'll be back some day." If nothing worse happened. Maybe when Lucie was dead and gone.

"Ma says you have a little girl. I'd like to see her."

"Her name is Evie, after my ma. She'll love you and your pretty place."

"Evie, I like that. Ma and Pa scared me when I was little, but if you bring Evie I'll make Ma behave if I have to shut her in her room. I'm sorry how she does things."

Wanda was sorry Piney had to stay with her. "Go with me, tomorrow. I'll take you all the way to Fargo. Ruth can come, too."

"Wouldn't that be nice? But Ma would never agree."

"Does it matter?"

"You see how she needs me. It works better to let her have the say. It's how we get along."

"She'll have you marry Hargis."

Piney dabbed the edge of her apron to her forehead. "I'd like some babies."

"Ahh. You're a sweet woman, Aunt Piney. You don't have to tie yourself to Hargis. There's lots of men better."

"Not hereabouts. Only old ones, the young all leave. And I'm not young neither." She giggled. "I loved a boy once. If I'd laid down with him like he wanted, I might have a big girl by now. Grandbabies, too."

"Come to Fargo and I'll find you another man."

Piney hugged her. "Would you do that? I believe you would."

"Don't tell Granny. In the morning, we'll up and go. Now do you want me to wash or dry?"

"You go along. You've got a hard trip tomorrow. With Ma gone, me and Ruth will work lighter. And I don't need a man. You come back and bring your little girl. She can be baby for us all."

Whose victory was it? Lucie had the last say, but might have put an end to future generations. Wanda had nothing to take home for Evie, and there'd been no chance to make Lucie pay for the ruin of her ma. She hadn't cured her fits, but she'd found Piney and Ruth. With them, she might have returned to herself.

She sat astride the mare and tied the strings of her straw hat under her chin. Ruth had convinced her not to travel alone, but to ride with Lucie and Hargis as far as Winkler.

Lucie stood beside the wagon and fumbled with a blanket on the bench. When it was arranged to her liking, she pulled herself into the wagon and sat beside Hargis. Piney set two bedrolls, a basket of boiled potatoes and a jug of Ruth's wine in the wagon bed.

"Get my shotgun," Lucie said. Ruth brought the gun and a handful of shells. Lucie propped the gun between her and Hargis and dropped the shells into her apron pocket.

More seemed to be going on than these people bothered to explain. There had to be a road out that a wagon could travel, but nobody said why Ruth and Piney, who were supposed to be staying home, rode ahead on their brown plow horse, double and bareback. Like Wanda, they wore trousers under their hiked-up skirts. They led the wagon past the pond, the field of young corn, and on across the meadow. One of the black and white dogs ran alongside.

Beside Hargis, Lucie sat straighter, looking in all directions, fidgety as a kid going on a picnic. At the edge of the trees, Ruth and Piney slid down from the plow horse and started moving a pile of dead brush. A downed tree lay underneath.

Lucie pushed Hargis's shoulder. "Don't sit there like a log. Evalena's Girl, you too. Get down and help."

Hargis flexed his shoulders and hefted the tree, a tall white oak about eight inches across. Wanda, Piney, and Ruth helped push it up and over the other way. They stepped back as it crashed down and cleared the entry to a roadway of straggly grass.

Piney and Ruth led them through a tunnel of trees and stopped at another pile of brush. Lucie ordered them down to clear it. This pile hid the entrance to a better-used road.

Hargis pushed back his hat. "Whadda ya know."

"Ruth, look out and make sure no one's coming," Lucie said.

Ruth made a show of spying up and down the road. "Don't see or hear a soul."

"Hurry then."

Ruth grinned at Wanda. "We been going this way off and on for years. Ma thinks nobody knows."

"A little concealment keeps out riff-raff," Lucie said. "Hargis, get in the wagon. Ruth and Piney will put the brush back after we're out."

Hargis drove through the opening. "This road is new to me. Which way?"

Lucie pointed left.

Piney wrapped her arms around Wanda. "Thank you for coming. Thank you for the salve. I haven't had a present since your ma left home."

Held close, Wanda blotted her damp cheeks on Piney's shoulder.

"Don't forget to come back," Piney said.

"Never fear, I'll see you in no time." The very thing she'd said to Evie, who'd run to May Rose like it didn't matter. "Aunt Piney, don't let anyone tell you what to do, including me. Decide for yourself."

"Let's get going," Lucie said.

Ruth and Piney began dragging brush over the opening, and soon they were hidden. Looking back for a landmark, Wanda saw nothing to show where the Bosell road began, only faint wheel marks in a ditch at the roadside.

Wanda let the mare lag behind. Time and again she'd argued with Homer that it was a lot more interesting to do whatever came to mind and not think about it too much. Thinking always brought up problems and set people worrying. But following her urge to resist Lucie in a small way had ruined her chance for a grander effect. Ahead, Lucie slumped on the wagon bench, a woman with a gun who appeared to regret nothing and grieve no one. It might take a disaster to make her say she was sorry.

At the first fork in the road, Hargis pulled back on the reins. "Which way?"

When Lucie pointed right, he turned the wagon onto a dirt road. "Ah." He twisted in his seat and sent a proud look to Wanda. "Now I know where I am."

The shaded slopes along the new road were like all the others: mossy rocks, ferns, and lichen-covered trees. She wished she could carry them home.

Lucie allowed no stop until they reached Winkler. When Will's barking dogs raced to meet them, the store door opened and a woman appeared on the top step, hands shading her eyes.

Hargis stopped the mules. "Why, I believe it's Virgie."

Lucie sat straighter as Virgie ran down the steps. "You two don't say nothing. I'll talk for myself."

He wiped his forehead with a kerchief and flopped it toward Virgie. "Lucie, this here's Virgie White."

"I've heard of you," Lucie said. "You're a pretty lady. I'm pleased to meet'cha."

Wanda lifted a stiff leg over her horse and dropped to the ground. Finding Virgie in Will's town was another irritation.

"I'm proud meet you, too, Miss Lucie." Looking past Lucie, Virgie stretched her arms wide. "Is that Wanda I see?"

"Wanda? Why yes, that's her, my Evalena's Girl."

Wanda did not miss the sugar in Lucie's voice nor the sharp look telling her to play nice. She stepped away from the horse to protect it from a possible collision of Virgie and herself. Sure enough, Virgie squeezed her in a hug.

Shading her eyes, Lucie checked the sky. "Hargis, help me down. I believe we'll stop here. Mrs. White, I'm glad to see you and my Evalena's Girl is friends."

Wanda smirked.

Virgie danced her over to Lucie's wagon. "We been through things together, Miss Lucie. Wanda was my only consolation when John…" She sniffed.

Wanda's horse walked off toward the river.

Lucie clung to Hargis's arm. "We was sorry to hear of your trouble, Mrs. White, but happy our girl was with you in your grief. You two have that in common—she lost her man a short while back."

Virgie's mouth dropped open. "Wanda, you never said. No wonder you was so understanding."

Wanda loosened Virgie's hold. "I gotta get my horse." She glanced across the valley. No sign of Will. She wanted to say goodbye, say she'd like to see him in Fargo. Maybe he'd come.

"Evalena's Girl, let Hargis get your horse. You come with me." Lucie wrapped her claw around Wanda's wrist. "Where's the outhouse?"

"Inside. Will's got a toilet."

"Better take me there now."

Lucie might be play-acting, but she leaned heavily on Wanda's arm as they climbed the steps. In the wash room, Wanda showed her how to pull the chain to flush the toilet.

Lucie backed to the toilet and pulled up her skirts. "Now, pay attention. Go out and tell Hargis to say nothing about us buying Virgie's still or getting back into the business." She paused halfway to the seat. "What you smiling at?"

"I'm on my way home. You told me to go."

Lucie sat. "I've changed my mind."

"Change it all you want, I told you I wasn't going to Virgie's."

"All right, that'll be fine. You can lay over here or go home and help Ruth and Piney. Right now, tell Hargis, and make sure he knows what you're saying. Sometimes he's like a mule that needs knocking in the head." Lucie flapped her hand. "Get along. I may need to sit here a while."

A small victory. Wanda liked it, just as she liked how Lucie thought she'd carry out her order, something she'd do by half. First, tell Hargis not to mention the still, then spoil Lucie's secrecy by telling all to Virgie. Then she'd go back to Ruth and Piney or leave for Fargo if the mood struck. Maybe out of the blue, just turn away from them and ride toward Elkins. Enjoy the surprise on Lucie's face. No, she wouldn't. Going before she had what she'd come for would be like Lucie, cutting off her nose to spite her face.

She found Virgie first, not outside with Hargis, but curled up on Will's lap, with her hair nearly hiding his face. Wanda breezed by, deciding Virgie deserved no warning of Lucie's intentions. "Pardon the interruption. Pay me no mind."

"Wanda!" Will jumped like he'd sat on a hot cinder, throwing Virgie into a stumble. They steadied her between them. His face was red again. "I didn't know you were here."

Virgie squeezed his arm to her side. "I see you've met my friend Doc."

Wanda gave each her sweetest smile. "Indeed I have." No reason to feel jealous—she hadn't known him long enough. And he wasn't the first man to be trapped by a silly woman, though if he were Charlie, she'd sit him down for a talk. "Excuse me. Lucie's in the wash room and I'm on my way to help Hargis."

Hargis was at the river, watering the mules. She delivered Lucie's message as ordered.

His face screwed up. "Don't Lucie want to buy Virgie's still no more?"

"I'd say she wants to bring up the subject in her own way. Don't blab about her getting into the business, neither."

"What do I say when they ask why we come all this way?"

"For heaven's sake. We came for store goods, we came to see about selling corn, or some such. You came along to drive."

When they brought the mules back to the hitching post, Lucie came to the steps with more orders. "Unharness them mules and turn them into Doc's field, then bring my goods inside. I've decided we'll stay awhile. Doc's gonna feed us."

It was time to choose. She was back in Lucie's favor, and her horse stood ready. She held the reins and leaned her forehead on its neck. No risk, no reward.

She led the horse into Will's fenced field and carried her saddlebags to the store.

CHAPTER 7

Wanda paced the store, listening while she pretended interest in items on the shelves. At Will's table, Lucie and Virgie sat with two glasses and the jug of Ruth's wine between them. Will worked at the stove, half-turned their way. From his perch on a counter, Hargis appeared fixed on Will's hands slicing onions and potatoes into an iron skillet.

After a while she settled on a stool that allowed a view of everyone. Will kept glancing around like he expected something bad to happen. He'd tried for a private word, but with so many present, it was easy to dodge him. He shouldn't think a few playful kisses at Lucie's meant he had to explain Virgie on his lap.

One of Virgie's hands clasped her wine glass; the other lay limp on the table. Lucie reached forward and patted the free hand. "Hargis says you and him's gonna carry on your business."

Virgie sighed and drained her glass. "What else can I do?" She didn't seem to be bothered by Lucie's habit of thrusting her head forward at an angle and peering from the corner of one eye.

Lucie motioned to Wanda and pointed to Virgie's empty glass. Wanda moved to the table, tipped the jug, poured, and returned to her stool.

"It's a hard life," Lucie said. "The business has always been full of trouble—not to mention thieves and tax men. I had more than one load emptied out and been reported by varmints who was in the business theirselves. But there was my girls to take care of, so I was like you—I had to go on."

Lucie brought a kerchief from her apron pocket, blew her nose and angled the other eye toward Virgie. "If I was you, Mrs. White, I'd worry about them revenuers." She tucked the kerchief up her sleeve. "Hargis says your setup is along a good road. If the tax men don't come after you, some other scoundrels will. They like those easy places."

Virgie turned her glass between her hands. "John talked about moving somewhere safe."

The room filled with the hearty odor of sizzling onions. Wanda liked how Will shoved a spatula and flipped the potatoes. She supposed he was used to feeding guests, like Roy at Jennie Town. He kept switching his attention from the skillet to Lucie. Or was it Virgie in his sights? Had he pulled her on his lap or had she dropped herself there?

Lucie and Virgie seemed comfortable together, one a mama cat, the other her pet mouse.

"I missed out on the good money like there is now," Lucie said, "but business has got more risky. Even so, I wouldn't mind making a turn of corn whiskey every few years, just for ourselves, times of sickness and all."

"Miss Lucie, I think you'd be a good partner for someone like me. You wouldn't have to do the work." Virgie covered her mouth for a quiet belch that heaved her shoulders. "Just be a guide for me and Hargis, tell what-all you know."

Lucie's head bobbed. "My memory ain't all that good, and like I say, I wouldn't get into selling, not rough as things are. But now and then I think of getting me a little still, just for my own self."

Wanda half-admired how proudly Lucie lied.

"Potatoes are ready," Will said.

She ate at the table with Lucie and Virgie. For a time the only sounds were forks scraping across plates. Then Virgie drained her third glass of wine and stood unsteadily, giving a wild look around the room and knocking her chair to the floor. "I gotta go home. I been away too long and my still ain't safe. It may already be stole or broke up!"

Lucie nodded like a wise old soul. "Dear girl, I hope to heaven you're wrong. But you're right about one thing. This business is a target for bad people." She pushed herself up. "You being a widow, I naturally want to help, so I'll take the whole kit out of your way, barrels and jugs, stir sticks and swabbers, what e'er you got."

Virgie fell on Lucie in a hug, unbalancing the tottery old woman, then let go and stumbled over her chair. Will hurried to help.

It was Wanda's hand that caught and steadied Virgie, but the new widow's smile was all for Will. They guided her to the door.

Lucie tapped her cane. "Hargis, you go with Virgie and help carry her equipment. Evalena's Girl and me don't need to go. We'll wait over."

"You don't mean today," Hargis said. "It's late to be starting."

Lucie arched her straggly eyebrows. "Go now, and you can get back here tomorrow night."

Hargis slid off the counter. "Yeah, maybe."

"She'll sober up on the way," Lucie said. "Make sure you cover the wagon and tie it down tight."

"Your wagon or hers?"

"Hers, a'course. No need to wear out our mules."

Hargis wagged his finger at Wanda and Will. "You-all be good, now." He slammed the door, rattling the glass and jangling the bell.

Lucie raised her voice. "Doc, maybe could you help Hargis harness up Virgie's mule?"

Will wiped the skillet with paper, hung it on the wall, and left without a word.

Lucie wagged a crooked finger. "I don't think Doc's friendly to the business, but him and me is gonna have a little talk. You say nothing."

Wanda helped Lucie outside where she clung to the railing with one hand and waved to Virgie with the other. When they came in, Lucie motioned Will to the table. "You sit down. She'll wash up." She motioned Wanda to take away the dishes.

"You're paying guests," Will said. "Wanda doesn't have to do that."

"She's glad to help. You and me's got business."

Wanda handled the plates quietly, not wanting to miss a word of Lucie trying to out-fox Will.

He brought a pencil and notebook from the counter. What do you need?"

"Three-four hundred pounds of sugar, Mason jars."

"Whiskey business." He tossed the book to the counter and stuck the pencil in a shirt pocket. "You lied to Virgie about making corn liquor for yourself."

"My thoughts on that has changed. Do you want to sell to me or not?"

"With a big load of sugar, revenue men will follow me all the way from Staunton. And revenuers won't be the worst of it. You said it yourself: risky business and bad people."

"Risky for infants and fools," Lucie said. "Them like Virgie. You've no need to worry for me."

"I worry for lots more than you."

Wanda rubbed a white platter till it shone.

"Doc, sit down here and think again." Lucie's voice purred. "You're not against liquor. Somebody's gonna supply the trade. You been supplying it all along."

"If I did, it was in a small way, and I didn't know about it."

"What's the difference? Whiskey ain't bad in itself. No doubt you take a drink now and then. What's bad is people that uses it wrong."

So in Lucie's judgment, Evalena was bad. Likewise, Ruth. Wanda stopped enjoying the argument.

"You're putting your family in danger," Will said.

"Don't be silly. Nothing is safe forever. I heard your own pa was shot, right in this town."

He took a frayed straw hat from a wall hook. "No sugar. Not more than five pounds at a time."

"All right. I can do without."

"I've a cornfield to hoe," he said. You ladies make yourself comfortable."

When he left, Lucie pushed herself upright. "I must of had too much wine myself, for that didn't go as I meant. I'm disappointed in Doc, but I believe he favors you. So it's your turn, Evalena's Girl. We don't want him calling the law on us. Be nice, anyhow he wants. Do you catch my meaning?"

"I like Will."

"I said, do you know what I mean?"

"I guess I do. I'm not sure he likes me that way."

"He's a man, and most of the time has no one but himself. He'll like you."

"Well, thanks for the compliment. Whatever he wants, then. Forget making a pet of Hargis."

"For the time being."

While Lucie napped in the back room, Wanda sat in the grass and watched Will hoe weeds in the long rows of his corn patch.

Halfway through, he flopped down beside her. "I didn't mean to get so mad."

She shaded her eyes against the sun. "You did fine. I liked it."

He had an unsettling smile.

"So," she said. "You and Virgie."

"I was in the storeroom, and when I came out, she surprised me."

"And then I surprised you."

He lay back and rolled to his side. "I don't like to see Lucie giving you orders."

Fresh air had sweetened his sweat. She leaned close, smiled. "I do what I want. Remember that."

After supper, Lucie claimed the washroom. Wanda sat on a one of the beds, weighing loyalties. First, to Evalena and Evie. Next, to other family, which included May Rose, Ruth and Piney, but left out Lucie. Then Will. She wouldn't use him to please Lucie.

Wanda finally had her turn in the washroom, but when she came out, the door to her sleeping room was locked. She pounded and rattled the knob. "Granny. Open the door!" Lucie didn't answer.

She put her face close to the door. "I know what you're doing."

From inside, a snore. Faked.

Will stepped out from his room. "Can I help?"

She had not yet undressed. The night had gone cool, but she could sleep in the store. "She's locked me out. Do you have another blanket? A cot?"

"I have a skeleton key."

She went to his door. "This is one of Granny's games. I'll play my own. Let her think I slept with you. She won't know the difference."

"Lucie wants...? I see. I'll sleep out front, you can have my bed."

She peered inside. Tall cabinets of natural pine stood against the walls, one with a padlock, one with trousers hanging on the open doors. His bed was also of pine, stout and four-postered. "Did you make all this?"

"I did. All plain. I have no time for fancy-work."

She took his stained, calloused hand. "Stay and talk. I'm lonely, too."

They sat on his bed while he spoke of raising goats and corn, digging coal, reading medicine, and his hopes for Trading Days. A kind, deserving man with never a brag. His hands rested on his legs. Every bit of him nice to look at. It was easy to think, "Why not?"

"This isn't for Lucie," she whispered, when they stretched out side by side.

Lying close after he fell asleep, she couldn't imagine leaving.

CHAPTER 8

With no window for starlight, Will's room was black as a cave, so when Wanda woke, she had no way to know if it was night or day. Fumbling for the bedcover, she touched a full-length source of warmth. Will Herff.

She pulled the quilt over her head and scooted closer, laid her hand on his hip bone and breathed against his back to warm her face. He rolled over and stretched, squeaking the bedsprings. They squeaked again as he sat up against the headboard. Warm hands reached under her armpits and pulled her beside him. The quilt dropped to her lap, baring her chest.

She dragged the quilt to her chin. "You've got no heat in here."

He yawned. "In winter, I put a cot by the stove, or let the dogs in—one at my back, one at my front, one to keep my feet warm."

She put cold feet against his leg. "That's only three."

"The other never comes inside. He's like a lot of folks, doesn't know what's good for him."

She laid her arm across his belly and tucked herself closer.

"Uh, oh," he said. He slid both of them down and pinned her with one arm and one heavy leg. "Got you."

Little by little they tangled themselves until she threw off the quilt to let the cold air dry their sweat. She woke again with Will curled to her back, one of his arms under her neck and the other draped over her chest. A thin strip of light at the bottom of the door made the room less black.

His lips brushed her ear. "I hate being grateful to Lucie."

"I'd of got here somehow." She closed her eyes and listened to the rise and fall of his breath.

He rolled over and sat up. "Don't go back with Lucie. When she leaves, I'll ride with you as far as Elkins. We'll have our photographs made. You can take one of me to May Rose."

A photograph? He was in a mighty hurry for her to leave. She put her legs over the side of the bed. She had a photograph of Homer in his coffin, no comfort at all. Maybe for Will, being alone was easy, maybe he liked his life empty.

She wiggled into her clothes and laced her boots. "Speaking of Lucie, you're not to call the law on her, and I'm to do whatever you want for the favor. I guess I've done that, so it's your turn." She left while she still had the last word.

In the hall, Lucie stood at the washroom door, smiling. "Ah, well and good. Now build us a fire—this place is wintery."

Wanda stirred the embers in the cook stove and added wood while Lucie huddled on a low stool. Will came out and poured coffee beans in the grinder. While he turned the crank, she set a pan of water to boil.

Lucie muttered about the cold. Aware of Will's every step, Wanda poured hot water over the ground beans in the top of the pot and listened while it dripped through.

He fried mush and they ate together at the table, neither saying more than "Pass the syrup." With her feelings torn up, mush and coffee settled poorly in her stomach.

After breakfast, she sat alone in the store, looking through Will's medical books at skeletons and people whose skinned-off bodies looked ropy as squirrels. In *Haydn's Dictionary of Popular Medicine*, she read a small note about fits: "a person suddenly falls down insensible." Nothing about a person raging like a demon. It helped to know she hadn't frightened Ruth and Piney, and hadn't shown that side of herself to Will.

She read a long passage about blood, but found nothing about blood poisoning. Homer's doctor had called it sep-something. Homer would know the name. So would Will.

She couldn't go home with nothing. The trip was too long and cost too much. Will hadn't said he'd be sorry to see her leave, but maybe he needed a chance to explain himself. With more time, he might ask her to stay and give the two of them a try. Not that she felt like it at the moment.

She gave up on understanding anything from books and followed a sound of tapping to the storeroom. Will sat below the high windows, fitting mirror glass into a cherry wood frame. Hunched on a stool nearby, Lucie squinted from him to Wanda. "This man's hands are never idle. I wish I'd had a husband like him."

He did not turn around. Wanda ambled among tall stacks of wooden boxes, clusters of wagon wheels, axles and oily machine parts, thinking of his hands. She stopped and pulled clothes from a cedar-lined trunk.

"Dead people's things," Lucie said.

"None of the dead's wearing them." She put her arms into the sleeves of a man's canvas jacket, double breasted, with wide lapels, a lining of red plaid, and a bulge in an outside pocket. The jacket was big enough for two of her. She shoved her hands in the pockets and felt a pouch of coins.

"Will. Is this your jacket?"

He tapped a finishing nail at the edge of the mirror frame and glanced over his shoulder. "Outa that trunk? Something I traded."

"Is it for sale?"

"Take anything you want."

Her fist wrapped around the coins. "Thank you, then, I will." She re-folded the jacket, linen shirts, woolen trousers, boy-sized knickers. "These are nice things. Where'd you come across this trunk?"

"I got it with other stuff from the Cotton brothers. They traded for coal and all the sugar I had." He paused. "Said they were buying for their neighbors."

Lucie wagged her finger. "See? People needs sugar, and there's lots of uses. Who's to know?"

Will set the framed mirror on a stack of three. "Lucie, I'm trying to grow a decent town here, and I want to be on the good side of the law. Plus it bothers me to lie."

"Well la-di-da," Lucie said. "I'm sure even the law lies on occasion."

The coins felt large and heavy enough to be gold. Wanda's thoughts warmed. "What other kinds of stuff did you get?"

"Knick-knacks, pictures, rugs. I sold all of that last Trading Day. I forgot to put out the trunk or it would of sold too."

"I might need wintery clothes," she said. "Piney's handy with a needle—she'll help me make these over."

Will frowned. "You're not going home?"

Like she should do what he said. "Not this exact minute."

She carried the jacket and knickers to the washroom and locked the door. The coins in the pouch were Liberty twenty-dollar pieces, gold. Ten of them. A small fortune.

Lucie rapped the washroom door. "My turn."

She brushed the coins into their pouch and squeezed past Lucie at the doorway. Will came into the hall as she ducked into Lucie's room. His steps stopped on the other side of her door. "Wanda."

She stuffed the pouch under a mattress and met him in the hall.

Lucie came from the washroom and passed between them into her room. "If you two don't mind, I'll have my rest."

Will took Wanda's hand. "Whatever I did, I'm sorry. Don't stay mad."

She bent her head. "I get moody." He might be no smarter about women than other men, but he was nicer than most. If she told him about the coins, he'd probably think she should find the owner.

Will left to shore up mine posts. Wanda lingered inside, listening to Lucie's snores, thinking what she could do with two hundred dollars in gold. She'd not part with it for no good reason. Maybe come right out and tell Will she wanted to stay with him, and if he liked that idea, show him the coins so they could decide together. Meantime, she needed Lucie to leave the room so she could hide them in her saddlebags.

Energized by these prospects, she went outside and walked to a street where he'd been fixing up houses. Making something better might be reason enough for all his efforts. She was not skilled like him, not even in womanly crafts of cooking and sewing, but she could be his helper. He'd said he was sorry. Anything was possible.

She stopped near a house with the upper story torn off. A bucket of bent nails and a claw hammer lay on the ground near a jumble of old framing lumber. He'd been pulling nails, sorting, and stacking this wood to use again. Sitting on an overturned bucket, she picked up the hammer and pried the claw against a nail. She liked how the nail resisted and then gave way, and how the sun was warm but the breeze cool. She wouldn't brag about her work, though maybe he'd notice some time and know she'd done it, and be pleased.

Pulling nails and stacking boards kept her busy until late afternoon. The smell of frying bacon drew her to the store.

Will turned from the stove when the doorbell jangled. "Thought you were lost."

She waved on her way to the washroom. "Not me, never."

Twice she opened and shut the washroom door, let the toilet cover bang on the seat, and sang while she washed, all to rouse Lucie from her nap. But Lucie didn't open her door until they called her for supper.

While they ate, Will talked about hiring a man and mule to haul railroad ties to the mine. She thought about being his helper and hoped he wouldn't expect her to dig coal. Before the meal was finished, Virgie and Hargis returned, and they all went outside.

Virgie's wagon was piled high with barrels. Hargis pulled one down and lifted the wooden lid to show the paddles, jugs and stir sticks inside. Another barrel held a sack of sugar and a copper coil.

Lucie lifted the cap of a blackened pot and thumped the bottom. "A good little turnip still. It'll do. Hargis, load all this in my wagon."

Hargis jumped down from the wagon. "It can wait till morning. Give me something to eat and show me my bed. I ain't had no sleep a'tall."

Shivering, Virgie hugged herself. "Miss Lucie, what're you offering to pay?"

Lucie leaned on Virgie's arm. "State your price. We'll get some serviceberry wine and talk; Evalena's Girl can unload the wagon. Doc, if you'll just go along and unhitch Virgie's mule…"

Virgie helped Lucie up the steps.

Wanda climbed into the wagon and Will drove it to Lucie's empty one. "May Rose wouldn't like to see you taking Lucie's orders," he said.

She balanced an empty barrel on the wagon edge. It was okay for him to take Lucie's orders, but not her? "You don't know much about May Rose anymore, and I see you know nothing about me. I do what Lucie says if I feel like it, and if I don't, I don't. Like right now, I feel like unloading this wagon.

Will eased the barrel to the ground. "So you're going back to her place?"

Straightening, she brushed dust from her skirt and tried to put a tease in her voice. "Do you have a better suggestion?"

"I'm not telling you what to do."

"You'll just let me know when you don't like it. So I think I'll bide with Granny a while longer."

He caught her wrist. "Because I've advised against it?"

She couldn't figure if he cared or needed to get rid of her. Maybe he was afraid to love a woman, or was holding out for a perfect, yielding woman. "I'm not being contrary, I have things to do, like helping my family. That includes Piney and Ruth."

Maybe he'd sent Virgie away too, and she'd married John as second choice. *Virgie.* Another reason she wasn't eager to go to Fargo. She pulled her wrist from his grasp. "Where will Virgie sleep tonight?"

He heaved the barrel into Lucie's wagon. "I don't know. Let her stay with Lucie."

"What about me?"

"Bed down in my room or double with her, whatever suits you."

Stay with him, but leave soon, the kind of man who'd drive her to fury.

"I'm not one to spite myself," she said. "It's gonna be another cold night."

He reached over the wagon side and whirled her to the ground. "I can always bring in the dogs. If you're just looking to be warm."

His hands at her waist made her weak, but she didn't care. "I'm sorry." Homer had never said a harsh word, though he'd had his silences. "I don't mean everything I say."

"How's a man to know?"

"I said I'm sorry. I don't often say that."

"I can tell."

"You're a hard nut." She stood on tiptoe and whispered close. He was grimy from the day's work. It didn't matter. "Do you want to fight or do that other thing?"

"Why would we fight?"

"I don't know. You're a dangerous man."

He took his hands away. "Maybe to someone with bad intentions."

They'd met four days ago, a short time for feelings to get so tangled.

The sky had darkened. She rested her head on his chest. So what if he didn't want a wife? There'd be no harm in another night of comfort.

They stretched and tied down the canvas, and she waited while he shoveled a bucket of coal from the pile behind the horse shed.

Shouts from inside reached them before they opened the door. Virgie pounded the table. "She's got no money! Me and Hargis whupped ourselves and about killed my mule to bring all this back in time, and she says she's got no money!"

"Doc, fetch us that wine," Lucie said.

Virgie shook her fist. "No more drink. Somebody make her pay."

Will pulled out chairs and urged them to sit. Wanda stacked the supper plates and eyed the path to the sink. Hargis sat on the store counter, eating cold beans. As she tried to pass, he pulled her skirt and patted the bedroll at his side. "Here's a nice warm place."

She frowned at his fingers.

He whispered. "I'm ready, honeybunch. Get out that belt."

She tested herself: no seize of breath, no heat, no crazy pounding heart. Satisfied, she tipped her stack of plates so one slid off and knocked his plate to the floor. It was a fool thing to do, for he laughed as beans flew and his plate rolled away on edge.

Behind them, Will shouted down the women's squabble. "A lot of us are tired. I don't tolerate fights or loud talk in here."

"Virgie." Lucie smoothed her voice the way people did when they wanted to show how nice and reasonable they were. "You got a choice—trust me or take back your junk. I thought I was helping."

"I gotta be paid," Virgie said.

"That'll happen. Come stay with us till we run off the first batch. When I sell some, you'll be the first I pay."

"You'll have to sell a lot to pay me."

Wanda snuck away to the room where she'd hidden the coins,

but as she fumbled under the mattress, Lucie stopped in the doorway. "I'll not have that woman coming with us." She shook a finger. "One of us has got to do something." She shuffled away to the washroom.

Upending the mattress, Wanda found the pouch caught in one of the coil springs. The toilet flushed. She lowered the mattress and pressed down on its top. With the pouch nestled in the spring, Lucie wouldn't notice. She turned down the lamp and left the room.

In the hall, Will put his hand on her back. "Time for us to disappear." He directed her into his room and shut the door.

Footsteps back and forth kept Wanda awake long after Will relaxed and his breathing calmed. Several times, doors to the back room and washroom opened and closed. The cooling air stripped her body heat, and she dressed in her clothes and scooted close, scolding herself for wanting him too much.

Sometime later, she woke to soft taps on the door and the rattle of the door knob. The skeleton key hit the floor. In the hall, someone whispered. "Doc. Sweetheart, let me in. Dammit, I'm freezing. Let me in."

She felt on the floor for the key, fumbled it into the lock and opened the door. Virgie's mouth gaped.

Wanda leaned her head against the door. "Not tonight, sweetheart."

CHAPTER 9

W ill sat on his side of the bed and pulled on long johns. Wanda had slept in her clothes. She lay curled under the quilt, watching him but listening for the others. A heavy tread in the hall. Hargis coughing, spitting. The toilet flushing. Footsteps back to the front, the push of a shovel into the coal bucket.

"I might close my eyes a while longer," she said.

"Do you want me to leave the lamp on?"

"I won't need it."

He buttoned his shirt. "I want you away from trouble."

"Me too." She had yet to confess the trouble in herself.

"I care what happens to you, and it has nothing to do with May Rose or old times."

She squirmed. "You can't help trying to save things. Even me."

When he didn't comment, she got to her knees on the bed and put her face against his. A kiss, she'd learned with Homer, bridged a lot of differences.

After Will left, she lay in her warm spot until Lucie's steps clunked past and her voice mixed with Virgie's at the front of the store. Then she laced her boots and tip-toed to Lucie's sleeping room. Its door stood open. Light from the hall windows showed the mattress slightly askew on its springs. She lifted the mattress, already angry, certain the pouch was gone. It was. She let the mattress drop. Lucie. Maybe Virgie. No, Lucie, half blind, but able to see the bulge in the jacket when she pulled it from the chest. Her own fault for not hiding the pouch far from Lucie's reach.

By the cook stove, she found Lucie the center of attention, gold gleaming in her outstretched hand. Lucie drew her forward with a rich smile. "My grandgirl gave me these to square my debts. Ain't she something?"

"Oh, she's something," Virgie said. Her glance at Wanda fell short of appreciation, but clearly she liked the sparkle in Lucie's palm.

Wanda clamped her lips and thought how she'd lure both Piney and Ruth to Fargo, with a stopover in Elkins to tell the law where to find Lucie Bosell.

Lucie let two coins clink into Virgie's hand. "Now you've been paid for your equipment, there's no need to bother coming home with us. For one thing, we ain't got a place for you to sleep. You're better off here, don't you think?"

Virgie winked at Wanda. "That's what Doc says, time to time."

Will's face was as blank as if he hadn't heard. He padded a cloth on the handle of the sputtering coffee pot and slid it off the stove's hot eye.

"We'll all stay friendly," Lucie said, "for who knows when we might need each other? For a start, Virgie, since you been paid over-generous, how about you settle with Doc what we owe for our food and all?"

The showdown with Lucie could wait. As for Virgie staying behind with Will, Wanda was well-practiced in pretending she didn't care, something learned when Winkler was a real town.

"Coffee's ready," Will said. He filled five white mugs and Hargis passed them around. Wanda stood near the door and sipped.

Lucie sat with her mug. "Be sure you and Virgie keep mum

about my purchase. If anybody strays onto our place, I might think you sent 'em."

"I won't be the one to put your family in trouble," Will said.

"Well and good. Now, Virgie, if any asks, you can say your still was stole."

Virgie smiled. "So it was."

When she'd drunk her coffee, Lucie passed her bedroll to Wanda and led the way outside. The valley floor sparkled white.

"Lord Almighty, we've had a frost," Lucie said. "What next, snow?"

Hargis grumped. "Killed our corn and beans, you bet'cha."

Everyone had a gloomy face but Virgie, who'd been paid in gold and might knock tonight on Will's door.

Hargis spat over the edge of the steps. "Doc, you got seed corn left?"

"Not a grain. And June is late to plant, unless the frost holds off till the end of October. This'll be hard."

"If they got seed, some will take a chance," Hargis said. "What grows will make fodder for the animals, even if it don't make ears. But think what this will do to prices. It's a good time for Lucie—she's got a full crib."

Lucie swatted her shawl across his face. "Keep that wisdom to yourself. It's bad enough 'shiners steal people's mash and whiskey without folks stealing corn to eat."

Will helped Wanda saddle her horse. She welcomed the excuse to stand close and talk in private. "I didn't give Lucie that gold," she said. It was too late to explain he'd recently owned it.

"I didn't suppose you did. Lucie seems fond of lying, and it's a gentle sample of what she'll do to get her way. Think on your dead grandpap. They say she don't like to be hindered in any way."

Like it or not, Granny deserved some hindering. She'd get the gold back and show Will she could take care of herself. Homer had never tried to talk her out of doing what she needed to do.

"Let's get going," Lucie said.

Wanda didn't like how Virgie slid her arm through Will's when they said goodbye, but she was plain disgusted at the interest in Hargis's eyes now that Lucie had made him think she was rich and generous.

The wagon load rattled and clanked.

"Hold up!" Lucie twisted in her seat. "All this commotion is a damn announcement." She pushed Hargis's shoulder. "Get down and fix it. Evalena's Girl, you too."

Will helped them untie the tarp, and together they wrapped metal pieces in blankets from their bedrolls and repacked everything.

Again they started. At the head of the valley their road turned toward the morning sun, and Wanda looked back at the mounds of boards and brush, Will's patches of progress. He might be wrong for her, but for sure, Virgie was wrong for him.

With the wagon loaded they traveled slower, giving Wanda more time to send evil thoughts toward Lucie's hunched back.

Mid-morning, a whistled tune rose above grinding wagon wheels and the clop of mule hooves, and a man on a high-stepping black horse rode up behind them. She noted his bedroll and saddlebags, the fiddle case strapped to his back, and his un-crumpled hat and shiny boots, too fancy for mountain travel.

On roads with lots of people, there was no need to stop and jaw with everyone you met on the way, but in the mountains, if you didn't exchange news and well-wishes, you'd be suspect. Besides, you never knew what might come from the mouth of a stranger. This one tipped his fine hat to Wanda as he passed.

Hargis stopped the mules. It was proper for him to do the talking, but Lucie jumped into the start of their conversation. "We're the Porters—back there is Wanda, my grandgirl, and this here's Hargis, my only boy."

Wanda couldn't help smiling at their new name, but looked down and patted her horse's neck when the stranger's dark eyes fixed on her.

His name was Price Loughrie, and according to his talk he

had nothing better to do than travel mountain roads, find music he hadn't heard before and make some along the way. As he and Hargis talked about fiddlers they'd met here and there, Loughrie's eyes studied like he was learning them. He drifted a finger toward the wagon bed. "You folks moving somewhere?"

Lucie touched Hargis's shoulder. "Sad to say, we are. We're headed for the lowlands in Virginia. Starting over where my boy can find work."

Loughrie nodded. "Paying work, never enough of that. Do you mind if I ride along for a while?"

"You're welcome," Lucie said. Hargis slapped the reins and the mules started.

Loughrie held his horse until Wanda reached him, then rode beside her. "You look like someone I seen before."

His long ears, long thin nose, and long brown beard drew down his face and made his eyes look sad. Curiosity got her. "Who would that be?"

"Well a girl, long time ago."

"A long time ago I was a kid, and since then I been in the State of North Dakota. Maybe you saw my aunt. Some say I take after her."

"Where's your aunt these days?"

"Over where we're going."

"Maybe I'll come along and see her."

Wanda smiled at the musical drone of his voice. "She's had two husbands and eight kids, and I don't think we look a'tall alike, but maybe that's 'cause she's lost her teeth."

Hargis gave a tight, sympathetic nod. When they approached the turn that would take them to Lucie's hidden drive, he snapped the reins and they rode on past.

The sad-eyed stranger whistled a lively tune, and Wanda wiggled a toe inside her boot and tapped a finger on her saddle. At the fork where the Bosell sign was propped against a tree, Hargis stopped the wagon and Lucie motioned Wanda forward.

"I need to go into the woods. Hargis, you stay till we get back, then you can go."

Wanda helped her down and held her arm while they climbed uphill over rough ground, with Lucie putting on a show of being feeble. "That man's a marshal," she whispered. "When you see Doc, tell him not to give us away if the marshal calls us Porter."

"I don't plan to see Will anytime soon."

"Leave that part to me."

"He said he's not gonna lie."

"He helped pack our goods, didn't he? Remind him of that."

Back at the wagon, Hargis and Loughrie looked to be swapping tales.

"Hargis, your turn, if you need to go," Lucie said.

"Might as well." Hargis jumped down and stood off the road behind a bush.

Loughrie helped Lucie into the wagon. "Bosells live on that road?" He pointed to the right fork.

Lucie shrugged. "Don't know. It's what the sign says."

"You going that way?"

"Nope, and never been."

"Then here's where we part." He tipped his hat to Lucie and to Wanda. "Maybe we'll meet again someday."

"We might just, if you're down Virginia way," Lucie said.

Hargis got back on the wagon seat and flicked the reins. Lucie watched Loughrie turn up the other road, then motioned for Wanda. "Hargis and me will go on. You stay here and watch to make sure our friend don't backtrack to follow us, but don't let him see you. After he's out of sight a while, come get us."

When Price rode over a rise and disappeared, Wanda caught up with the wagon.

"Up ahead's the horse trail down to our place," Lucie said. "You go that-a-way and tell the girls to clear the brush from the road. Tell them to wait there. Then you go on back to Winkler and tell Doc about us being the Porters."

Wanda didn't object to seeing Will again, but Lucie's hiding her name was silly. "What if Loughrie gets to Doc first, or comes while I'm there?"

"You're right," Lucie said. "If he sees you, he might think I wasn't truthful. Tell Ruth to go."

"He might be no more'n a fiddler," Hargis said.

"He's the law—I got a nose for it. If Virgie tells on us, one of you remember to shoot her in case I'm dead or locked up. It don't have to be right away, just sometime."

"Virgie's my family," Hargis said.

"She's no family if she tells on you. Remember that, Evalena's Girl."

Hargis turned the wagon around, and Wanda rode on. The path that dipped off the road still bore skid marks from her trip down with Will and Hargis, visible to anyone who might stop to piss or peer for any reason over the edge of the road.

When she reached the cottage, she found Ruth sprawled unconscious on her bed. "She's been drinking since you and Ma left," Piney said. "Finished off all her new wine, so when she comes out of this she'll be sober for a while. And mean."

Wanda went with Piney to uncover the road entrances.

Lucie grumped when Piney told her about Ruth. "Best of it is, there won't be nothing to make wine till the summer berries come on, so she'll be happy to work on the still. You, Evalena's Girl, get on to Doc's place and keep outa sight of that marshal.

It was mid-afternoon when Wanda came again to Will's valley. She found Virgie on the store steps, drying her hair in the sunshine. Virgie beamed. "Doc's gonna take me home for my goods, and I'm gonna have a house right here in Winkler!"

Wanda stayed on her horse. "Won't that be nice. Is he inside?"

"Digging coal up the holler."

She followed a path marked by coal dust to the mine entrance, a low opening framed by railroad ties. When she called, Will crawled out, his face and miner's cap black and a carbide light burning on a tin headband. He turned a screw to douse the light and wiped his face with a rag. "Ah. You're a nice sight. Had enough of Lucie?"

"I can take her." She slid down from the horse and peered into the mine. "This is bound to fall in on you someday."

"Don't worry about me. I'm greatly against risk to myself." He waved a hand toward the entrance. "I don't go too far inside. Working with Lucie is risky too. I'm hoping you've had a change of heart."

She resisted the urge to say how her heart felt when he was near. "We met a man Lucie says is a marshal, and she gave our name as Porter. Could you and Virgie play dumb if he asks about the Bosells?"

"Come here." He didn't wait for her to step closer, but passed a rough hand beneath her hair, drew her forward by the back of her neck, and wiped his lips on her forehead. Coal dust dropped from his cap to her eyelashes, cheeks, nose. She liked the smell of his sweat.

For devilment, she slipped her tongue between his lips then laughed at the surprise on him. "So. Virgie's gonna live here. Won't that be handy."

"I told you I want to build up the town." He squeezed her so hard it hurt.

"Do you plan to move the goods of every poor widow, or just the pretty ones?"

"I won't deny I've spent some time with Virgie, days past. She was about the only woman around. I never could live with her."

"You should have more control."

"Look who's talking."

"I'm always in control. Did you lay with Virgie?"

"None of your business."

"I'd say you did. You must like something about her."

"She's womanly."

"I'm womanly."

He looked down at the trousers showing beneath her hem, and her boots, dusty as his were black. "You kind of hide it."

"It's plain we're not suited. I won't have a man who's a fool for a silly woman."

He wiped her face with the underside of his shirttail. "As long as you're here, Virgie has no chance."

Was this an offer? He'd told her to go.

"I'm safer with Lucie. She don't pretend to like me."

Will dropped his hands to his sides. "What have I pretended? I like you as much as any woman I've met."

"You don't know me that well."

She'd lain awake at night, thinking how the fits felt when they were coming on. If she learned to hold off Hargis without getting crazy, she might be safe for Evie and Will. "I need to stay with Granny a while longer." Until she had the gold, until she taught Granny a lesson, until she stopped being crazy. Or maybe only until Will made a real offer.

He pushed the coal cart and she rode beside him. "Remember about that marshal. If he trails after us again, I think Granny will shoot him. Price Loughrie's his name."

"Ah, poor Price. Lucie may be right—he's been connected to the law in his day. But last I saw him, he was flat-out drunk."

At the store they found Virgie on the steps, still brushing her hair. Wanda leaned down and kissed Will for Virgie to see. "Remember, we're the Porters, and you don't know any Bosells. Tell Virgie, too."

He grabbed the ankle of her boot like he was going to pull her from the saddle.

She caught her breath, hoping he could see how much she wanted to stay. "I have to go."

He released her ankle and walked away.

~

When she reached the Bosell sign, the sky darkened and rain pounded down. Putting on her hat and the canvas jacket, she decided against the path, likely slick as snot, and turned back to the fork that would take her to Lucie's hidden road.

Greatly to her relief, a pile of brush at the roadside looked unnatural, and with a close look she saw an impression of wagon wheels. Instead of moving the brush, she rode between trees. Finding the road lifted her spirits, and she thought how easy it was to be satisfied with a small thing. She'd always lived day to day, never with big goals. Now she had a few, and they weren't easy to keep straight.

She came out from under the trees and rode toward a light across the meadow, snuggled into the big jacket so when she reached the horse shed, only her cheeks, hands, and the lower parts of her dress and trousers were wet and cold. She left the hat and jacket on porch pegs.

Inside by the pot-belly stove, Piney helped strip off her sodden clothes and scurried away to heat up supper.

Lucie peered from her usual chair. A crocheted rug was spread over her lap. "Well, did you see him?"

"Which?"

"Did you see that marshal feller, did you tell Doc?"

Will. What might have happened if she'd walked past Virgie and settled herself in his room to stay? Her stomach growled. "I didn't see your marshal."

"Did you tell Doc?"

"I always do what I set out to do." She opened her palm. "I'll take the rest of my coins."

Lucie pulled the rug to her chin. "I guess you won't. You was dumb to leave them where they was. Anybody could of stole them. Lucky for you, they're put to good use. You've bought a share of the business."

Fury spread up Wanda's neck, and she stepped away from the stove to chill down. She kept her lips shut until she could open them without screaming. Then she bent close to Lucie's face. "A share in the business. Lucky me."

Lucie never wavered.

Piney came back with a bowl of potato-fish hash. Wanda smiled for Piney, but ate like food was the enemy.

Lucie hunched under her lap rug. "Piney, stir up that fire, I've caught cold."

Wanda shook her spoon. "You should of took the jacket instead of my gold."

Lucie laughed until she had a coughing spell. Piney rushed out and brought back a glass of water.

Lucie waved the glass away. "Evalena's Girl, you're mine, through and through."

Wanda set down her bowl and left the room. She didn't have the gold, but she'd held off a fit.

CHAPTER 10

Wanda dragged Lucie's cot up a wooded ravine toward the still. Lucie had picked a site that might kill her, but no one suggested she stay at the cottage.

Ahead, Lucie leaned hard on her cane and grunted as she walked and talked. "Hargis wants to know for a fact that he's gonna get something for his effort. You see how he works, strong as a mule and smart enough to do only what he wants. You be the carrot and I'll be the stick."

"I won't marry him," Wanda said.

"What's that?"

Wanda set the cot on end. "Stop and turn around so you can hear me."

Lucie rotated herself with three prods of her cane.

"I said, I don't know why you think someone has to marry Hargis."

"'Cause I've picked him, and 'cause he wants a legal connection to my legacy. 'Cause there's blockheads who won't do business with a woman."

"You might have picked someone more agreeable."

Lucie grunted. "There's only two other kind, the ones worse

83

than Hargis, and the ones that think they're better'n us. Doc, for instance."

"You said you wished you'd had a man like Will."

"Somewhat like him. He's got no more heart for this business than Piney."

The kind of man Homer would like. "I'll not marry till I bring my girl back from Fargo." And it wouldn't be Hargis.

Lucie smiled. "Well and good. You work it out, but keep him hot and hopeful. There's heavy jobs ahead, and I need him to sell the product." She trudged uphill, shouting in gasps. "From now on...climb up here a different...way each time. We've mucked outa regular...highway. This here path needs to grow over."

"Yes, Ma'am."

Yesterday they'd carried the equipment to a spot where a fallen tree bridged the slopes of the ravine. Brush and vines trailed over it, making a natural roof that would filter smoke and help disguise the still from any who might approach from the cliffs above. Since the place was already isolated, Lucie's caution seemed extreme, but only Ruth complained, saying the site didn't have enough good water to make the mash and to cool and condense steam from the boiler.

Lucie stopped where they'd spread equipment on the facing slopes. In the narrow crease, Hargis shoveled clay from a mud hole. Uphill, Ruth sat on a rock and dug soft pulp from a branch of sumac for a water line. Two dogs sprawled near her feet. Beside her was a pile of carved-out sumac, each piece about the thickness of her wrist. The line was supposed to carry water down from a spring to the barrel with the copper coil.

"Where do you want me to set your cot?" There was no level ground.

"Someplace it won't tip over."

Wanda set the cot down, and Lucie plopped herself in the middle with the cane between her feet. "We'll level up a platform later for sleeping and such, and build a roof for it. Once we start the run, someone has to be here day and night. I don't need you now, so get back to the house and help Piney shell corn."

Wanda ran downhill in a new direction, glad to work alone with Piney, who might tell something about Lucie's plans. Latching onto saplings to avoid tumbling head over heels, she felt wild as a kid. Without Lucie and Hargis, she'd love this place.

She came out near the corn field where young stalks drooped, cooked black by frost. Lucie had forbidden them to seed the field again, saying the plants wouldn't mature before frost, and they had better things to do.

Piney was shelling corn on the porch that connected the cottage to the cellar house. "We had a corn sheller at the old home place," she said. "I figger it's still there, since there was nothing much to it that would burn."

Wanda sat beside her and pushed her thumbs over a cob of hard kernels. "A sheller might be worth the trip. This will take the skin off our fingers."

Piney flexed her fingers and picked up another ear. "It takes a full day to get there and a day back. Ma won't spare the time, long as she has us to do this."

Kernels plunked into Wanda's bucket. "How much does she want?"

"Two bushel, enough to sprout and grind for malt. More will go to the mill to be ground fine for mash. That'll take another day, if the miller can do it soon as we get there. Two days, if not."

"Will we go, you and me?"

Piney kept looking toward the woods, like she expected to see Lucie bearing down. "Wouldn't that be fun? But I suppose Ma will send Hargis."

"Might be good to let him do it," Wanda said. "There's talk of corn thievery."

Piney tossed a cob into a basket by the cellar wall and reached for the next ear. "Honey, I keep thinking how you said I shouldn't marry Hargis. But now Ma says him and you's gonna marry."

"That's your ma's idea. I'm not marrying anybody."

"I'm sorry I asked. I didn't think you'd do me wrong. But don't get Ma against you, and be careful near Hargis. If he goes to the mill and hears there's a traveling preacher near, he'll want to haul you off to stand with him and say the wedding words."

"I'm good at dodging."

Piney kept her frown.

"I won't fight him like before," Wanda said. "I'm getting a hold on myself."

"If you start feeling bad, just run to me."

Learn to ignore Hargis. Think ahead, and choose how to act. Easy as turning inside out.

"Aunt Piney, your ma has a plan to get back her old home place, some way to raise money beyond whiskey-making. Has she said what that is?"

"Ma never says what she's gonna do until she does it. I've learned not to ask."

Wanda bounced a corncob off the cellar house wall and into the basket. "We need to stand up to your ma."

Piney lifted her eyes toward the woods.

The work went faster when Piney started telling stories about her and Evalena as kids. When she judged they'd shelled enough, she leaned a ladder against the porch roof. Wanda climbed first, and Piney handed up burlap bags and buckets of corn and water. Together they spread a layer of kernels on the bags and drenched them with water.

From the roof they had a good view of the ruined cornfield. "When our kernels sprout, I'll plant a handful," Piney said. "If summer lasts long enough, we'll have ears for the table."

"Good for you," Wanda said. "Will Granny make you plow it under when she sees it growing?"

"Likely she'll forget she told me not to plant. Or I'll tell her she didn't say that."

"Sneaky," Wanda said.

Piney's face reddened. "Ma doesn't always know best. If we

did everything her way, this place would be no better than the old."

When they came down from the roof, they carried hoes and bean seed to the garden, dug under the dead plants, and planted new hills. Later they carried provisions for lunch to the ravine. Lucie's cot sat more evenly—someone had set rocks under its downhill side. Ruth squatted at the base of the slope, mortising layers of stone with clay.

"That'll be the furnace," Piney said. "The fireplace for the boiler."

Lucie sat with her hands propped on her cane, watching Ruth's every move. Hargis went up and down the slope, pounding forked sticks into the ground and laying sections of Ruth's carved-out water line in the v of the forks.

"About time." Lucie pointed to a spot close to her cot. "Piney, clear a place for the cook fire over here. Evalena's Girl, your job the rest of this day and tomorrow is to haul in the biggest pieces of hardwood you can handle. Chop off the limbs so we have straight logs to push under the boiler."

Wanda began to see how Ruth's circle of stones suited the turnip still. Standing, Ruth rotated her neck and cracked her knuckles. She toed a sheet of tin on the ground. "When I get the stone built up so high, we'll set this tin on it, like a stove-top for the boiler. We don't want fire touching the boiler and burning the mash."

With a hatchet and handsaw attached to her belt, Wanda ranged over the slopes to find fallen branches that fit Lucie's requirements. Plenty of wood lay on the ground, most with at least one branch too thick for her saw. She felt like a mule, tugging the first stout limb toward the smell of coffee, and didn't see Hargis until he grabbed her from behind. His hat rolled downhill.

"Gotcha!" His bristly face pressed her neck and his hands squeezed her waist.

Angry that she'd let herself be surprised, she tried to swing the tree limb against his legs, but it was too heavy to swing uphill. She struggled to stay on her feet and keep the fury down.

With one thick arm, he squeezed her waist and with the other he tried to knock loose her hold on the limb. He grunted. "Go ahead, fight me. I like it!"

She dropped the branch and fumbled at her belt to unhook the hatchet and handsaw. He stumbled over the branch, then came around, face-to-face, laughing, dancing like a boxer.

Think. Don't be the ax head flying off its handle.

As soon as she loosened the hatchet, he seized and flung it into the brush. When she raised the handsaw, he snatched it away with a force that pulled her off balance. For a minute she twirled and staggered downhill with Hargis catching, losing, and catching her again. They came to rest with a scrape of her elbows on stony ground and a bump of her forehead against his. She lay on his chest, crushed in his thick arms, his breath hot on her face.

"Whee!" He rolled her over. "Let's have a kiss."

Crushed beneath his weight, she let him press his mouth on hers while she fought bad memories and rising rage. He liked her to struggle, so she must be calm. Talk him away. Frighten him off. Her knife had done that before. Breathing hard, he ran his hands down her sides and grabbed her rear. She pictured her fingers wrapping around the knife and bringing it out, a warning. Her hand slid into her pocket.

He lifted his head and widened his eyes when the knife tip touched his back.

"Get off."

"You wouldn't."

She tightened her grip, felt the knife pierce his skin. "Get off!"

His arm whipped out and hit hers away, scraping the knife across his back.

Howling, he stumbled to his feet. She rolled to a crouch.

"Hargis! Wanda!" Piney ran between them and helped Wanda up.

He showed his ripped shirt. "Look what she done! I'm bleeding!"

Wanda sheathed the knife. "You're lucky it's a scratch."

Piney put her arm around Wanda. "Leave her alone or you'll get worse from me and Ruth."

"I wasn't gonna do nothing." Hargis side-stepped down the slope, picked up his hat and squared it on his head.

Piney put her head against Wanda's. "I'm sorry this happened."

"Don't be." She brushed dirt from her arms and face. "Hargis doesn't think I'm fun anymore."

"That's for damn sure," he said. "You're crazy."

The last time she'd been crazy. This time she'd done better.

She sheathed the knife and retrieved the hatchet and hacksaw. Piney helped her drag the tree limb to the site. Pausing her stonework, Ruth gave them a look that asked if they were all right. Piney nodded.

Wanda held a tin cup under the waterline. "I'll be all day trying to get a drink."

"That spring used to run good," Lucie said. "Hargis, you and Ruth see if you can dig it out."

Ruth rose from her squat and stepped away from the circle of stones, skirt and arms coated with mud. She grabbed a pickax and started up-slope.

Piney lifted a bucket. "Honey, there's drinking water here."

Wanda sat on a log and held the cup in both hands to keep it from shaking.

Hargis stopped at Lucie's cot. "So far I've give a lot and got no more'n grief. I'm going home to my place to see if my corn was frosted."

"If corn is all you want in life, you go," Lucie said. "But if you're smart, you'll stay here and do my bidding. I keep my promises."

Piney lowered her eyes and stirred potatoes in the skillet.

Wanda drained the water in her cup. Nobody talked sense when they were angry.

Hargis and Lucie were locked in a stare-down. Finally Lucie thumped her cane. "All right. You can check your place when you take our corn to the mill. That'll be day after tomorrow. I'll give you three days, round trip."

"With a load of corn, I may need someone to hold a gun. Or a knife." He shifted his eyes to Wanda. "I'll take Piney."

"No you won't," Lucie said. "Stop and pick up Virgie. Likely she's handy with a gun. You can bring her back with you if she's interested. We'll need more lookouts for when our mash starts to work and the smell of it drifts every which way."

"Me and Wanda can take the corn to the mill," Piney said.

"Not this time. Next few days, I've special work for Evalena's Girl."

CHAPTER 11

The rest of that day and into the next, Wanda worked in a glow of victory. She'd frightened Hargis and avoided a fit. And Lucie wanted her for a special task, one that might reward her with what she needed to go home. She listened for clues, but Lucie said no more.

Hargis stayed out of their way, disappearing for long stretches of time, occasionally dragging in wood. Ruth resumed work on the furnace while Wanda and Piney wore themselves down, digging and carrying clay mud.

Her aunts were full of speculation about Virgie White. "There's not a spare inch in our room," Ruth said. "If she comes, she'll have to sleep with Ma."

Piney giggled. "Hargis says him and her don't get along, so I think I'll like her."

Ruth glanced toward the shaded platform where Lucie napped. "Virgie better be a strapping big girl, with long arms and hands like a man. If she comes, Piney, you're not to treat her like company."

Wanda laughed at the thought of Virgie doing any of their work. "She's small-sized and talks too much, and I'm sorry to say she has little hands, which I think she likes to keep pretty."

"I don't know what gets into Ma," Ruth said. "She could of asked help from the Porters."

Wanda swiped at her mud-splattered arms. "Porters? That's what Granny called us when we met that man she thought was a marshal."

"The Porters lives at the next place up the road," Ruth said. "Two brothers and their sister. They've done some distilling in their time. They're old now, but not too old to ride and hold a gun."

Lucie's shotgun lay beside her on the platform. Ruth and Piney might think it ordinary as a broom, but Wanda was bothered by a gun in the hands of a half-blind woman who couldn't steady a fork. "There better not be shooting."

Ruth stood, arched her back, and flicked mud from her fingers. "Guns are for show, like a dog growls and shows his teeth. Though now and again a dog gets excited and bites." She and Piney shared a look. "And guns go off accidental."

In the morning, Wanda wrenched awake, damp with sweat. Jamie Long, her pa, had moved in and out of her dreams—a man who'd killed another with his knife. He'd come to a worse end than her ma. She turned to face the wall. No wonder she had fits. She could only hope Homer's blood was stronger in their child than all the bad from her side.

Life was easier to bear when she could do something about it. She rolled out of the hammock. The aunts were already up and gone, and the cottage was quiet. Last evening she'd helped them bag corn. This morning Hargis was to drive it to the miller's.

She chewed a piece of cold fish on her way to the corn crib. Lucie sat on a keg in a sunny spot, her face shaded by a farmer's straw hat, watching Hargis harness the mules. "Remember now, three days, and bring Virgie back here."

Hargis climbed to the wagon seat. "Virgie's always ready to go someplace. 'Less she's cabined up with Doc." He smirked at Wanda and winked at Piney. Already he'd switched his attentions to her, poor soul.

He pushed the lever to release the wagon brake. "Lucie, three days ain't enough to go and come back. I need to find someone to watch my place before squatters take over."

"Four, then," Lucie said. "Don't lay over at the miller's if he can't grind the corn right away. Leave it there and take care of your business."

"I'm a grown man."

Lucie leaned forward. "What's that you say?"

Mumbling, he flicked the reins.

Ruth and Piney came around the building on the plow horse and started across the field toward the hidden drive. One of the dogs ran alongside.

When they left, Lucie pushed herself up with the aid of her cane. "Evalena's Girl, pack your bedroll and food for two-three days. You and me's gonna ride to the old home place."

This might be Lucie's promise to make her trip worthwhile, but Wanda was leery of riding off with her alone. Until they'd convinced Lucie to ride a mule to the still site, she'd had several hard falls. And it took three people to get her on the mule.

"Could we take Ruth?"

"She's got work to finish here."

"You're putting a burden on me, old woman, namely yourself, and I'm not in a mood to go." The last part wasn't true, but she couldn't help stretching the truth with something contrary. "I wouldn't be surprised if you're leading me into an ambush."

"Why ever would I do that?"

"I got no idea. Maybe you'd sell me off."

"Don't pride yourself. You ain't worth that much."

"It takes a day to get there? How long's it been since you spent two days in a saddle?"

"Don't fuss about me." Lucie's voice shook. "I'm making this trip, and I'm choosing you to go along, and if you want any part of my legacy you'll help me get there and be glad of it."

Evie's legacy. "My horse won't carry double, not all day long. You'll have to ride the plow horse."

"That's my plan."

When Ruth and Piney returned, Lucie told Ruth to saddle the old horse. "Me and Evalena's Girl is going to the old home place."

Ruth blinked. "Just you two? Is this some kind of sentimental trip?"

"Have you ever knowed me to be sentimental?"

"Buried treasure, then."

"Something like that." Lucie licked her lips and brushed them with the back of her hand, like a satisfied cat.

"Please don't go," Piney said. "The trip could be the end of you."

"Now listen here," Lucie said. "If I die before I come back, make the mash and run it best you know how, then get out of the business. And nobody has to marry Hargis, how about that?"

With a wicked smile, Ruth leaned close and whispered to Wanda. "I hope you won't let temptation get the better of you, but if you do, we'll understand."

Wanda shrugged. "You'll see us back here in an hour or two when her tailbone's numb and the rest is jarred to pieces." When that happened, Lucie might tell her where to find the treasure and let her go alone.

They saddled the plow horse and strapped on Lucie's bedroll and a bag of boiled potatoes, then hoisted her onto the horse. Ruth tied on a coil of rope. "In case you have to fasten her."

When Wanda looked back, Piney's hands were folded in prayer, and one of the dogs was following. Ruth waved them on.

Lucie was either made of iron or unable to feel pain, for they reached Winkler a few hours later, with no stops to rest. Will's pack came running and circled with Ruth's dog, all wagging tails and sniffing butts.

Wanda needed a stop. "Granny, would you like to use Will's toilet?"

"Be all right. Get me down."

Wanda tied the mare to a post and led Lucie's horse to the steps. Will came out, looking from her to Lucie and back again. To Wanda he mouthed, "Sick?"

Lucie held out her arms and slid down. "We're traveling to my old home place."

"Is that right?" He scowled at Wanda, a dark look that pulled her like a magnet.

She took Lucie in the washroom and came back to where he sat on the middle step. He raised his arm to tuck her beside him. "Come here."

"I'm tired of sitting. You get up."

He stood and pressed her against the door. "See how agreeable I am? You say 'get up' and that's what happens." He kissed her neck. "You and Lucie shouldn't make that trip alone."

"She'll take care of me."

"There's a scary idea."

She nosed his cheek, loving his skin. "I was there once, but don't recall the way."

He ran his hands down her back. "The road follows a creek around the mountain past Russell Long's place, where you and your ma stayed, way back. You ford the river here, right below where your boardinghouse was."

"Does anybody come and go that way anymore? I mean, what's the road like?"

"I only know this end, and it's clogged with brush. I've not heard of anyone moving back there."

"I wonder if I'll remember anything."

"If Lucie didn't have those cloudy eyes, she might know the landmarks."

"If they aren't burned up." She glanced up and down the

empty street. "So, now your town has two people. Is Virgie all cozy and happy?"

"I helped her move into a house, for which she's paying rent. She'll be great for the town."

"What does that mean?"

"People like her. She'll be a good neighbor."

"She wants you."

"Not permanent. Virgie's like your granny, always on the lookout. She left here an hour ago with Hargis, said she's got an invitation to your place."

"Granny's place."

"Whatever you say."

"So, nothing new between you and Virgie."

"I'm not saying we wouldn't comfort each other on a winter night, if I didn't have you."

"You figure you have me?"

He unfolded an envelope from his shirt pocket. "If I can't tie you down on my own, I'll get May Rose to persuade you. My hired man brought the mail yesterday. This letter is mostly for you, lots of it about your little girl."

"Oh." She took the envelope and held it at her back to hide her shaky hand. "Can I keep it?"

"Sure."

She wanted to go home right now. "Did you tell May Rose about us?"

"I haven't wrote back. What should I say?"

She pressed her face against his, wishing she could let him decide everything. "How about, you're crazy for me?"

"How about the other-way-around?"

Lucie's cane pushed open the door. "Evalena's Girl, do you have to piss?"

Will warmed her neck with his whisper. "This meeting isn't very satisfying."

"I'll agree. Help Lucie on her horse while I visit your washroom. We've a long ride ahead."

"You think you'll get her there?"

"She's set her mind."

"Tomorrow night, then, I'll see you back here. Stay over."

"I do like you, Will Herff, though you're as bossy as Granny."

"Likewise."

She and Lucie forded the river, found the creek that came into it from the west and almost immediately entered a region of lifeless trees. With the road choked by thorns, they rode in the creek, a tumble of rocks and shallow pools.

The mare placed its hooves with care, but they slid now and again, jolting her side to side. The plow horse splashed behind.

"It's going to be hard going," she called. "Might take longer than you thought."

Lucie did not answer.

Wanda looked back and shouted, "Do you want to go on like this?"

The dog sat down in a sandy spot. Lucie lifted her head. "Keep moving."

The day grew warm, and the dead trees gave no shade. Wanda tied on her hat and watched for something familiar. Half a lifetime ago she'd come this way in a wagon with her ma lying sick and wrapped warm and Uncle Russell and Homer on the wagon seat. It was the winter Russell had taken them in. Then Ma had died, and she'd attached herself to Homer.

She closed her eyes against the sun in her face, let the mare pick its way upstream, and listened to the slow splash and plop of eight hooves in water.

Her eyes might have been closed for only seconds when she realized the mare had stopped, and the plow horse was drinking from the creek. Lucie slumped over its neck. Dead? Wanda rode back.

Lucie's mouth was open and twisted, with slobber at the lower side. Puffs of air lifted strands of the horse's mane. Wanda touched her arm. "Granny. Do you need to be tied to the saddle or can you stay awake?"

Blinking, Lucie sat upright and pulled the reins to bring up the horse's head. "I'm fine. Get along, get along."

"I don't recall. Does this stream follow the road all the way to your place?"

"Nearly. I'll say when to leave it."

If she stayed awake.

A rabbit jumped from a bush, and Ruth's dog chased it for a few yards. Ahead, a family of finches lifted into the air. Wanda turned her horse upstream again, glad for each small sign of life.

Getting to Uncle Russell's place from Winkler had taken the better part of daylight, but they'd traveled in winter, when days were short. Lucie's home place was farther, but on a long summer day like this, they might reach it before dark.

Lucie rode with her head down. Uneasy, Wanda circled her horse in the creek.

"Granny. You doing all right?"

"Quit your worrying."

"Do you recognize anything?"

"I know it all."

"You'll know when we get there?"

"I'm not dead yet."

She grew accustomed to the unevenness and uncertainty of their course and to the sameness of the terrain, green brush on the banks, charred trunks fallen over the road, tree skeletons on the slopes. She got used to the jolting rhythm as her horse picked its way through shallow pools, hooves clicking and sliding on the rocky bottom, jarring softly in mud.

She opened the letter and cried quietly, reading about Evie, who played well with other children and liked to help with the babies, but lacked a strong appetite. The letter did not condemn Wanda for coming so far—after all, it was written to Will. But it set her to worrying. Anything could happen. They could get lost and starve in this abandoned territory. Something could happen to May Rose, then what would Evie do?

"I need to relieve myself," Lucie said.

Wanda needed a rock or stump to help Lucie off her horse. The best choice was a boulder jutting into the stream, half as high as their horses' backs. She held the plow horse by its bridle while the old woman slid to the boulder's flat top.

Lucie surveyed the distance from the boulder to the roadbed. "I need my cane."

"You didn't bring it."

"Nobody gave it to me. Find me a walking staff."

Every piece of wood on shore was charred or rotten, but in the creek Wanda found a stout stick that would do for a staff. With her fingers wrapped around it, Lucie wobbled across the boulder and squatted, half visible, behind a bush. Wanda tied the horses where they could graze, then pulled potatoes and water canteens from her saddlebags for their late day meal.

The dog came and sat beside her.

"That there looks to be Old Henry's Dog," Lucie said. "But I never would've thought it to come this far."

"Who's Old Henry?"

"Old Henry's the horse I'm riding. That dog follows it most everywhere."

Wanda gave the dog half of her boiled potato. "Lucie, it's time to say what this trip's about."

Lucie wiped her mouth with the back of her hand. "Russell Long's place is upstream a little way. Don't you want to see it?"

"We've not come to visit Russell's place. Why are we here?"

"I want to see my old home."

"The real reason."

Lucie handed her a canteen. "Find a pool we haven't stirred to mud and fill this up."

Wanda set the canteen on the boulder. "I'm not going farther till you tell me why."

"It'd be nice if you was more trusting."

"It'll be fine with me if we turn around and go home."

"All right." Lucie lowered her voice. "There's greenbacks buried on my place, from before the fire. I never had a chance to get them out. They'll buy back my land."

"And pay me for the gold you stole."

"Nonsense. The land's your legacy, supposing you outlive the rest of us. Now, don't make such a face. There's more."

"If you had such a stash—*and more*—why didn't you get it long ago? You could of easy kept the taxes paid."

"There's good reason. When we was burned out, we stayed in Virginia with cousins. We tried to come back about a year later, but everything was ash. The going was awful and the air foul to breathe, so we settled where we are now. Every year I thought about going after that stash, but I figured it was safer where it was than where Ruth could get her hands on it. If she had money, she'd drink all day. I waited too long."

Growling, the dog stood, hair bristling on its back. Wanda seized Lucie's walking stick and held it like a club. An intruder in all this quiet was scary as one popping up inside a house.

Old Henry's Dog splashed into the water and raced up the creek. Wanda ran onto the boulder to see. The dog stopped halfway between her and a black bear with cubs. The bear went up on its hind legs and studied the dog.

"Dog, here! Get back!" She jumped up and down on the boulder and waved her arms.

Lucie pushed herself upright. "What's this fuss?"

While the mother bear sniffed the air, her cubs hurried out of the water and disappeared in brush. Old Henry's Dog leaped forward, barking.

The mother bear dropped to all fours and followed the cubs out of the creek. The dog stopped where the bears had left the water. Wanda called again, and he came back.

"Bears," Wanda said. "We chased them off."

"Uhmph," Lucie said. "That dog's got big ideas. He'd never handle a bear by hisself. Why did you let me forget my gun?"

The dog lay down beside Wanda and licked his paws. "There used to be a den near Russell's," Wanda said.

"I told you we was close."

"I crawled into that den one day with Homer and there was the ma bear in her winter sleep, two black handfuls of fur sucking on her."

"Now you're storying. The den would be pitch black and you wouldn't see a thing."

"Homer had a torch. The bear never blinked."

"I'll believe what I believe," Lucie said. "When we get to Russell's place, do you want to stop and look around?"

"Not if everything's burned."

"It will be. But it's good the bears have come back. That means fish in the streams, grubs in the ground. People will come next. I've got here just in time."

CHAPTER 12

T here was more. Lucie had dropped the hint like a lure. Lurching through the creek on horseback, Wanda tried not to think of riches. She couldn't take Lucie's legacy if it meant being her slave.

Late in the day, Lucie shouted, "Up there's Russell Long's place."

Wanda saw only another overgrown slope, but she stopped mid-stream. Russell and Homer had dug a shallow grave for Evalena in the hard earth. She'd helped mound rocks on top.

"You said yourself, no use stopping," Lucie said.

No use.

The sun dropped lower in the sky and a cooler breeze riffled the water. Old Henry's Dog disappeared into the brush. The horse whinnied, and soon the dog splashed into the water, circled Old Henry, and left them again. Riding on, Wanda had glimpses of the dog running above them on the roadbed. Then it barked, and seemingly on his own, Old Henry climbed the bank to the old road.

Lucie motioned her to follow. "The dog and Old Henry has the right idea. Road's good here."

Wanda directed her horse to the bank. Old Henry led through

grass up to its belly, and the dog ran behind in the path tramped by the horses. With better footing, they moved along faster, and she began to hope they'd reach their destination before dark.

The valley had darkened and a red sunset glowed on the western ridges when finally Lucie said, "This is it."

"Where?" Wanda saw only another brushy slope, but it was time to camp for the night, whether Lucie was right or not.

Lucie pointed. "Up there. Let's go."

Wanda dismounted. "It's near dark. We'll camp by the water." She walked along the shore, picking up scraps of wood and discarding them, looking for pieces not too badly charred to burn again.

"We can camp up at the old home place," Lucie said.

Wanda tossed wood in a pile. "You go ahead, but don't call if you get into trouble, 'cause I'm gonna be right here in my bedroll."

Old Henry's Dog circled round and round, then settled on the grass, laid his head between his paws and closed his eyes.

"All right," Lucie said. "Get me off this horse."

Wanda saw no likely stepping rock.

Lucie waved her arm toward the hillside. "I'll get off easier on the slant."

Wanda walked the horse uphill and turned him so Lucie could get off on the shorter side.

Lucie leaned from the saddle. "Here I come." Heedless as a child, she held out her arms and fell from the saddle, catching Wanda around the neck. Wanda stumbled backwards and sat down hard with Lucie sprawled on top. "Good," Lucie said.

Wanda held her breath against the stink of her closeness. She rolled Lucie off and pulled her to her feet. Old Henry stood motionless while Lucie leaned on him and Wanda untied the walking stick from the rope on her saddle.

Holding onto a stirrup, Lucie prodded the ground with the stick. "Go real slow and lead him back down to where we're gonna sleep."

Old Henry chose a pace Lucie could manage, and Wanda let him pick his path around rocks and ruts.

Lucie waved her stick. "Hard to believe. This was our road."

When they got back to the level strip along the creek, Wanda tied Old Henry to a bush. "Don't do that," Lucie said.

"Don't tie him?"

"Old Henry won't go nowhere. Let him graze."

"All right, but I have to tie this mare—I don't know what she'll do."

Lucie sat near Wanda's pile of kindling. "She'll stay with Old Henry. Let 'em be, they'll eat and drink and find a nice spot to lay down."

Wanda left the horses free to roam, too tired to worry about anything.

Her dewy blanket woke her before dawn, and she threw it off and pulled charred wood away from the tiny ember glowing in the campfire.

The starlit sky was deep blue, lighter than the blackness below. She scraped a handful of dry litter from under a bush. In a crouch, she added bits of leaf and blew gently on the ember until one caught. When the snap of burning was louder than the gurgle from the stream, she added kindling. By the time the fire grew enough to show the lump of Lucie under her blanket, morning edged the mountains.

In the clarity and quiet of dawn, she thought of good things. Evie, and how she'd like Will, Old Henry's Dog, and these horses. *Which were nowhere in view.*

"Granny, get up."

Lucie rolled over like she might have been awake for some time.

"The horses are gone. Dog too." She could walk out of here, but not Lucie.

"No, they ain't. Old Henry's just visiting his favorite spots."

"You know that for sure?"

"Here's where he was raised. We'll find him bye 'n bye."

Wanda chewed her cold breakfast potato, hoping Lucie was right, hating to take her word. "I'll see if I can find them."

"There's a lot of territory. Likely you'll get lost. I'll show the way."

"Your choice," Wanda said. "But this better not take all day. I don't want to sleep here another night. Are your pockets deep enough to carry down your treasure?"

"Some of it," Lucie said.

Wanda slung two bridles on her shoulder and put a potato in her pocket to lure the dog.

"Give me your arm," Lucie said.

They struggled uphill, Lucie bracing her steps with the walking stick on one side and Wanda on the other. Ten steps, and Lucie paused to catch her breath.

If she hadn't been bearing part of Lucie's weight, Wanda might have taken pleasure in the old woman's ordeal. Thirty steps farther, Lucie pointed to a rock where she wanted to sit. While Lucie rested, Wanda studied the land's emergence from the big burn. Berry bushes flowered. Poison vine and Virginia Creeper twisted up trunks and limbs of blackened trees.

When they started uphill again, the morning cloud layer parted, and the sun shone through. Beads of sweat stood out on Lucie's forehead, but she kept lifting and thrusting a foot forward, leaning on Wanda's arm.

Finally, Lucie stopped, looking confused. "Did we pass it?"

"How am I supposed to know?"

"Find me a place to sit down."

Wanda led her toward a mossy log. "You should of brought Ruth."

"It all looks different." She pointed to deep ruts. "Even the ground's moved. Look for a chimney. And tombstones. We had a little burial plot."

CAROL ERVIN

"Which way should I go?"

"Over that-a-way." Lucie gestured vaguely to their right.

Wanda cursed her own foolishness with every high step through prickly weeds. Old Henry might indeed have left to find his former home, but that place could be miles away. There was nothing to do but expect to find it. If she didn't, she'd never get there.

Lucie's sense of location might have depended on something other than her eyes, or maybe they'd reached a different homestead, for not too many paces into the charred pines Wanda saw a chimney. She heard a whinny and saw the red mare. Her heart settled.

The horses and dog came to her, and she stroked each, then bridled Old Henry and tied the reins to a sapling near the chimney, eager now to have Lucie find her treasure so they could go home.

When she brought Lucie to the chimney, Wanda was irritated and pleased to see sadness in her face.

"I always thought some of it would be the same."

"We need to leave soon. Where's your stash?"

"We have to dig it up." Lucie pointed to a brush heap. "Right about there was a tool shed with spud bars and such in it. I forgot the shed would be burned, but metal parts should be left."

"I'm not digging into that with my fingers," Wanda said. "Why didn't you bring a shovel?"

"Why didn't you?"

"You never said there was to be digging. Where's your stash supposed to be?"

Lucie raised her arm and pointed to a treeless knoll. "Buried in the graveyard up there between Pap and Granny."

"Ain't that sweet," Wanda said. "Let's hope you can dig that ground with your fingers."

Lucie picked up a rusty wedge of tin roofing. "Use this."

Wanda took the tin scrap and walked off to find the graveyard. Lucie followed, grunting with every breath. The gravestones were overgrown too. Wanda ripped runners from tilted slab markers until she found the names Lucie wanted.

Lucie pointed to a crust of ash between two markers. "Dig right there."

Old Henry's Dog sat beside Wanda as she scraped with the bent piece of tin. "This is soggy ground."

"It never was before."

The tin struck something. Wanda tossed aside a rock the size of an apple and dug deeper. When the tin struck again, she pushed her fingers into the ground and pulled up a chunk of mud stuck to a thick piece of pottery.

"Give it here." Lucie held the shard in both hands. "Not the one, praise be. Dig some more."

When the tin proved too flimsy, Wanda dug with her knife and uncovered the top of a crock.

Lucie gripped the top and pulled. "It won't come loose. You do it."

Wanda pried again and pulled out a squat, wide-mouthed crock plugged with a cork.

"Break it open," Lucie said.

It fell apart when she struck it with a rock, revealing a dank, soggy mass. Howling, Lucie squeezed the mass in her fist and let it drop to the ground. Old Henry's dog got up and slunk away.

Wanda picked apart a clump that looked and smelled like rotting leaves. "Is this money?"

"Greenbacks. Near two thousand dollars, ruint!"

The ruin of Lucie's stash felt like justice. But two thousand dollars—a fortune for Evie, rotten. A hard trip for nothing.

Lucie braced herself on a gravestone and pointed to a brushy ravine, a crease between steep slopes. "I've one more hope, and it's in a cave up that holler. Go up there, find the cave, and tell me what you find."

Wanda hesitated. "You'll have to tell me what I'm looking for."

"Oak barrels of the finest whiskey my family ever made, a true fortune. It'll take a wagon team to get them out."

"Not to mention a road," Wanda said.

"True enough. I didn't plan to disturb the barrels till I redeemed my land and things was better out this way. We'll have to put the whiskey in kegs and pack them out on mules. Those sure-footed Mexican mules if we can get 'em."

"If the barrels are there." Fire might have ruined everything. Greenbacks would have been easy.

Back at the chimney, Lucie sat on the lower of two stone steps, the entry to a house replaced by brambles. "I'll have to get them out soon. Go along and see."

"I'll put you on Old Henry and you can show me the way."

"I'll wait here. As I remember, a horse will have a hard go over them rocks."

In shape, this narrow ravine was like the site of Lucie's still, except it had thorny brush instead of living trees and ended in a tumble of rocks and boulders. She stood at the base of the rock fall and surveyed the brushy cliff at its top. Curiosity pulled her forward.

Water dripped from the cliff. She trampled brush and pulled away vines, rewarded finally by a rush of cooler air and a glimpse of a dark recess. Her matches were in the saddlebags by the creek, but she was encouraged to hear no flap of bat wings. She didn't push on, but probed with her boot, then traced her fingers along a wooden curve to a crusty iron band. A barrel. She tried to rock it, but it did not move, either full or stuck in mud. Her hand, when she brought it into sunlight, was black—char or fungus or both, she couldn't tell.

"I found something," she said, when she came back to the chimney. "Touched a barrel, couldn't budge it."

"Was it full?"

"How would I know? It's time we're going. Can you ride bareback down to where I left the saddles?"

"How many barrels?"

"Granny, it was pitch black. I didn't crawl in there."

"All right," Lucie said. "We'll come back soon."

Not *we*. She might have pretended ignorance about the source of Lucie's buried greenbacks, but she couldn't carry and sell illegal whiskey. And she'd been stupid to think Lucie would give anything without chains.

She knew what her ma would say. *Get out.*

Riding bareback down the long slope, leading Old Henry and gripping the mare's sides with her knees to keep from sliding forward, Wanda decided animals were better than people. And it was time she gave her horse a name.

CHAPTER 13

"Evalena's Girl!"

At Lucie's call, Wanda glanced to each side of the creek for robbers or bears or whatever was making the old woman's voice rise in fear.

"Help."

Wanda circled back. Lucie clung to Old Henry's neck, about to slide into the creek. Wanda pulled her upright.

Lucie's hands gripped the saddle. "Take that rope and tie my wrists to the horn. It'll wake me if I start to fall."

Tied wrists would not keep her from falling off the horse. Wanda imagined her slipping, pulling the saddle so she dangled under Old Henry's belly, smashing her brains on creek rocks. From a distant place, like Fargo, she might have felt satisfied to hear it. Close-up, she did not enjoy the prospect.

She loosened Ruth's coil of rope. "You better let me fasten you to the saddle."

"Just my wrists."

Wanda clamped her jaws and did as Lucie ordered, as Piney or Ruth would have done, feeling more like them, more like Evalena's Girl, less like herself. Then she trailed last to keep Lucie in view. The mare followed Old Henry without direction, and Old

Henry followed the dog back and forth from the creek to passable sections of the old road with Lucie nodding and dozing on its back.

The animals traveled with waning energy, but Old Henry and his dog seemed to encourage each other. Laying hand on the mare's rump, Wanda was heartened by the strength and rhythm of her muscles.

"Ginger," she said. "I'll bet that's your name." The mare flicked her ears. Wanda patted her neck. "Good girl."

It was nightfall when they reached the store, Will helped her get Lucie to the small room in the back. Lucie waved them away.

"I'm about as done in as her," Wanda said.

"Sit." He poured coffee and set a cream pitcher on the table. "Drink it down while I settle your horses."

She laid her head on the table. "Would you feed our dog? He's a good one."

"Milk in your coffee?"

She lifted her head and nodded, and he poured a stream into her cup then emptied the pitcher into a long-handled pot of moldy bread. "I'll have to feed your dog separate from my pack or they'll fight over this."

One moment the door slammed and the next she smelled sizzling meat. Will set a plate of ham on the table and gave her a fork.

She didn't look up until the ham was gone.

Will tilted his chair and laced his fingers behind his neck. "I thought you might turn around and come back yesterday. But I guess you got there?"

"We did."

"Lucie do all right? Anything special happen?"

"We saw a bear. And cubs."

"People?"

"No sign."

"The roads are still grown over?"

"Mostly." She propped her head on her hand, uncertain what

to confide. He might suspect a dark purpose to their trip, or know more than she thought. He might have heard of the cave.

"Anything left of the old place?"

"The chimney. Gravestones."

"I should have gone with you. I worried."

"Lucie wouldn't have allowed it." There were risks in telling and not telling, but she was too tired to know which was better. "Lucie says there's barrels of whiskey up there in a cave. She wants to sell them and buy back that land."

"Barrels?" He scratched his fingernails on the table. "A cache of old whiskey means trouble from both sides of the law. You don't want to be caught in the middle."

"Have I said I was going to take them out? You act like I don't have good sense."

He stared like that was exactly what he meant.

She stared back.

"So will you go home now? Before Lucie starts a war?"

Piney and Ruth would be caught in that. "I don't like to be told what to do."

"Then you've got a problem."

She wiped meat grease from the plate and licked her finger. "I'll go soon. When I've done Granny a bad turn. Tit for tat." It was more than she'd meant to say, but she was tired and cross.

Will leaned back in his chair. "That's why you've come?"

She felt scolded. "Partly."

"You better get over it. First off, revenge brings no comfort. Second, if you stay with Lucie you risk getting killed—with her or by her."

She studied the table without objecting or agreeing. He covered her hand with his. "Wanda, why bring trouble to yourself?"

"Not to me, to Lucie. You knew about my ma? You were just a kid when we lived here, but you knew about Ma?"

"I don't know as I ever saw her."

"You knew she was a whore? Sure you did. Ma was the

world's sweetest person, but not strong enough to live with Lucie. After Pa left us and our house burned, Lucie wouldn't help Ma unless we lived under her thumb. So we came to Winkler, and Ma did what she did."

"I'm sorry. But that's done and gone. Your ma's not living, but your daughter is."

"My daughter's in good hands."

"Tell me about her."

"I don't want to talk about Evie. Someone has to stand up to Lucie. Maybe I can't make her admit she ruined Ma, but she'll feel what it meant to me."

He pulled his hand away. "Wanda, be sensible. You bother me about as much as I can take."

Tired though she was, she left her chair and sat on his lap. "In what way bother?"

He pushed her to her feet. "Forget that. If you can't listen to good advice, you're as bad for me as Virgie."

She squared her shoulders. "You know, it's a mistake to let Virgie settle here if you don't intend to give her everything she wants."

"The town needs people."

"Oh, that's right. Here's an idea—if you want to live in a town, go find one." She blew a kiss and strode away, head up, toward the room where Lucie snored.

"Get up and saddle them horses," Lucie said. It was barely dawn, but Wanda was ready to put space between her and Will for a while.

On her way to the horse shed, they greeted each other like strangers. She came back to the store and bought gifts for Piney—coffee beans, a hock of ham, a poke of eggs, and fresh peas Will had taken in trade. She paid without lifting her eyes to his face. Funny how a little argument made her crave his good opinion.

Mid-morning she followed Lucie and Old Henry down over the edge of the road to the valley with its sparkling pond. For the first part of the trip, she'd fussed silently about Will. For the last part, she wondered if she should confront Lucie or do something sneaky, like getting her aunts to leave.

Piney's face was joyous, but Ruth's was full of questions. Lucie slid from Old Henry onto a stool. "Let me hear what's been done."

"The furnace is laid up and the water line's running," Ruth said. "That means, dripping. We'll have to carry water for the mash. Did you get what you went for?"

Wanda hung the saddles and her saddlebags on the fence rail, wondering how much Lucie would tell.

"Evalena's Girl, walk me to the house."

"Ma," Ruth said, louder. "Did you get what you went for?"

Lucie made no sign she'd heard. Ruth turned to Wanda. "What happened?"

Wanda raised her voice so Lucie would hear. "We dug up her stash, but it was rotted."

"Oh, Ma, I'm sorry," Piney said.

"I always thought there was more than what she brought out from the fire," Ruth said.

Piney offered her arm, but Lucie brushed her away. "Evalena's Girl, get me to the house."

"Let Piney help. My back's broke from you hanging on me the last two days."

"I want to talk about what we're gonna do next."

"I can tell you what I'm gonna do next. I'm gonna brush down my horse and have a bath in the pond."

Smiling, Ruth let down a fence rail, and she and Wanda led the horses into the field. Lucie let Piney walk her toward the cottage. Old Henry's dog flopped onto its side in the shade of the horse shed.

"I like how you take care of yourself," Ruth said. "I was afraid there for a while you'd turn out like Piney."

Wanda slipped the bridle from Ginger's head. "And I'm afraid you'll die of drink, like my ma. Leave poor Piney with nobody but Granny and Hargis."

Ruth's eyes sparked. "I'll get a brush." She came from the shed and tossed a brush to Wanda. Ruth pried mud from Old Henry's shoes with a pick while Wanda scraped the brush against Ginger's hide. Then Ruth motioned her to brush Old Henry.

The mare held still while Ruth picked at her shoes. "All of us is glad you're here."

"I guess I am too, though most of the time I wish I hadn't come. Do you and Piney know about the whiskey in the cave?"

Ruth straightened. "It was special runs from Grandpap's day. I thought it would've burned with everything else. Did you see it or did she tell you about it?"

"She sent me to find it. The cave is grown over and I had no light, but I touched the side of a barrel."

"I'm surprised she told you," Ruth said.

"She was too wore out to go to the cave herself. It was a hard trip, and I'll not take her out there again. It'll take years to clear that road unless a whole bunch of people get busy on it."

Ruth lifted a hat from a post and set it her head. "Coal companies will do it. The thought drives Ma crazy, but I don't care. Me and Piney don't want the old home place, nor anything to do with the business. Piney's against liquor in every way. 'Course you know I like doing a run of whiskey for our own selves, but Ma will have us do it time after time till she has enough to buy back that worthless scrap of land. Hargis won't like it—he'll want his cut of every run. She'll have to convince him there's a bigger pot of gold at the end of that rainbow."

"Like what's in the cave."

"It'll kill her if she has to tell him about that."

Telling Hargis about the cave was an interesting possibility, easy and sneaky, but telling a lawman would be a stronger blow.

Old Henry and Ginger trotted away, stopped in a bare patch of the field and went down on their knees. Ruth replaced the fence rails. The horses flopped to their sides and rolled in the dust. Old Henry's Dog got up and nosed Ruth's hand, and she scratched its ears.

"Does Lucie really think your place here is secret?"

Ruth chuckled. "All that cover-up is for strangers. Folks about here know of us like we know of them. Nobody hands out information."

"I wonder why you've stuck with her," Wanda said.

"I'm past wondering. She made us quit school in the sixth grade, and after that we almost never saw anyone but Pa's old cronies, and them not too often. She never wanted us to leave."

"But Ma got away."

"She did. Boys sniffed out Evalena like she was a heifer in heat, she was that pretty. And just fourteen when she run off." Ruth leaned her back against the rail. "She didn't come back till that time with you. I can see it's good you didn't stay."

"Ma said she couldn't abide to live with Granny, and Granny wouldn't help her start somewhere else."

In the shade of a tree, Old Henry and the mare stood head to rump, their tails switching away flies.

"That was only half of it," Ruth said.

Wanda had heard Evalena screaming. She didn't need to hear the other half. "Did you know how Ma kept us after we left?"

Ruth nodded. "We got word. Ours was never a good family, but we wasn't raised to know better. In our house, if you bucked, you were out."

"I heard your pa was found in a sinkhole, shot."

Ruth's hat shadowed her face.

"And I heard Lucie's the one shot him," Wanda said.

"It wasn't her shot him, though she's never tried to stop the talk."

Killed by a rival, Wanda imagined, or by the law, with Lucie letting rumors add to her reputation. "Did you ever find out who did it?"

"We always knew." Ruth took off her hat and fanned herself.

"It was me. Now, don't look like that. I'm not dangerous to the rest of the family, not even to Ma."

Piney called them from the cottage door.

"We better go," Ruth said.

Wanda's tongue felt stuck to the roof of her mouth. Ruth had shot him? She picked up her saddlebags and followed a step behind, afraid to know why, trying to shake off her aunt's confession as easily as Ruth had let it fall. Near to stuttering, she searched for a different subject. "Did you ever know a Price Loughrie?"

Ruth slowed and walked beside her. "That's an odd name, ain't it? I don't figger there'd be two with it, unless one was the son of the other. There was a boy ahead of me in school, used to walk part way home with us girls, a quiet boy. His family left the territory, but I never forgot him."

"I think, Aunt Ruth, he never forgot you."

CHAPTER 14

No doubt, she carried bad blood. At least she knew why she found it hard to be good. It would be easy to give in and be her natural self, but for Evie she had to do better.

Since Ruth's off-hand confession, she'd been wondering about her Bosell grandpap. She knew only three things—first, he was not a Bosell but a Crabtree, a branch so poorly regarded that Lucie had refused to have her daughters carry his name. Second, he liked to sit on his porch and shoot crows. Third, he'd been shot by Ruth.

She brought him up that evening when she and Piney were cleaning fish. "I don't remember much about Pappy Bosell. When did he die?"

"I don't recall, exactly."

Wanda picked a scrap from the cutting board and threw it to Old Henry's Dog. "What was he like?"

"I don't know." Piney smiled like she wanted to change the topic. "Ma managed him. I guess you have to do that with men. I'd be no good at it."

Managed by Lucie, shot by Ruth. Wanda rinsed the cutting board at the pond's edge. "How'd he die?"

"How?" Piney swished her hands in water and dried them on her apron. "He failed, same as most everyone. I nearly died of typhoid when I was a girl, did you know that? I lost my hair."

"Did your pa die of typhoid?"

"I don't remember what took him. I was sick a long time, but Ma and Ruth took good care of me. We always looked out for each other." Piney handed her the pan of fish. "You take this to the house—I'll get potatoes from the cellar."

Piney wasn't a good liar. Wanda chose not to press.

At bedtime, Wanda sat on the bedroom bench and watched Ruth unbraid and brush her hair. Ruth stared into the mirror like she was looking for something long gone. She'd avoided Wanda since their talk, either sorry she'd confessed or confused about Price Loughrie.

Memory was a strange thing. Sights and sounds did not come back in full, but feelings could rise afresh at the mention of a name. Shame and regret, anger. Even love.

"Aunt Ruth."

The mirror reflected Ruth's lifted eyebrow.

"Do you think Granny's right about that Loughrie being a marshal?"

"He was a quiet boy. I can see him favoring law and order." Ruth laid her brush on the dresser. "It'll be best if he keeps away from us."

Wanda wasn't sure what to do next. Telling Hargis about the cave wouldn't keep Piney and Ruth safe from trouble. Reporting the cache to a revenuer might be wiser. If the whiskey was there, she might even earn a bounty. If it was gone, nothing would change. Lucie wouldn't redeem her land, but she'd still have her ambitions and her daughters to do her bidding. Until Evalena's Girl took them away.

By noon of the next day, Lucie decided it was time Hargis and

Virgie got back. Wanda and her aunts were washing barrels and stirrers in the pond, a job neglected earlier in Lucie's haste to move the equipment into the woods. Lucie supervised from her seat on the rock at the water's edge.

"Evalena's Girl, you ride on out to the road and wait. Don't uncover the opening until you see 'em, and don't show yourself if there's anybody else on the road, just let Hargis drive on by."

Wanda was glad for a job that took her away from all of them, Piney wanting to please everyone, Lucie shouting orders like a blind general, Ruth quiet, maybe guarding her feelings. She saddled the mare and rode along the hidden drive to the screen of brush near the public road. Ready for leisure, she tied Ginger and sat against a tree where she'd hear anyone approach.

Her shady rest was too soon interrupted by a rattle of wagon boards and tackle. She peered through the brush. Sure enough, it was Hargis, but the person beside him was not Virgie, it was that dark, long-nosed marshal, Price Loughrie.

Trouble.

If Loughrie had invited himself along for the companionship of the road, Hargis would drive on, maybe pretend to be lost. But Hargis had a satisfied look on his face. He stopped the wagon and invited Loughrie to help him uncover the entrance. Wanda backed Ginger farther into the trees. Either Loughrie wasn't a marshal like Lucie thought, or he'd recruited Hargis to expose her. Either way, Lucie would be crazy-mad. Shots would fly.

She stepped on a log to get into the saddle, pushed the mare to a fast walk among the trees and a gallop when they came onto the meadow. At the pond, she shouted from horseback. "Hargis! Hargis is coming, but he's brought that Price Loughrie."

Lucie motioned to Ruth. "Get my guns." Ruth slopped out of the pond and ran, shaking her skirt, toward the cottage. Piney dragged their barrels from the water and upended them on grass.

Wanda tied her horse to the pasture fence, then ran back to the pond and tugged on Piney's sleeve. "There might be shooting. Let's get to the horse shed."

"I can't leave Ma," Piney whispered. "We'll be all right. She almost never has to shoot."

The moment felt like Will's prediction coming true. Ruth handed her ma the shotgun as the wagon of fat sacks came into view, two men on the seat and Loughrie's dainty black horse tied behind. Wanda stayed at the waterside with her aunts, Lucie, and three barking dogs. Ruth held the rifle loosely over her arm.

Lucie raised the shotgun.

"Granny." Wanda laid her hand on the cold gun barrel. "Don't shoot yet. I'd like to hear Hargis try to talk his way out of this."

Hargis stopped the mules well within shooting range. Loughrie stood in the wagon and removed his hat. Compared to Hargis, who wore his usual grubby overalls, Loughrie looked fancy in a white shirt, leather vest, and fine wool trousers.

"You remember Mr. Loughrie," Hargis called. "He's friendly. We got everything worked out."

Lucie wrenched the shotgun from Wanda's touch. "You're not supposed to work out anything."

"Easy, Ma," Ruth said.

The dogs stopped barking and sniffed the wagon wheels.

Loughrie fingered his hat. "I understand the need to keep yourself private. All that about you being the Porters is fine with me."

In answer, Lucie raised the shotgun and pulled the trigger. Hargis dove to the ground. The gun made a feeble click. Lucie pumped the action and swore. "Ruth, you get him!"

Ruth raised the rifle, then lowered and held it against her hip.

Hargis lifted his head above the wagon side. "Let the man talk. He's got an offer."

Ruth kept her stance. Wanda saw her own fear in Piney's wide eyes.

"He ain't a marshal no more," Hargis said. "He buys for boot-leggers."

Bootleggers. More bad company.

"Nice to see you-all again," Loughrie said.

Lucie handed the useless shotgun to Piney. "Hargis, you're a fool, but double's the shame on me, for I knew that already. Ruth, keep your rifle on the marshal while me and Hargis has a talk." She motioned to a swing under an oak. "Evalena's Girl, help me up there."

Lucie leaned on Wanda's arm until they reached the swing, then let go and dropped to the seat.

Lucie shook her fist at Hargis. "I said you should bring Virgie. Nobody else."

Wanda glanced back at the pond. Loughrie had stepped down from the wagon, but Ruth still held the rifle. Piney stood close beside her, and the dogs had settled in the grass. Whatever the marshal was saying had not made Ruth put down the rifle. Wanda took a step backwards to hear him, but Hargis was too loud.

"Look here, I've done you a favor," Hargis said. "Price Loughrie can get top dollar for our product. He knows what it's worth 'cause he's heard of you. And he'll help with the making, just for a pleasant place to rest over."

Lucie gripped the swing's chain. "This ain't gonna be no pleasant place. How many other vagrants and thieves did you excite by blabbing about my product? And where's Virgie?"

"Well you see, Virgie rode along with me to the mill and all, then changed her mind. I dropped her off back at Winkler."

This news went down like a swallow of bad medicine, but Wanda couldn't be distracted by Virgie now. She kept one eye on the pond, where Ruth, Piney, and Loughrie had moved closer together.

"It's true he's been a marshal," Hargis said, "but you know even lawmen get tired of seeing what can be had on the other side. Did you see his nice clothes? That don't come from playing the fiddle or hauling folks to jail."

Lucie grumped. "I can shoot him or work him. But I warn you Hargis, if I have to shoot, it'll be him first and you right after."

"Miss Lucie, I promise you'll be thankful."

"Ruth," Lucie called. "Load up my gun."

While Ruth took the shotgun to the cottage, Wanda put Loughrie's horse in the field with the others and had a private look in his saddlebags. They carried jerky, folded shirts and finely-woven union suits, scraps of printed music, and wrapped in paper, a family Bible.

She returned to the pond as Ruth gave Lucie the shotgun. Lucie pulled back the action bar and peered at the shells. "All right. You get the rifle from Piney now and watch the marshal. Piney and Wanda will tote the barrels and all up to the still."

Was Loughrie friend or foe? His face showed nothing. Wanda spoke close to Lucie's ear. "It'd be nice to eat something." Lucie gave no sign of hearing.

Loughrie took off his vest and string tie and rolled up his sleeves. He and Hargis packed sacks of corn meal on the mules and went back and forth to the site, followed by Ruth and her rifle. Lucie watched from her rock. As she and Piney worked, Wanda stayed alert for any sudden movement of the gun in Lucie's hands and any change in Ruth.

When finally they gathered at the site, Lucie invited Loughrie to sit beside her on the cot. Wanda waited at a distance for Loughrie to reveal himself.

Lucie directed his gaze to overhanging brush and trees. "What do you think, Marshal? Are we hid good enough here?"

"Nothing's a hundred percent, Miss Lucie. Somebody wants to find you, they will." He sounded sad.

"That's for certain. You, for one. I suppose you could of found us on your own."

"True enough." Wanda followed his gaze around their circle. Hargis looked proud. Piney's face was eager, Ruth's hidden.

Lucie nodded. "Do you know of any who wants to find us?"

"I've heard your name spoke in rough company."

"Rough is usual here. If company comes, are you prepared to fight?"

"I carry no gun."

Lucie waved to Hargis. "We should check that. Hargis, give a look in the marshal's pockets."

Ruth's forehead puckered.

Hargis grimaced. "In his business, he has to carry something."

"He claims he's not in business no more. If you was a smart feller, you'd take his weapon away before bringing him to me. Get to it."

Loughrie stood and raised his hands. "Some say my fiddle playing's a killer."

Wanda smiled in spite of herself. Hargis pulled out Loughrie's pockets, revealing coins and paper money.

"Roll up his trousers," Lucie said.

Hargis inspected Loughrie's ankles and the open tops of his riding boots.

"Ruth, see if he's got anything under that shirt."

Piney gasped. Loughrie averted his eyes while Ruth unbuttoned his shirt and felt his chest, his underarms and back like he was no more than the trunk of a tree. "Nothing," she said.

Lucie pursed her lips. "Did any of you think to look in his saddlebags?"

"I did," Wanda said. "No guns or knives."

"Well, Marshal, you're a brave one, roaming the world with nothing to save you."

"Not brave at all. When we walk in faith, we find our salvation. Do I pass inspection?"

"We'll see. Let's make the mash." Lucie gathered them to the copper boiler, now seated in the circular furnace and sealed to the stones above its widest place with Lucie's special paste.

"Here's what's gonna happen. We'll work in pairs to make the mash, run the liquor, and act as lookouts. Once we start the run, only one pair will sleep at any time." Lucie pointed a crooked finger at Hargis. "You'll be with me, because I don't trust you. Ruth with the new man, same reason. Piney and Evalena's Girl."

"Put me with Piney," Hargis said.

"I've decided this already. At times, four will work together, and when we start the run, two or more will stay overnight at the site. Nobody does anything but what I say."

Wanda smiled to herself. Clearly Ruth did not do everything to please her ma, or there would have been shells in that shotgun.

Lucie pointed toward the eight barrels on the slope. "Ruth, you and the marshal level more spots for them barrels and scrape out a place for one under the slop arm of the still. Hargis, fill the still with water and build the fire, then help Ruth and the marshal dig."

Hargis frowned at the steep ground.

Loughrie got a pickax and Ruth a shovel and they set to work. Hargis looked to be thinking about it.

"Piney, you and Evalena's Girl go now and grind your corn sprouts. Get 'em fine. Hargis, get to it!"

Starting downhill, Wanda checked again on Ruth and Loughrie, their heads bent close as they picked and scraped the rocky soil.

Piney grabbed Wanda's hand. "I hope Ma won't scare Mr. Loughrie off. All this company makes things interesting."

"He won't be company for long," Wanda said. Loughrie looked tired and dirty as any of them.

"Oh, my. Do you think he'll leave us? Ma don't really mean to shoot him, but it won't be good if he gets away."

Piney didn't think Lucie would shoot him? She'd tried it once.

"I hope Ruth treats him decent," Piney said.

"She'll be fine." Sometime during the afternoon, Ruth had set her rifle aside.

"I like his eyes. Don't they look deep and kind?"

"There's no way to tell from eyes if someone's good or bad." Or because they carried a holy book.

She and Piney dragged the sausage mill from a dark corner of the cellar house to a table under the porch roof. The corn kernels, now dry, had white spindly roots, pale green sprouts, and a slightly sweet odor.

Piney attached a coarse blade for the first grinding. "This is gonna take us to the end of daylight. You start grinding while I run out to the corn patch and put some sprouted kernels in the ground. Pull the sprouts off yours afore you grind."

It was tedious business. Wanda threw sprouts in the grass and seeds in the hopper and cranked the handle of the sausage mill, wondering if Ruth often removed shells from Lucie's guns, or if this time was special. Price Loughrie, solemn and sad-eyed, claiming something about salvation: had he come to buy liquor or confiscate it, or—most interesting—to find an old sweetheart?

Piney came back and took a turn at cranking the mill. "I can tell Ruth likes Mr. Loughrie. Wouldn't it be grand if he stayed here with us? 'Course Hargis wouldn't like that. He plans to be top dog when Ma's gone."

Wanda's belly rumbled. Work here was hard and they had less to eat than May Rose's orphans. "Will they be a long time up there?"

"Hours more. They'll heat water and meal in batches, let each batch bubble in the still then drain it through the slop arm into one of those barrels. When they're done, we'll have seven or eight barrels."

"Of whiskey?"

"Wouldn't Ma be glad of that? No, barrels of mash—the start of the beer. Not beer like folks drink, though I've known Ruth to get thirsty and drink some. The mash works for four or five days before it's ready to run. Then we dip it into the boiler. This sprouted corn will make the malt—it gives our product a good taste, Ma says, though none of it tastes good to me."

Piney put the cracked corn back through the grinder until she judged it might satisfy Lucie. By then daylight was gone. And when finally the others came down from the site, Loughrie no longer looked like company and Lucie did not ask where Piney had acquired the meal for corn cakes. Ruth, however, came to the table freshly washed and combed.

It was another dinner without talk. Wanda planned what she'd say to Loughrie if she could catch him alone. While she and

Piney washed dishes, Loughrie sat outside and tuned up his fiddle, then played sweet, troubled tunes. Wanda hummed along. She wasn't ready to trust Loughrie, but couldn't help liking his music.

Lucie peered into the kitchen. "Tell them out there to get to bed. You too."

In the moonless night, Wanda followed the glow of a cigarette to a stump where Hargis sat, smoking. Beyond him, the swing moved. Ruth.

She leaned against a porch post and didn't speak until the tune ended. "Mr. Loughrie, I'm curious who you were looking for, that day we met you on the road."

Loughrie laid his fiddle on his knees. "I spoke true that day, though maybe I should have said I'd been traveling around, looking for signs of folks I used to know. When I saw 'Bosell' spelled out on that board, I figured I'd found some. Then I met Hargis again."

"I'd like to hear about that," Wanda said. "How you got him to bring you here."

"He already told it to Lucie," Hargis said.

"But not to me. If you don't mind, Mr. Loughrie."

"I don't mind. I met Hargis at the mill. He was in a spot of trouble. Some men were about to take his corn. They'd heard things about me."

"Cottons," Hargis said. "Small-time rascals. They backed off 'cause Price is a buyer."

Loughrie plunked a string. "No more. I've turned over a new leaf." He spoke almost too quietly to be heard.

A breeze ruffled branches of the oak tree. Wanda broke the silence. "A new leaf, as marshal?"

"I'm done with that, too."

If he was a marshal, he wouldn't admit it in front of everybody. But since Hargis had introduced him as a buyer, why not claim that? He'd have a better chance of Lucie's favor.

Time would tell. "Well good luck, Mr. Loughrie. Lots of us

would like to reform ourselves. But now Granny has sent me to say all of you are to get to bed."

Hargis stamped out his cigarette and disappeared in the dark. In the room she shared with Piney and Ruth, Wanda stayed awake long enough to know that Ruth did not come directly to bed.

CHAPTER 15

There was no easy way to discover Loughrie's true nature, for unlike Hargis, he worked steadily and offered no opinions. One thing Wanda knew. If he wasn't what he claimed, he was brave or stupid.

They went to the site after breakfast the next morning. Wanda came last, behind Hargis, who held the lead rope of Lucie's mule. He stopped at the top of a bank and let the mule take its time. She kept her eyes on Lucie, who lurched on the mule's back as it scrambled up the bank, and farther ahead, on Loughrie, who paused now and then to give Ruth a hand up the slope.

"We don't need to climb up here a different way each time," Hargis said. "It's not like this land is along the National Road."

Wanda agreed, though she didn't like to hear Hargis make sense. Lucie didn't favor him with a reply.

When the site was in view, Ruth seized Wanda's arm and pulled her away. "Stop watching us."

Wanda shrugged her off. "I'm real sorry if it irks you, but if your ma don't trust Mr. Loughrie, why should we?"

"Most of the time, Ma is a fool."

"So if I suspect him, I'm a fool, too? What if he's really a marshal, come to put your ma out of business?"

"I wasn't born yesterday," Ruth said. "First, Ma is hardly in the business, yet. And second, if Price was here to spy, he could do it a lot of different ways than all that digging and hauling."

"So he's here for…what? Hard work? To take over the business? Run off with the product?"

"Watch yourself, you're talking ugly as Ma."

Wanda followed her gaze to Loughrie, who waited near Lucie and the mash barrels. "I know he's a pretty man. Well-spoken, like a gentleman. Just the kind to make a woman believe anything."

"He's been a lot of things. He wants to change for the better."

"By making whiskey?"

Ruth walked away.

Lucie beckoned, and Wanda joined the others at the barrels, where the air was faintly sweet and full of gnats.

"Look over here and see what we're to watch for," Lucie said. "Lift them boards."

When they'd set aside the barrel covers, Lucie pointed a crooked finger. "See, some of these mixtures has got no bubbles— they're not working good as the others." She handed a long-handled dipper to Loughrie.

"I'll do that," Hargis said.

Lucie waved him away. "The marshal's got it."

Wanda took notice of Hargis's scowl.

"Now, let's dip a little from the working mixes into the ones that are lazy," Lucie said.

Loughrie dipped and Ruth stirred. Lucie motioned to Piney. "Pour in the malt."

Piney poured the meal from their sprouted corn and Ruth stirred again, eyes on the stir stick in her hands. Loughrie stood back, watching her face, while Hargis studied Loughrie like he might be having second thoughts.

"Tonight we'll keep watch around the property," Lucie said. By then the mash will be working strong enough to notify more than gnats."

Wanda followed Loughrie downhill, seeing how he steadied

Ruth by latching onto her arm, though Ruth was strong and sure-footed and would have shrugged off anyone else.

When they reached the cottage, Lucie ordered Hargis to build another bunk in the horse shed, Ruth and Loughrie to dig a pit for a new outhouse, and Wanda and Piney to catch fish, fix lunch, and then sleep if they wanted because they were to do the watch that night.

Wanda kept reminding herself why she was here, and why she had to stay.

An hour later, she stood with Piney at a board nailed like a shelf between two trees at the water's edge. A catfish big enough to feed them all lay on the board, and a bucket of water sat at their feet. "I'm glad Ma's paired me with you," Piney said.

Wanda had sharpened her knife, and with Piney pointing, she made slits through the tough skin. "And I'd say Ruth is glad to work with Mr. Loughrie."

Piney pressed down her hand, steadying the slimy catfish. "Now grab the skin with those pliers and peel back. Wouldn't it be wonderful if he stayed? I'd take him like a shot, but I see he favors Ruth."

Wanda pulled back the tight skin a little at a time. She paused and glanced toward the site of the new outhouse where Loughrie was swinging the pick. "I suppose what a man has been is no proof of what he'll do next."

With deft swipes, Piney cut two long fillets from the fish. "Ma's always had a notion of getting a marshal on her side. She used to say they're no different from us, just haven't had our opportunities."

Wanda raised her skirt to her nose and sniffed. "Time to soap this off. And I hope you're right about Mr. Loughrie." So far he acted pure as Piney.

~

CAROL ERVIN

When everyone gathered for their lunch of fish soup, Wanda took a seat across the table from Loughrie.

"I don't suppose, Mr. Loughrie, there's any danger of those men following you and Hargis from the mill?"

Hargis stopped slurping his soup. "We was careful."

"I'm asking, Mr. Loughrie, because I run across the name of those men before, and I've not been here long enough to hear many names, so it's odd to hear that one twice."

Lucie tapped her spoon on Wanda's bowl. "What name you talking about?"

"Cotton," Wanda said. "We heard that name at Will's store. Remember? He took a trunk of fine clothes and other things in trade from some Cottons, and gave me a jacket from that trunk." She watched to see if Lucie might follow her thought, that the gold coins might belong to the same Cottons who'd tried to steal their corn.

"Uhmph," Lucie said.

"Probably things they stole," Hargis said. "Cottons don't worry about thieving in broad daylight 'cause the law around here is nothing. For one thing, there ain't enough lawmen, and for another, what there is can't stand up to bootleggers with motor trucks and sharpshooters."

"We don't need lawmen," Lucie said. "We take care of ourselves." She gave a narrow look to Loughrie. "Pity's the man who tries to steal from me."

Hargis scraped up his last bit of soup. "The big time is coming. Bootleggers go where they want, haul whiskey outa these hills to places where they pay better than them poor fellers in mining camps. Big-city bootleggers is the connection we need, Lucie."

"Maybe the Cottons would like to take over Mr. Loughrie's connection," Wanda said.

Loughrie's eyelids drooped. "They're welcome to it. I've worked both sides of the law, and Hargis is right, these days the threats are mighty."

"I'd like to hear again what side you're on," Lucie said.

"Neither, like I said. When I was a marshal, I got tired of hauling people to jail, poor fellers selling a few jugs to feed their children. I got to drinking myself, then got mixed up with the bootleggers and put them onto a couple of good distillers. They always wanted more. I've come a long way to get away from all that."

"Yet here you are," Wanda said, "making whiskey." For Ruth's sake, she wanted to believe.

Loughrie straightened. "If there's other work, I'd rather do it. I don't want to be drawn to drink again, so it's best I'm not around those who do."

Lucie lifted her bowl and swallowed the last of her soup. "I approve of that. Drinking spoils us for the work."

Wanda caught Piney's quick glance at Ruth, who sat with her head bent. If he was telling the truth, maybe he and Ruth would influence each other for the better.

"Mrs. Bosell," Loughrie said, "I've seen an attachment at some stills that makes the work lighter. I can tell you about it if you're interested."

"Does it change the product?"

"Not at all."

"I'm always glad to hear a new trick." When Lucie rose, Hargis hurried to help. Loughrie and Ruth followed, but Wanda stayed at the table, thinking how those gold coins had slipped through the hands of several thieves. Including hers.

Wanda and Piney refused to carry Lucie's shotgun and rifle while they rode night watch, but each wore a wooden whistle on a ribbon around her neck. If the whistle wasn't loud enough to alert those at the still, at least the other should hear it.

She made her first round while there was light to see, riding toward the slope that led to the still, continuing past the cornfield and the hidden road, and circling back to the sheds and cottage.

The sky was overcast, and when night fell with no moon and no stars, she had to trust Ginger to step over groundhog holes and other pitfalls.

Old Henry's Dog had followed Piney, but the other two dogs ran near Wanda, and she was glad to hear them sniffing through the grass. They yipped when the others returned from the still, like it was their job to signal night movements. On a later round, as Wanda and Piney passed each other near the dark cottage, all three dogs whirled and raced toward the pond, barking like fierce beasts.

"We should take a look," Piney said. "Don't worry, nothing sets them off like a stray dog. If it's something wild and nasty, our pack will catch it or chase it off."

Wanda set the whistle between her lips. Unbidden, Ginger trotted off after Old Henry.

At the edge of the valley they found the dogs whining and circling something in the grass.

Piney jumped down.

"You shouldn't," Wanda said. "Whatever it is might bite."

"It cried, did you hear?" Piney pushed the dogs away and knelt in the grass.

Wanda stayed on her horse. "Aunt Piney, please."

"Sweet Jesus," Piney said. "I think it's a child."

Wanda jumped down, stumbled on dark rough ground and nearly collided with Piney, who struggled up with a bundle in her outstretched arms. Wanda touched a cold leg. The leg kicked, then was still.

Piney gasped. "It's so limp. I think it's close to dead."

"You get on Old Henry and I'll hand it up to you."

Piney set the child in Wanda's arms. It was very still, its dress wet and crusty, and though the night was warm, its skin was cold. When Piney settled in her saddle, Wanda lifted the child to her arms. Left alone in the dark, she struggled to mount her horse without some kind of step up, but finally Ginger stood still long enough for her to get her foot in the stirrup and swing into the saddle.

She arrived at the cottage in time to see Ruth and Loughrie standing close on the back porch. Piney passed the child to Ruth, and Loughrie took their horses. In the kitchen, Ruth laid the child on the table and pushed tangled, matted hair away from her face. The child was barefoot, her dress muddied and torn, and every bit of skin that showed had red scratches and bruises.

Lucie entered the kitchen in her nightgown. "What's this ruckus?"

Wanda and her aunts kept their attention on the child. Loughrie stopped inside the door. Piney poured water from the teakettle and wrung out a cloth.

"Ruth," Lucie said, "what's that dirty mess you got on my table?"

"It's a little girl, Ma. A lost child."

Snot and dirt smeared the child's face. Trembling and sniffing, Piney dabbed the cloth on the child's cheeks. "Somewhere there's a mama who's beside herself for the loss of this little one."

Loughrie looked down at the child. "Poor pitiful thing. Tomorrow I'll ride out and check with everyone along the road. "Several of us should go, we'll see more people that way."

"You're going nowhere," Lucie said. "We've work here to do. I'll think on this and decide."

"I suppose we might wait until folks come looking for her," Wanda said.

Lucie's face took on a bit of worry. "Evalena's Girl is right, we don't want strangers here. First light, you get the child away. Set it up on the road, someone will come by."

Ruth opened her mouth and clamped it shut. Piney wrung out the cloth, ran it over the child's legs and feet and carried her toward their bedroom.

"All right then," Lucie said. "If you won't take it, Hargis will."

Loughrie touched Ruth's arm. "I'll say goodnight. Holler if

you need me." He closed the door softly. Wanda and Ruth followed Piney.

Lucie thumped her cane. "Piney and Evalena's Girl, get back to your watch. Piney! Evalena's Girl! Did you hear me?"

In their room, Piney laid the child on the bed and slid the wooden bar to lock the door.

Ruth looked at Wanda. "How old?"

"Four, maybe."

Lucie's cane pounded on the door.

"Don't open it," Piney said.

CHAPTER 16

Wanda woke in the night, aware of the lantern's dim glow, of Ruth and Piney whispering over the small figure on their bed, of the door softly opening and closing, of the scent of fish soup, of murmuring as they tried to spoon nourishment into the child who lay so still.

Thankfully, they were too busy to notice how the hammock shook as Wanda harkened back to other whispers in the night, a baby born dead, then another. She laid her arm across her eyes to soak up their tears.

The lost one's screams woke her at dawn's light, and she rolled out of the hammock to see Ruth looking happy with a flailing, red-faced child in her arms. "This means she's better, doesn't it?"

Piney rushed into the room with a bowl of steaming soup, and Ruth sat down with the child on her lap. Piney dipped a spoon and held it toward the child.

"Test it on your wrist," Wanda said.

Piney dabbed the spoon on her wrist and blew gently to cool it. The child stopped crying and opened her mouth. The child tried to swallow and made a face, then wailed and reddened again.

"Oh, dear," Piney said. "It doesn't seem too hot. Wanda, what can be wrong?"

"I'm sorry, I don't know."

Lucie opened the door. "Ruth! Piney, shush that child. It's gonna wake the dead."

"Good," Ruth said. "They'll be glad to rise up."

The child cried harder, then held her breath.

"Wanda?"

Her aunts looked panicky. "I'm sorry, this is beyond me," she said.

Lucie snorted. "Don't let it holler no more. Piney, see to breakfast."

When Lucie left, Piney locked the door.

The child's eyes rolled back in her head, and she went limp in Ruth's lap. Ruth laid her on the bed and put an ear to her chest. "Bring the mirror."

Piney held a small mirror to the child's nose, then turned it for the others to see. "She's breathing." She gave the child a gentle shake, and then a harder one. "Why doesn't she wake up?"

"Get dressed," Wanda said. "We'll take her to Will."

The women moved quickly, pulling on trousers under their nightgowns, then boots, then dresses in place of their nightgowns.

"Wanda, let us use your horse," Ruth said.

"Can't—I want to go. Take the wagon, or ask Mr. Loughrie for the loan of his horse, or Hargis."

"Horses will be faster," Piney said. "We can go out by the trail." She doubled a bed sheet and wrapped it around the child.

In the kitchen, Lucie swung around from the table and blocked them with her cane. "Hargis will take it now."

"She's sick," Wanda said. "We're taking her to Will."

Ruth jerked the cane from Lucie's grip and tossed it across the room. Pulled off balance, Lucie fell against the wall and stared at Ruth like she didn't know her. "All right, then. I suppose it would go hard on us if it got out we left a sick child on the road. But one of you has to stay to help me manage those men."

"Wanda and me will go," Piney said. "Ruth, help us with the horses."

Lucie shook her fist. "Be sure you're the only ones to come back. Leave it with Doc or somebody."

Wanda opened the door and they hurried past.

Loughrie helped saddle and bridle Old Henry and Wanda's mare. She draped the sheet around Piney and tied it at her shoulder like a sling. When Piney got into the saddle, Ruth handed her the child, now sleeping or unconscious, and she and Loughrie secured her in the sling so she was bound to Piney's chest.

Ruth touched the child's cheek. "Get her well. Bring her back."

Wanda mounted and leaned over to Ruth. "If we're not here at the end of the day, come after us."

"That I will. If you have to take her somewhere else, leave word at the store."

Piney turned Old Henry toward the steep trail to the road. Old Henry's Dog ran ahead.

Most of the way to Winkler, Wanda and Piney rode side by side, speaking only to warn of an overhanging branch, the condition of the child, and their hopes that Will would know what to do.

About halfway, Wanda suggested she carry the child for a while, so when they came to a rock big enough to serve as a step, Wanda got off her horse and took the bundle. Then Piney tied the sheet around Wanda and held the child while she mounted.

At Winkler, they found Will on the street, setting up tables of boards and sawhorses.

"Doc," Piney's voice rose like a sob.

He showed no surprise to see Wanda's bundle, only untied her sling and took the child in his arms. She warmed with relief. They followed him to the store.

Inside, he laid the child on a high, padded leather bench against the wall. She marveled at the calm in his face as he laid his ear on the child's chest, lifted her eyelids one at a time and placed three fingers on her wrist, not telling why or saying what he found.

He straightened. "Tell me what you know."

"We found her last night, in our meadow," Piney said. "I mean, the dogs found her. She was very dirty and didn't wake till this morning, then she cried and held her breath, and ever since she's been like this."

He turned each limp arm and leg. "I wonder, did she get these bruises while she was lost, or before?"

The child's skin was painful to see. Will sat and leafed through his medical books. Wanda kept finding new reasons to love him.

He came back to the bench and ran a finger down the sole of the child's foot. The child's leg flexed and her eyes popped open. Whimpering, she shifted a glance to each of them. Piney closed her in her arms.

"She seems okay for now," Will said. "The fit could be a lack in what she eats, or something more serious. I took bread in trade yesterday, and I could soak some in milk if you'd like to feed her."

"Yes, please," Piney said.

Wanda offered to fetch the milk. She hurried to Will's spring house, where water flowed into a stone basin with crocks of butter, fresh meat, and a pitcher of milk. Returning with the milk, she fingered the money pouch sewn beneath her skirt. "Will, could we buy one of your milk goats?"

"There's one I'll give you, an old nanny with her milk almost dried up. She's a sweet thing, and I hate to butcher her."

They all smiled when the child grabbed Piney's spoon and fed herself. "We'll take the nanny, thank you," Piney said.

Will lifted a small halter and a coil of rope from a hook near the door. "She'll be a nice pet, too."

Wanda followed him outside, hurrying to keep up. "Where's Virgie today?"

"She's on a buying trip to Elkins, wants to sell ladies' clothes in the store, maybe at Trading Days too."

"I guess she learned to handle that wagon."

"I guess she did." He walked into the herd of white and spotted goats, put the halter on one and led her toward the horses.

Wanda hurried behind. "Piney loves all kinds of creatures. She'll take good care of your goat."

"I wouldn't give her to just anybody. Which horse should I tie her to?"

"Old Henry will do best."

When he'd tied the goat, Wanda tried to slip her hand into his. "I'll be going home soon."

"That's smart." He turned for a handshake. "You know I like you, Wanda, but I think we'd be bad, together all the time."

His hand was warm, but his face was as blank as when he'd examined the child. She lifted her chin. "You've judged me too quick."

"Could be. I try to know myself and do what's best, even if I don't like it."

She found a bit of comfort in the thought that he might not like sending her away. Often Homer had gone cold at some little thing she'd done.

"I might get May Rose to come, next time," she said.

"I'd like to see her." He shaded his eyes against the sun as his dogs raced off, barking, toward a horse-drawn wagon approaching from the valley head. "I believe this is my miller."

Wanda scratched the goat's head. It would be all right, living here, even if she couldn't win him. Evie would like the goats and dogs. Piney and Ruth could visit. Her gold coins would help, soon as she stole them back.

The wagon drew close. The driver had reddish hair, a feature that always made her look twice. When he stopped his team and got down she saw how the hair thinned over his red scalp. His face was dense with freckles, like Homer's, and long white hairs curled from his eyebrows and the back of his neck. Beside him on the wagon bench, a young woman held a swaddled infant.

Will extended his hand. "Simpson. I'm pleased to see you." Wanda envied the welcome on his face and in his voice.

Simpson's grin crinkled the skin at the edges of his eyes. His hand was plump and hairy, and maybe the largest she'd ever seen. "Doc, I thank you."

Will nodded to the woman. "Ma'am, welcome to Winkler." The woman's eyes were wide and shifty, and like a shy child, she did not reply. A small boy perched beside her. From the table and chairs turned upside down on the wagon load, Wanda judged the family to be on the move.

Simpson got down, took the infant, and extended his hand to help the woman to the ground. Sand-colored hair straggled over her face, her dress was soiled and her mouth limp. As soon as she stepped from the wagon, the boy leapt at her, and she wobbled, catching him. He wiggled out of her arms to the ground.

Simpson took hold of the boy's arm and gave him a shake. "Here, now, Robert, you can't jump at folks like that. Blanche, take his hand. Doc, this here's my daughter, Blanche. She and her children will be staying with me."

Will nodded. "Pleased to meet you, Mrs. …"

"Her married name's Cotton. She's suffered a tragedy."

Cotton.

Blanche's shoulders heaved.

The little boy sat in the dirt, and Simpson pulled him up. "We'll tell you about it once we've settled. It's shook us all. Could you spare some refreshment?"

"Come in and rest, then I'll take you to your house."

Simpson gave a nod of greeting to Wanda, but Will walked the family up the steps without an introduction. She didn't let it bother her. He'd find she wasn't easily put off, not by a slight, not even by words.

She followed them inside in time to hear Blanche Cotton's scream.

"My Dear Lord," Simpson said.

Blanche seized Piney's lost child.

Piney stood stunned, her arms outstretched and empty. Wanda hurried to her side.

In the middle of their circle, the miller's daughter moaned as she rocked the child side to side.

Simpson stepped toward Piney. "Ma'am, we thank you dearly for bringing back my daughter's girl."

Wanda's hopes fell as the child squeezed her thin arms around Blanche's neck. Piney would not be taking her home.

"How..." Piney's voice broke. "How do I know it's hers?"

"Miss Piney," Will said. "This is Simpson Wainwright. If he says the child belongs to his daughter, I'd say it does. Simpson, this is Piney Bosell. It was her that found your grandbaby."

Simpson jiggled the infant. His blue eyes sparked. "We're in your debt, Miss Bosell."

Piney let Simpson Wainwright shake her hand but kept her eyes on the lost child.

"My daughter's name is Blanche," Simpson said. "Mrs. Blanche Cotton. Honey, say 'thank you' to Miss Bosell."

Blanche buried her face in the child's tangled hair.

"My daughter's not herself... been through too much, but she's eternally grateful," Simpson said.

Near Wanda, the boy Robert toddled to a set of shelves, prodded a can with a red wrapper and watched it drop and roll on the floor. Then he lifted his arms to climb up. She hurried to stop him, but the shelf swayed and crashed down. He howled.

Simpson dropped the swaddled infant into Piney's arms and came to help Wanda and Will lift the shelving. Underneath, Robert thrashed and cried like he was more angry than hurt, though there was a red gash in his forehead and blood running into one eye. Will carried him to the bench where he'd treated the girl. Blanche set her daughter down and picked up a can near her feet.

Without a word or glance, Piney returned the infant to Simpson and walked to the door. The girl was now wandering about and touching everything in reach while her mother stood at the bench by Robert.

Outside, Piney bawled until she was red. "The baby smells

sour and dirty. And the ma stood right there and watched a child who barely walks climb up that shelf. She's not fit."

"We can't be sure," Wanda said.

Piney would not be consoled. "There's something wrong."

"The ma has bruises on her arms, like the girl's," Wanda said. "But I think Will trusts Simpson. Maybe with him they'll all be safe, and the ma will do better."

Piney mounted Old Henry. "We never knew her name." Her tears flowed again. "Leave the goat for them."

Wanda retied the goat to the hitching post, then got a leg up on her horse and followed, troubled by that word *trust*. She'd given Will every reason not to trust her.

CHAPTER 17

S ide by side, Wanda and Piney rode out of Winkler, away from their lost child, away from Will. Wanda looked back at his restored houses. One for Virgie, one for the miller and his daughter's family, a town grown this week from one to seven souls. She hoped Will's dream came true. He didn't need a woman whose ideas blew this way and that until they lit on trouble, and she didn't know how to be different.

At the head of the valley they turned up the road to Lucie's.

"I wish we'd brought the goat after all," Piney said.

"We can go back and get it."

"I'd feel bad. Those children need milk."

They stopped and drank from a stream where water oozed through cracks in a rock face. Below it, sunlight sparkled on a clear, rocky pool. "This is a pretty spot," Piney said. "I'm grateful for pretty sights, aren't you?"

"I've never paid a lot of attention to prettiness, Aunt Piney. But I'm grateful for you. And you're a pretty sight."

Piney's lips broke in a smile. Wanda put one foot in a stirrup and swung into the saddle. "You're getting better at that," Piney said.

One accomplishment. Wanda patted Ginger's neck. "I'll find a way to earn money in Fargo so I can come back with Evie." Say goodbye to the house where she listened for Homer.

"I've never been anyplace but Virginia that one time. I wish I could go with you."

Wanda touched the flat money belt hidden against her skin. She might have enough for one young goat. "Do you have money for train fare?"

"Ma keeps the money."

And eight stolen gold coins. "When I come back, we'll live together in Winkler, you, me, and Evie." If May Rose followed, Will would be pleased.

"Could we keep goats there?"

"Why not? But let's not tell anyone we're leaving till they see us going through the door." And after a look-around for those coins.

For the rest of the trip, she let herself imagine a distant time when, like a miracle, Will would trust her again.

They reached the cottage in late afternoon. Ruth met them at the horse shed, hammer in hand. "Where's the child?"

"We found her folks," Wanda said.

"Oh." Ruth blinked. "I guess that's good. Did she get okay?"

Wanda wasn't sure. "She was walking about when we saw her last."

Piney dismounted and loosened the cinch on Old Henry's saddle. "Someone beat her."

"Yes," Ruth said. "All those bruises." She and Piney shared a grim look.

"I don't think the ma did it," Wanda said. "She's bruised too. But they have a new place in Winkler with the grandpap, so maybe it won't happen again. Have you heard of Simpson Wainwright?"

Ruth hung the hammer on her belt and took the saddle from Piney. "I've heard the name. I think he helps the miller at Crosscreek, where Hargis took our corn."

"The child's ma is Simpson's daughter," Wanda said. "He's gonna be miller at Winkler."

Ruth took the saddle from Piney. "Good. We'll keep an eye out, make sure the child's all right."

They turned the horses into the field, and Piney hustled off toward the cottage. Wanda followed.

The kitchen was as clean as they'd left it. "I'm tired of this," Piney said. "Nobody has cooked a thing today, and in a minute they'll come in here wanting to know what I've fixed for supper." She tossed wood into the firebox and slammed the door.

"I'll help," Wanda said, "soon as I get rid of these hot trousers."

"Peel a potato or two first," Piney said.

They peeled side-by-side until Piney judged they had enough for supper. While Piney sliced potatoes into a skillet of meat grease, Wanda left to change. She stopped at Lucie's door. Reforming herself to Will's liking would have to wait a while.

Lucie's room was the smallest in the cottage, with a narrow bed and a home-made table with pitcher and basin. A dress and a coat hung from hooks on the wall; other garments lay folded on two shelves. Wanda stuck her hands in the pockets of Lucie's clothes, upended the mattress, checked under the bedding and under the bed. Not even a fuzz of dust. Likely the old woman wore the coins in a money belt. In the aunts' bedroom, Wanda shed her trousers and got back to the kitchen before the potatoes were ready.

"Give them a holler," Piney said. "Supper's near done."

"We should eat ours and go for a walk till bedtime. Make them wonder."

"Wonder about what?" The screen door slammed behind Hargis.

"You're all over sawdust," Piney said. "Get yourself outside, and tell them it's time to eat."

"Ain't you the sassy miss. I like it!" He squeezed between

them. "This is nice. I been sawing boards for the outhouse. Lucie wants you to come and hammer them on."

"Supper first," Wanda said.

He circled his arms around both waists. "We ate already. Price fried a mess of corncakes just a while ago. Cleaned the kitchen, too."

Wanda pushed him away. "Seems the marshal is getting himself in good with Lucie."

"I'm beginning to wonder." Hargis said.

She liked Hargis's doubt. Loughrie had worked harder, proved himself smarter than Hargis, won Ruth's and Piney's admiration, and now maybe Lucie's. If Loughrie showed signs of deceit, Hargis would let everyone know.

He pinched Piney's cheek. "When I'm head of this family, I'm gonna treat my wife like a queen. No hammering, no hauling water or hoeing corn. You can rest in bed all day."

Piney struck her spatula against the side of the skillet. "Your bed, now who could pass that up?"

Hargis hitched up his trousers. "Piney, let's set our date. You know it's what Lucie wants."

Piney took her plate to the table. "I've changed my mind. I don't need a man, and Wanda don't neither. We're gonna leave here and live in Winkler." She glanced at Wanda. "I'm sorry."

Wanda shrugged. "We were only saying how nice it would be to live in a town. We've got no plans."

"I don't believe it anyway," Hargis said. "You two couldn't get along on your own."

Piney's face twisted. "That part about not wanting to marry is true."

"Then march along and tell it to your ma."

"I'll march where I please. You tell that to Ma."

"I'll say you're coming this minute." He slammed the door.

For the remainder of the day, she and Piney indulged their whims like girls playing truant. They were lying on their backs in tall meadow grass when Ruth tramped by, searching. Seeing them, she nodded and went on.

"When we live in Winkler," Piney said, "we'll see those children all the time and make sure they're all right."

"We will." How many years would she have to scrub dirty underwear to travel back, rent one of Will's houses and start a herd of goats?

To get her mind off Will, Wanda thought about money. Lucie owed her, and not just for stolen gold, but she wouldn't get anything if she left too soon. Next morning, when Lucie ordered her and Piney to help at the still, Wanda pulled Hargis aside.

"If it comes to Lucie choosing between you and the marshal, I'll be on your side."

Hargis kicked the dirt. "Him and Ruth's getting thick. I'll be chucked out if you or Piney won't have me."

"You won't be left out," Wanda said.

"How do you know?"

"I'm the future here. Trust me."

Hargis gave his gummy smile. "I think you appreciate me after all."

"Everybody's good for something," Wanda said.

Lucie's cane clicked on the paving stones. "Wanda, Hargis! Let's get to work. Piney, you too!"

"There's something new here," Piney said, when they reached the site. A barrel sat between the boiler and cooling flake, connected to both by pipe.

Lucie tapped the barrel with her cane. "The marshal built it. It's a 'thumper,' meant to shorten our work. Pay attention now."

Hargis caught Wanda's eye. He mouthed, "The marshal."

"You-all," Lucie said. "Take the lids off the mash."

They set the lids on the ground. The foamy heads had nearly disappeared.

"It's time. Piney, plug the slop hole."

Piney bent into the empty boiler and pushed a knot of rags into the clean-out hole at the bottom.

"Stop," Lucie said, when the rags plugged the opening. "All of you, now, dip outa that first barrel and fill the boiler near full. Then put three or four buckets' worth in the thumper."

"I'm mystified about that thump thing," Piney said.

Hargis gave a sober nod. "Could be your marshal's way of ruining you."

"Don't be a fool," Lucie said. "He's done us a good turn. I've known of a thumper, but we never made one. See, the steam coming off the boiler will heat the beer in the thumper and pass on through the coil. It's a faster way to double the run. You'll get the hang of it. Now, Hargis, build the fire gradual. If it gets too hot too fast, you'll scorch the mash."

His face was dark but he hustled to do her bidding.

When the beer was hot, Hargis and Piney sealed the cap with Lucie's special paste.

"Hargis, set a rock on that cap," Lucie said. "The marshal said we might get blowback from the thumper.

Wanda and Hargis exchanged another look.

Not long after boiling began, the thumper startled them with sounds like something inside was pounding to get out. Hargis and Piney stepped back, but Lucie did not, so Wanda stayed beside her.

"Good," Lucie said. "That's the steam from the boiler hitting the cold beer in the thumper. It'll set that beer to steaming too."

Lucie pointed her cane to the spout at the far end of the box of water with the coil. "She'll be coming outa there pretty soon."

As they watched the spout, there was a burst of steam, then liquid spurted into a small crock. The spurt soon became a trickle, and Lucie picked up the crock and tossed the liquid on a bush.

Hargis explained for Wanda. "The first bit is poison. She'll keep what comes after the second big spurt."

"Mind the fire," Lucie called.

"Yes, ma'am."

As the first run dripped into a clean crock, Lucie sometimes held her finger under the spout and touched her finger to her tongue. Finally she said, "There ain't no more kick to it. Stop now. Hargis, pull the logs out of the firebox and we'll let the boiler cool."

Wanda smelled and swirled the liquid in the crock. "Is it whiskey now?"

"Not quite," Piney said. "We'll run it back through."

"But not the old way," Lucie said. "The old way was to save all these firstlings till all the barrels was run, then run them through the boiler again. This new way is to put the firstlings in the thumper box and double each run as we go."

Lucie sat on her cot while they cleaned the boiler and thumper for the next run. After a time of observing their quiet work, Lucie whacked her cane on a rock. "Piney and Wanda, let me hear now, in the presence of this man. Which one of you is gonna marry him?"

They all stopped. Wanda squeezed Piney's hand. "We were talking of it this morning. We'll let you know."

"All right then." Lucie said. "Soon."

Hargis gave Wanda another secret look. Piney poured the newly-distilled liquor into the thumper, then all three carried buckets of beer to the boiler.

"My trouble," Wanda said, "is I need to go back and get my girl. I have money to get to Fargo, but none to get back here. And I have debts to settle there."

Lucie pointed her cane toward Hargis. "Get what you need from your new man."

"That won't be fair, 'cause I think he and Piney want each other. Granny, if you want me to come back, hand over those coins you took."

"I'll think on it," Lucie said.

At the end of the second run, Lucie ordered Piney and Wanda to go the cottage and send up Ruth and Loughrie with supper.

"You girls ride the watch tonight. The marshal and Ruth will stay here and help me and Hargis."

For the watch, Piney suggested they take turns sleeping and riding. Because the night air was more comfortable outside, they tied Wanda's hammock in its old place from a hook on a tree to the corner of the cottage.

"I'll ride first," Wanda said. She drew her dress up and let her legs hang bare, enjoying the soft air against her skin.

The horse made the rounds without direction. "Good horse," she said. "Ginger." She could not get used to the name, or think of the horse as female. It plodded on in the dark, slower and slower, with pauses that made her think it might be napping.

Her thoughts rambled. Someday she'd build a grand house on the old boardinghouse site, if Will would sell that to her. She'd get along fine without him—maybe she didn't even love him. It was possible to admire something without having to have it. Still, it would be nice to have a man she admired love her more than anything. And losing him made her want him more.

She came out of her wishes when the horse stopped at the cottage.

Piney sat up in the hammock. "Put her in the field and get your rest. Me and Old Henry will do the watch."

Lulled by the monotony of her ride, Wanda swayed in the hammock and drifted toward sleep. She woke in a fright, with fingers creeping beneath her dress and fat lips pressing against hers. She wrenched her head to the side and bit hard on a bristly ear, clamped her teeth and tossed her head like a dog with its jaws on a groundhog. The man who belonged to the ear howled and slapped at her head until she let go. She tumbled out of the hammock.

"Hargis, are you crazy?"

"Wanda? I thought you was Piney!"

A gun blast shocked the air.

The dogs barked, Hargis ran off, and Piney galloped out of the dark on Old Henry.

Another gun shot. "It's Ma," Piney said. She rode off toward the site.

Wanda pulled on her boots and took time to get her horse, in case she needed to ride from trouble or go for help.

The site was dimly lit by the glow of the furnace, the reflected shine of the boiler, and a lantern in someone's hand. Ruth's. Three other shadows wavered in the glow of the furnace—Lucie, Hargis, Loughrie—and there was a strong smell of burn. Wanda brought Ginger close to Old Henry.

"They've scorched the mash," Piney said.

Lucie whacked her cane against Hargis's butt, throwing him into a stumble. "He let it burn while he was who-knows-where." She prodded Ruth and Loughrie. "And they let it burn, sitting back there, drinking doublings. Do you smell it? The mash puked into the cap. If that puke reached the coil, you'll all pay."

Ruth giggled.

Lucie whisked her cane in the air. "You'll not think it's funny tomorrow when you're scrubbing and scraping with your fingernails."

Hargis pushed himself to his feet. "Lucie, maybe you should take notice of your oldest. She's sweet on the marshal, and who knows what he's up to."

Loughrie's shadow moved closer to Ruth's.

Lucie grumped. "I know what I know."

Ruth raised her lantern, showing the trail of blood down the side of Hargis's head. "Where you been, and what's been chewing on you?"

Hargis took off his shirt and pressed it against his torn ear.

"All right," Lucie said. "From now on, the pairs is changed. Piney, you'll be with the marshal, and Ruth and Hargis can devil each other. Evalena's Girl, you're with me."

Ruth stumbled against Hargis and laughed in his face. "Watch yourself, or you might get shot. Even Piney might do it."

CHAPTER 18

Hunger brought them together at the breakfast table, where they ate like sullen strangers.

Finally Lucie spoke. "Much as I hate to say it, Ruth's in charge today. Unless one of you thinks you can do the job better. I trust she's got her senses this morning."

Ruth stared into her coffee cup. Hargis's face got red.

Wanda shrugged. "Fine with me." Loughrie's drunken spell with Ruth showed a weakness she hadn't expected, and somehow made his story believable. Unless he'd pretended that too.

Lucie brushed her hand in the air like she was turning them out. "Get on. I can't stand the sight of you."

Piney whispered, "That means Ma needs to go back to bed."

Stoney-faced, Ruth ordered them to the site and said what needed to be done. Wanda set about scraping the inside of the boiler with her knife, while beside her, Piney scratched hardened mash from the boiler cap. A few paces uphill, Ruth and Loughrie again dug out the spring. Hargis lounged on the slope like he dared Ruth to scold.

Bent into the boiler, Wanda was aware of Hargis speaking quietly. She caught one word. "Stash."

She lifted her head.

He sat on his heels between her and Piney, chewing on a grass blade. "I got it figured. Price is after your granny's stash."

Piney stopped scraping and whispered back. "Why would he think Ma has a stash?"

"It's a point of common knowledge." He flicked a fly from the clot of blood on his ear.

"It's also common knowledge," Wanda said, "that only half of common knowledge is true.

Hargis nodded like a wise man. "That stash is said to be gold."

She swiped her knife blade on the sole of her boot. "You might as well know. Granny had a stash, but it was greenbacks, not gold."

"Greenbacks? We'll, they're lighter to carry."

"I dug them up. Rotten."

"What?"

"All gone."

His voice rose. "Lucie don't act like she's lost her fortune."

Ruth stopped and leaned on her pick. Hargis spoke louder. "I guess you and the marshal want me to think Lucie's got nothing."

Loughrie picked a rock from the spring and tossed it aside.

"Hargis, nobody's against you," Ruth said. Ma had a lot of paper money buried in a crock on the old home place. Over time, it took on water."

He switched his glare to Piney. "Give me a look at your face. Is that a lie?"

Piney frowned. Hargis kicked the dirt and swore. "She might of told me!"

Wanda stepped away from the still and sat on the slope to rest. She understood Lucie's devotion to her craft, and why Ruth and Piney accepted it, but more and more she questioned herself. "Hargis, if you're looking for easy money, find a different family. There'll never be anything here but work."

Both Piney and Ruth gave her a look that made her wonder what she'd said.

"It ain't work," Hargis said, "it's bad-tempered females that make life painful. Marshal, I recommend you watch out for this bunch." He stretched out on Lucie's cot. "You won't get rid of me that easy. The old woman's right about one thing—there's good money to be made. These will be better times."

Loughrie swished his hand in the spring hole and threw out another rock. "Bad times, not better. You don't want to meet the people I know."

"The old woman will have you meeting them whether you like it or not," Hargis said. "You gotta be tough, that's all."

"Huh," Ruth said. "That's all."

Loughrie stooped at the spring and appeared to wait for the water to clear.

Wanda thought again about trust. If Loughrie was telling the truth, he'd not kept faith with the law or the bootleggers. She felt more at ease with Hargis, who was poor at deceiving. You never knew what to expect from a smart man like Loughrie.

She wiped grit from her arms and face. "I been bothered by the idea of those men that tried to steal our corn. Where they from?"

"They got a place a couple o'hours up the road," Hargis said. "You see one Cotton, you've seen them all, they're that much alike, big and yellow-haired."

Piney sent Wanda a frantic look. "The little girl we found was a Cotton. Do you suppose one of them's her pa?"

"That'd likely be Raz, the middle one." Hargis rolled to his side and leaned on one elbow. "He's the fanciest of the bunch, and the only one I've knowed to have a woman. The youngest is Duck, and he's just crazy."

"What a comfort," Wanda said. "Mr. Loughrie, are these Cottons a fair sample of people you know?"

"There's worse."

"Those boys is known all over," Hargis said. "Do most of their work where their ma won't hear of it. Raz and Duck get distracted by women and such, but Coyne's serious about business. He's oldest, maybe meanest. When you see them together, you can tell Coyne 'cause he's getting bald on top."

The Cottons wouldn't have traded the trunk if they'd known about the coins. "I get the idea the Cottons make whiskey," Wanda said.

Hargis nodded. "They do some o'that on the side, but theirs'll rot your gut, and the work of making it is likely more than they care to do. Though I know for a fact they'd kill for Lucie's recipe."

"Blanche Cotton has come to live in Winkler with her pa," Piney said. "He's building a grist mill."

"It's good to hear about the mill," Hargis said, "but Winkler won't improve if the Cotton boys gets to hanging around."

Wanda was sorry to agree.

Late that day, Lucie returned to the still and they re-started the run. Every one of Will's cautions now snuck into Wanda's thoughts: getting between bootleggers and the law, caught in a whiskey war, shot by Lucie or with her. She also worried about Will, who might have troubles of his own if Blanche's husband didn't like her living in Winkler.

Lucie had them leave the distilled backings in the thumper. "It's all too precious," she said. "Every bit we've made, except what went down the throats of Ruth and the marshal. The product's gonna taste of scorch, but nobody will notice after the first sip."

"Bootleggers will be glad to get it," Hargis said.

"Not this time they won't," Lucie said. "We'll sell it in the coal camps, for it won't be a true sample of Bosell whiskey. Marshal, you might notify one o'your big buyers there's something's special on the way."

No one seemed interested in something special, and Wanda figured she might be the only one who knew Lucie intended to sell the whiskey in the cave. Loughrie did not look up from patting paste around the boiler cap. But he nodded.

After their talk about the Cotton brothers, having lookouts seemed a proper caution. That night Lucie dispatched Ruth and Hargis to ride the watch, and kept Wanda, Loughrie, and Piney to run the remainder of the beer. In the dark, they spoke less, and had to be careful of their footing. Thinking of Evie, Wanda did her part with growing unease. If trouble came, would she run away or stay to help Ruth and Piney?

The night passed with no intruders. At dawn, Lucie shook a small portion of liquor in a medicine bottle and approved the resulting bubbles as evidence of two-hundred-proof whiskey. Piney and Loughrie tied the jugs to the backs of the mules and led them down to the cottage. Wanda waited in the woods with Lucie.

"When I get back, I'll see if I can buy kegs from Doc," Lucie said.

Wanda was irritated by Lucie's habit of speaking like everyone followed her thoughts. "Back from where?"

"Back from the coal camps," Lucie said. "I ain't sending Hargis by hisself—he don't know who's safe to sell to. On our way back, I'll get kegs from Doc. Then we'll trail our mules to the old home place and haul out what's in the cave."

"Heavy hauling," Wanda said. She'd be home before then.

"We can't bring it out all at one time, though I wish we could, 'cause we pretty much have to go through Winkler, and every trip's gonna bring us more notice. We'll take Ruth and Hargis or Loughrie, whichever seems best at the time. I haven't made up my mind."

"Take Hargis," Wanda said. "But maybe take the marshal too, so you'll know what he's doing."

"Smart thinking."

Encouraged by this bit of approval, Wanda decided to ask outright. "Granny, you've had time to think. I need my money."

Lucie studied her sideways. "How about if you get the cash from this run? Or wait till I sell what's in the cave? It'll be a lot more."

"I want what you took."

"Well, we know the coins wasn't yours in the first place, was they?"

"They were mine when you took them." Wanda opened her palm.

"I'll give over the coins when we get back from the camps."

"What's wrong with now?"

"I don't like to travel with nothing, 'case of trouble." Lucie coughed. "This smoke's about done me in."

Wanda was thinking about wrestling Lucie down and finding her money belt when Ruth came back with a mule. They put Lucie on it and took her to the cottage.

Lucie directed as they cut the strong liquor with spring water and put the final product in Mason jars. Everyone had been up all night, yet when the jars were filled, she told Hargis to hitch the mules to the wagon.

They wrapped the jars in strips of blanket cloth and tucked them among dry grass, old tools, broken chairs and cracked crocks in the wagon bed. On top, they tied some of Lucie's baskets and Piney's rag rugs. "For decoration," Lucie said. "And mystification. Now, give me a hand up." She held out her hand to Hargis.

"Ma," Piney said. "What're you doing?"

"What does it look like? Get my gun."

Hargis helped her climb to the wagon seat.

Ruth handed up the shotgun. "Ma, it ain't safe for you to go. When folks see you, they'll know what you're hauling."

Lucie set the shotgun at her side. "Only the right ones in them coal camps knows me."

"You're Lucie Bosell. You've been talked about for ages, and no doubt described."

The edge of Lucie's cheeks crinkled in what was nearly a smile. "I can take care of myself and Hargis too. Well? What are you staring at? Go along and clear the road."

Wanda and Piney rode ahead to clear brush from both ends of the hidden road.

"I'd like to keep going," Piney said, when they'd done their work and started back to the cottage.

"Full moon's on the way," Wanda said. "Let's ride over to Will's Trading Days. It's time we have some fun."

~

"We'll go too," Ruth said, when Wanda announced she and Piney were going to Trading Days. "But first we'll clean the still and barrels."

Wanda's hammock looked inviting. "You're getting 'bout as bad as Granny," she said.

Ruth tossed her a wire brush. "You too."

Being hard as Lucie was nothing to admire, but at least the old woman thought ahead. To be fair, if she sent a revenuer to the whiskey cave, she'd share the bounty with Piney and Ruth. They wouldn't have to know where it came from.

After they cleaned the still, her aunts dragged a roll of canvas from the horse shed and spread it on the grass.

"It's one of them army tents," Ruth said. "We lived in it while we built the corncrib and the wash house. Then we lived in the wash house for a year while we built the house."

Wanda and Piney swept dead spiders, cocoons and mud-dauber nests from the canvas. It smelled like mold.

"It'll freshen when it's set up at Winkler and air blows through," Ruth said. "Be better than sleeping in the open with a bunch of strangers."

She hadn't thought of sleeping anywhere other than in Will's room.

Next morning, they packed the tent on Hargis's pony, along with baskets, rugs, and needlework to sell or trade. Starting out, they argued briefly about who would ride double, for they had only three horses. Loughrie said they should switch around so no horse carried two for the whole trip, and none should carry double up the trail. For that portion, he'd walk. Both Ruth and Piney smiled like they'd follow him anywhere.

When they started, Piney looked back. "We've never all been away at one time. Do you think everything will be all right?"

"The dogs will hunt and keep off varmints," Ruth said. "The geese can feed themselves, the mules are gone with Ma, and we've got all the horses. The garden will sprout new weeds for when we come home."

Going forward lightened their spirits. Even Ruth seemed happy.

When they reached the road, Piney gave Loughrie his horse and rode with Wanda. Old Henry's Dog ran circles around them.

The day started cool and turned drizzly, making Wanda glad she had the canvas jacket, large enough to button over both her and Piney. For the last part of the trip, they switched riders once more. It was Old Henry's turn to carry two, Loughrie and Ruth.

The sun came out when they reached Winkler. The grist mill looked to be half-built, and a few people strolled in the street.

Piney chattered about seeing strangers and earning money to buy something. Wanda dwelt on buying a nanny goat for Piney and meeting Will again. All she needed was a smile that said, in spite of all, he was glad to see her.

They set up their tent by the river and staked their horses among wagons, mules, and foundation stones of the former sawmill. She left her riding trousers, the canvas jacket and bedroll in the tent with Piney's trade goods. Old Henry's Dog stretched out at the tent entrance with his head between his paws and his ears pitched forward.

Will had blocked off most of the street for trade tables and had arranged church pews around a low platform. Small children hopped on and off the platform while men in clean bib overalls and women in faded dresses talked in clusters.

They waited while Piney claimed one of the tables by covering it with a sheet and a rock to keep the sheet from blowing away. Then they strolled together through the makeshift market. In front of the store, a few customers waited at a table where a man sold sausage links.

A boy in knickers and a newsboy cap delivered a pan of sizzling links to the table, then ran up the store steps. Wanda climbed three steps to see better over the growing crowd. If she found Will, she'd say she was proud of him for giving folks a place to gather and trade. Which she was. Would he like that, coming from her?

She waved to Piney. "Go on. I'll catch up in a minute."

Inside, the store smelled of baking bread. The boy greeted her. "Something you want? I know everything we got, prices too."

"Are you the clerk today?"

"You bet. Me and Pa mind the store when Doc's busy. I'm frying sausage and that's my granny over there baking bread. Are you looking for something special?"

"Just looking." Better to meet Will by accident. She nodded a greeting to the boy's granny.

On the street, she joined Piney, Ruth and Loughrie at a table where a stooped and wrinkled woman was setting out corked bottles.

Ruth touched a bottle and the woman gave her a narrow look. "Have you bought my fruit liquor before?

"No. Could I take a sniff?"

The woman pulled a vial from her pocket and untwisted the cap. "You can sniff my sample but don't sip, and don't snort into it, neither."

"Why would I snort?"

"You'd be surprised what some folks does."

Ruth held the vial under her nose. "We'll have a bottle."

Wanda and Piney stood back while Loughrie dug in his pocket and laid coins on the table. Ruth hid the bottle in a harvesting bag that hung from her shoulder.

"Don't make use of that around folks you don't know," the old woman said.

Ruth leaned close. "You be careful, the sheriff may be here today."

The sheriff. Wanda looked along the street for a sign of Will. He'd like her better if she told a lawman about the whiskey cave.

The old woman winked. "The sheriff's bought before."

Ruth and Loughrie drifted away toward the river. Piney stared after them. "I didn't think Ruth would need liquor, now she has a nice man."

"Ma drank, even when she had Pa and me both," Wanda said. She put her arm through Piney's. "Should we set up your table?"

"Oh, no, I want to see everything first. It's so exciting to be here. I feel like something nice is going to happen, don't you?"

For Piney's sake, she agreed. "Something nice." A beginning or an end. Already Ruth had gone off to drink. Wanda's hopes went up and down.

At the next table, a man laid out items of ladies' clothing: skirts, dresses, aprons, and a long gabardine coat. Piney lifted the coat.

"My wife made all these," he said. "See the fine stitching? Everything's new."

Wanda fingered the neat tucks of a mutton sleeve. The stitches were small and neat and the clothes on the table appeared to be clean, but every piece showed some sign of wear: grease spot, frayed cuff, cloth faded and thinned from the wash. Wanda understood—she'd sold Homer's things. The man didn't want to say the clothes belonged to a dead woman.

Piney slid her arms into the coat, but it did not meet across her front. "I'm too fat for it. Wanda, it'd be nice for you."

Wanda held it to her shoulders. "I think you're right." Leaving Piney at the table, she went to the tent and brought back her canvas jacket. The seller admired it, and they traded. The long coat was a comfortable fit. When she put her hands in the pocket, she found not gold, but a folded handkerchief embroidered with yellow flowers. She pressed the handkerchief into the seller's palm and looked away to avoid his eyes.

They put the new coat in the tent and strolled arm in arm to the site of the old boardinghouse, so Wanda could show Piney where she'd lived. Then they turned around and walked to the school building at the upper end of the valley. On the way back, they stopped at the grist mill, where a familiar-looking man hammered floor boards. He lifted his cap and wiped his pink forehead with a kerchief. "I remember you ladies." He shook hands with Piney, then Wanda. "Simpson Wainwright. Grandpap of the little girl you found."

"We hope she's well," Piney said.

"Her and her ma are doing better, thanks to you."

Piney shaded her eyes from the sun's glare. "How about the nanny goat? Does she give enough milk?"

"Well now, I hate to say this. My daughter's man said the goat was worthless. He butchered it."

Piney gasped. "How did he get the goat?"

"He comes around, God help us. If I had sons, we'd drive him a long ways off, but I got only Blanche. I been buying a little milk from Doc."

Wanda put her arm around Piney. "Mr. Wainwright, we're glad your girl and her children have you. We'll not delay you longer. Good luck with your mill."

"If you have corn to grind, bring it to me." He went back to hammering.

Wanda had to take Piney's hand so she'd walk on.

"I better not see those children, or hear about them neither," Piney said. "I'll just worry all the more."

"How about we look over Will's goats and see if there's a young one you'd like to take home?" A goat seemed small comfort, like kissing a wound to make it better, but Piney perked up.

When they crossed the footbridge, two shepherd dogs stepped away from the herd and growled.

"I guess we better wait for Will," Wanda said.

When finally they spotted him at a market table, they had to wait in line to speak. He shook Piney's hand, then Wanda's. "Good to see you here," he said, like they didn't know each other.

"We'd like to buy a young nanny," Wanda said.

His eyes narrowed. "The other you took didn't work out too good."

"Not because of us."

"I'll think on it." He turned to the next person in line.

Piney glanced back as they left. "Doc's not very friendly today."

"My fault," Wanda said. So far, Trading Days wasn't much fun.

CHAPTER 19

"I'm scared," Piney whispered.

"Scared of...?" Wanda stood with Piney behind her table of baskets, doilies and rugs. Along the street, men and women crowded around tables of trade goods or stopped to greet each other, women with kids hanging on, old people as eager-eyed as the young. Nothing scary.

"What will I do if nobody stops to look? Or buy?"

Wanda set a laundry basket under the table. "You can enjoy the sight of folks passing."

"But if they do stop? What do I say?"

"Be your sweet self." Wanda nodded to three women in old-fashioned bonnets who'd paused a few paces away. "Good afternoon."

The women bobbed their heads and hurried on, in close step, like geese.

"Thank goodness," Piney said.

"Aunt Piney, they were shy. Folks will stop, look and walk away, but some will want to talk and some will buy. Just talk like they're friends."

"Oh. What do I charge?"

"Think of a fair price, what you would pay."

166

"I'm not used to paying. I wish Ma was here."

"I can tell you what I'd pay in Fargo, but let me ask one of the other sellers."

"Don't leave me," Piney said.

"I'll be back in a minute."

"Hurry."

Threading through the crowd, eager to see Will again, Wanda bumped into the chest of a man who, like her, seemed to be searching for someone. His hat fell to the ground.

He pushed her away. "Watch where you're going."

She was about to scold his rudeness when he picked up his hat, revealing, when he bent, his bald top and long yellow hair. He strode off, big, tall, nasty.

At the fruit liquor stand, the old woman sat on a keg, watching a younger one talk with buyers. Wanda waited her turn to get close, then spoke to the old one. "Would you come and advise my aunt about her trade goods?"

The woman pushed down on her cane and stood. "Glad to do it if it don't compete with my own."

"It's rugs and baskets and such," Wanda said.

The old woman followed her to Piney's table and proceeded to turn baskets and hold up needlework. "Ah, pretty," she said. She beckoned to the crowd, spoke of the fineness of the rugs and doilies and then haggled about prices while Piney stood back, surprised pink.

When a young woman 'in the family way' pointed to the laundry basket under the table, Piney lifted it and ran her hands over the smooth weave inside. "With a lining, it could also be a baby bed," Piney said.

After Piney took payment for the basket, Wanda said, "I have an errand. Is it all right if I leave?" Maybe she'd ask Will to introduce her to the sheriff.

"I'm fine now," Piney said.

Not far from Piney's table, Wanda found Virgie with a display of sheer dresses and pointy-toed shoes. Virgie wiggled her hand in the air. "Come see if you don't need one of my dresses."

Wanda lifted a skirt of filmy silver cloth. "I'd take this, but it doesn't match any of my jewels."

Virgie's laugh bobbed her curls. She glanced from Wanda's mud-crusted boots to her frayed collar bow. "I'm trying to get Doc to sell pretty things in the store. He's got no idea what women want."

Wanda let the dress fall to the table. "I hope a lady of leisure happens by."

"Oh, dear," Virgie said. "I've never met one of those."

"Your best customer for these things is young fellers. If they got any money, they'll spend it all on their sweethearts."

"I believe you're right." Virgie eyed the crowd.

Moving on, Wanda sidestepped running children, then stopped where two tiny ones stood still. They held hands, a boy barely able to walk, and a girl with a pale face, a dirt-smeared dress, and straggly yellow hair. Piney's lost child and her brother, Robert. There was no sign of their mother or Simpson Wainwright.

The girl tugged on Wanda's skirt.

Wanda took her hand. "Where's your ma?"

The girl whimpered like she didn't want anyone to hear. Her brother gave a noisy bawl. Wanda lifted him and took the girl's hand. "All right. Let's get your pap."

The boy sniffed. "Pap."

At Piney's table, Wanda peered between the backs of two stout women. "Aunt Piney, see what I've found." Piney hurried around the table.

"If you see Blanche Cotton," Wanda said, "tell her I've taken her lost children to their grandpap at his mill. Be sure you say 'lost.'"

Piney set a basket into the hands of one of her customers. "Mrs. Wise, I have to help these children. If you stay here and watch my table, you can have this basket." Without waiting for the woman's answer, she took the girl's hand, freeing Wanda to hold both her arms around the wiggly boy.

"They were in the street," Wanda said, as she and Piney went on together. "No sign of their ma."

"Ma," the boy said.

Piney took a handkerchief from her pocket and wiped the girl's nose. "Honey, where is your ma?"

The girl's face puckered.

"It's all right," Piney said. "Grandpap will find her."

When they neared the mill, Simpson Wainwright came running. "Now what?" He reached for the boy.

"They were lost in the crowd," Wanda said. "I didn't see your daughter anywhere."

"Ruby," he said to the child. "Where's your ma?"

Ruby spoke in gasps. "I...couldn't...find her."

"Is the baby at the house?"

Ruby nodded.

"But your ma ain't there?"

"Ma said 'take care of Robert.' I tried." She sniffed back tears. Piney blotted and kissed her face.

"Ruby took good care of her brother," Wanda said. "She wouldn't let go of his hand till I picked him up."

"Good girl. Miss Bosell, if you'll kindly stay with them a minute longer, I'll get my things and take them home." He handed the boy to Wanda and hurried toward the mill.

"Pap," the boy called.

"Ma!" The girl pointed.

Wanda's mouth dried. Blanche Cotton ran toward them, ahead of a burly, yellow-haired man taking his time. He was fancy-dressed in bowler hat, high-collared striped shirt and white waist-coat, and he was a look-alike for the man she'd bumped in the street. If this was Raz, the man she'd bumped into was Coyne, the oldest brother.

"What are you doing with my children?" Blanche snatched the boy from Wanda's arms and kissed his cheeks.

Wanda put her arm through Piney's and whispered, "Let's go. This isn't our business."

Piney stood fast, clutching Ruby's hand.

Simpson came on the run, carrying a toolbox in each hand. "Blanche, where were you? These ladies found Ruby and Robert at the market."

Blanche's hair was curled and girlishly tied with a red ribbon, and she looked cleaner and more alert than when they'd first seen her. Any bruises that might still be on her arms were covered by long sleeves. Her daughter wore a dress with long sleeves too.

Blanche set the wiggling boy on her hip. "Impossible. Little Robert couldn't walk all that way."

In an attempt to get down, little Robert threw himself backwards. Simpson set his toolboxes on the ground and held out his arms, but Blanche gripped the boy tighter.

"I found them on the street, lost in the crowd," Wanda said.

"Lies." Blanche frowned toward her daughter. "Raz, get Ruby."

Ruby hid her face in Piney's skirt. Instead of taking Ruby, Raz peeled the boy from his wife's arms and handed him to Simpson. "The kids are all right. Time to go."

Blanche whined. "Please, Raz, can't we take them?"

"I got one horse and one room at Ma's, and she won't have kids underfoot. If you want us together, tell your pa to let me stay."

"Pa, please."

Simpson shifted the boy to his right arm and clasped Ruby's other hand so the child was between himself and Piney. "You and the children are welcome. Not him, and you know full-well why not."

Raz spit a plug of tobacco that hit the miller's boot. Simpson glared. Wanda took a half-step back, afraid a fight was coming, but Piney stood fast.

"Pa, don't keep us apart," Blanche said.

Simpson kicked the tobacco from his boot and ground it in the dirt. "Make your choice. But I swear, if you leave these children again, you won't get them back."

"Raz," Blanche said, "let me go home and get the baby."

Raz walked away. Blanche hugged the boy and pushed him back at her father. Then she bent to Ruby and sobbed. Both children cried as she hurried after her husband. Simpson hung his head.

"I'm sorry for your daughter," Wanda said, "but she's chose the wrong side of duty."

Simpson wiped his eyes. "I've tried to save her. Now I gotta deal with what she left. Ruby, are we ready to go home?"

"We'll help you get them there," Piney said. "Let Wanda carry the boy."

"I'm grateful." Simpson transferred the boy to Wanda and lifted his toolboxes. "Most times I could leave my tools here, but with all these folks in town, and one of them my son-in-law, I need to lock them up."

The boy squirmed to be down, and when he was down he wouldn't hold Wanda's hand, so on the walk to Simpson Wainwright's house she took slow steps while the boy toddled on his own, following Ruby. When distance grew between them, Piney and Simpson stopped and waited.

Simpson's house was the highest of the six scattered along the hillside.

"It's amazing the boy walked all the way down," Wanda said.

"I tried to bring him back," Ruby said. "He wanted Ma."

The house smelled of soiled diapers, and somewhere an infant cried. While Simpson hurried up the stairs, Wanda kept the door open and stood there to keep Robert from running outside. Simpson returned with the infant and sat in a rocking chair. He looked from child to child, then from Wanda to Piney. "Whatever am I going to do?"

Piney took the infant and spoke to Wanda. "Put my trade goods in the tent. I'll find you later."

Wanda was not surprised. "Can I help?"

CAROL ERVIN

"Tell Ruth where I am. I'll send word if I need you."

Instead of closing Piney's market table or looking for Ruth, Wanda spent the rest of the afternoon selling baskets and rugs and worrying about her own child.

When she'd sold every item, she tied Piney's coins in a kerchief and left them in the tent on Old Henry's saddle. She found Will near the store at a table of mixed goods—dinted cooking pots, hand tools, cherry-framed mirrors, and the Cottons' trunk. She waited for a chance to make peace.

Seeing her, he nodded toward the store. "If you need anything inside, there's a boy will take your money."

Being humble didn't come natural, and was harder with him putting her off, but it felt like a last chance. "I'm sorry you've seen the wrong side of me."

He straightened the stack of mirrors. "Wanda, I'm tired. We'll be better friends when there's long miles between us."

"If you say so." She meant the words to sound polite, but their tone didn't seem to matter, for he was already looking at the next customer.

She paused on the top step, where she had a view of his back. His white shirt was still wrinkled from being folded. Someone had trimmed the hair on his neckline. When there were long miles between them, she'd write friendly letters, and when he saw her again, she wouldn't be the granddaughter of Lucie Bosell, but Evie's mother, a woman good for the town.

In the store she bought strips of deer jerky and a tiny carved horse for Evie. Outside, she paused again on the top step. The clouds were dark with rain. Will was shaking his head at two stout men, one a copy of the other, both with yellow hair, one pawing through the trunk and throwing clothes on the ground. Cottons, Raz's brothers, no mistake. As each garment hit the ground, Will picked it up and laid it across the table.

Straining to hear over the babble of the crowd, she caught the word "jacket." Will shrugged. She didn't move until the Cottons left.

When she reached his table, he spoke in low tones. "That was Coyne and Duck Cotton, asking about a canvas jacket. I believe it's the one I gave to you."

"It was too big. What did you say?"

"I said I sold a lot of their stuff last Trading Day. They wanted me to remember who'd bought the jacket. I said I didn't remember. Seems their other brother hid something in it without telling them."

"Then I guess that brother is in trouble." As she'd feared, the gold had passed through their hands. She hoped they wouldn't think Will was hiding it.

"Was there something about the jacket you didn't bother to tell?"

When she had something bad to confess, she liked to get it over with, so she said it fast. "Gold coins in the pocket. Lucie took them, paid them out to Virgie for the still. You saw the whole thing."

Will looked right and left, like he was making sure no one else was close enough to hear. "Stolen money, for sure. I'm sorry you didn't tell me. I'd of turned it over to the sheriff. I hope you left the jacket at Lucie's."

"I traded it earlier today."

"I'm sorry to hear that too. I pity anyone who wears it here, and pity you if the Cottons learn you had it first." He began laying clothes in the trunk. "You need to go home to Fargo before something bad happens."

He was right, and maybe with practice she'd learn to admit it. "Thanks for not giving me up."

"I wouldn't give anyone up to the Cottons. I asked if they wanted me to notify the sheriff. They said they'd handle it."

"I'm going soon. May Rose will write."

"I reckon she will." He closed the trunk lid.

Wanda plucked his sleeve and spoke in a half-whisper. "Will, tell the sheriff about Lucie's cave of whiskey. Claim the bounty."

It felt good to surprise him. "I'll tell the sheriff if you say so, but I don't want a reward."

"Give it to Piney, from me, but don't tell her what it's from."

"You're not coming back, then."

"Would it bother you if I settled here?"

"All law-abiding folks are welcome."

Because she could not steady her face, she turned away without saying goodbye.

CHAPTER 20

Waiting for Lucie's promises no longer felt smart or safe.

Wanda was halfway to the river before she allowed herself to glance back at Will's table. She glimpsed the top of his head, no way to tell if he'd watched her all the way, full of regret. Or relief. He hadn't even offered a dry place to sleep.

Up and down the street, sellers looked to the threatening sky and covered their tables or packed trade goods in crates and sacks. Wind swelled to a low roar, sweetening the air. Men chased their hats and women seized their children's hands and hurried them along. Every sight of a mother guiding her child was painful.

At the camp area, Wanda led her family's horses one by one to drink at the river. She borrowed a shovel from a man scooping manure into a pile and added clods dropped by their animals. When rain fell in sheets, she ducked into the tent, followed by Old Henry's Dog. Ruth and Loughrie stumbled in, each clutching a new bottle, adding body heat and alcohol fumes to the trapped odors of mold and wet dog. Taking her long coat and tin canteen, she left to find a better place for the night.

The last of the crowd hurried toward the church building.

With the coat draped over her head, she let herself into Will's spring house and dipped the canteen into the water basin. Then she ran to the church, drawn by the odor of sizzling meat.

The church floor slanted down toward a platform across the front, just as she remembered, but the pews were in the street and the piano and pulpit were gone. Men and women with damp shoulders and hems stood in a line stretching to the platform where the granny was selling small loaves stuffed with meat.

Wet hats, blankets and jackets hung from hooks on the back wall. Wanda reached to hang up her dripping coat, but stopped midway, spooked by the sight of the canvas jacket beside the only empty hook. With a glance to see if anyone was watching, she moved a damp blanket beside the jacket and put her coat in its place. This caution made her feel no better.

She stepped to the end of the food line as Will's helper carried in a tray of crisp sausage. By the time she reached the front, the sausage had sold out.

"More's coming," the old woman said, slicing open one small loaf after another.

Waiting, Wanda surveyed the crowd in line and against the walls for anyone tall and hefty with yellow hair. Seeing none of that description did not take away her unease. Will's helper carried in another tray, and she left the platform with a greasy sausage tucked into a small bread loaf.

She found a place against the wall to eat and watch. The floorboards were damp, the air smothery and noisy, and rain dripped from a spot or two in the ceiling. But people laid babies down on blankets and sat on the floor with their legs stretched out like they might stay the night. Even with no Cottons in view, it felt like a risky place to close her eyes.

As she passed through the crowd toward the wall of coats, someone tapped her shoulder. Ruth smiled, her eyes glazed. Loughrie wavered behind her.

"Piney," Ruth said. "Piney came by the tent and said she won't be sleeping with us tonight." Ruth's hand covered her laugh. "Piney's found a real bed."

Wanda leaned close to Ruth's ear. "Tomorrow I'm going home. To Fargo. I'll say goodbye to Piney."

Ruth laughed and clung to Loughrie. Wanda was through worrying about him. Drunk or sober, he and Ruth might do all right together. She kissed Ruth's cheek and moved on, thinking of the old school building, a quieter shelter for the night. She'd take Ginger inside, and in the morning they'd be dry and ready to go.

The sight of an empty hook where the canvas jacket had hung gave her a spurt of relief. She folded the coat over one arm and edged through the crowd to the doors. Outside, she halted on the stone steps. A garment with a red lining lay in the street, soaked and muddied. The jacket.

Water dripped from the eaves onto her neck, and she took another step down as carefree as she could pretend with a thumping heart. Only a careless drunk—or a man angry to find no gold coins in its pocket—would leave a fine jacket in a puddle. She surveyed the sky's patch of blue and the muddy street as an excuse to let her eyes roam over the store and church fronts. Two Cotton brothers slouched against the church wall.

A woman came outside and shook a wet shawl.

"It's good the rain's stopped," Wanda said, loud enough for the men against the wall to hear. She wanted to hide herself in her long coat, but did not, because the sun was hot, and now the coat felt treacherous. The seller might not remember her, but he'd be able to describe his wife's coat. Had the Cottons taken the jacket from its hook or ripped it from the new owner? Were they watching for him or did they already know what she'd done?

She and the woman stepped together into the street. Beside the puddle, Wanda said, "Look at that." She lifted the jacket by its lapel and held it out with two fingers.

"Take it," the woman said. "Finders keepers."

Wanda gave the woman a considering look. It was like being in a school play, speaking for an audience, yet pretending the audience wasn't there. "I believe I will. It might fit my pa." With a goodbye nod, she dragged the jacket across the street, through the weeds and toward the river, resisting the temptation to look back.

Old Henry's Dog stood and wagged his tail when she drew close to the tent, but she walked on like she didn't know him. Farther along, she let the jacket drop to the ground, bent and wiped her hands in the grass. As she stood, she glanced back the way she'd come. Sure enough, the brothers sauntered behind, a distance of about three wagons.

Whatever she did with the jacket should not look suspicious. So she shouldn't drop it in a sinkhole or toss it in the river.

Near a campfire where people were shaking water from their hats and shawls, she held up the jacket. "Hey, y'all. Anybody lose this?"

Some laughed at the state of it, but a man took it from her hands and held it to his shoulders. "You giving or selling?"

Afraid the music and crowd noise hadn't let his words reach the brothers, she cupped her hands at her mouth. "Say again?"

He shouted, "I said, you giving or selling?"

"I found it. I was gonna give it to my pa, but he don't need a jacket like this. 'Course if you ask enough folks, plenty will say it's theirs."

The man tossed the jacket toward a woman by the fire. "Mary, stow this somewhere."

Uncertain if the brothers were following her or the jacket, she ambled on in a wide circle past tents and wagons and came back to the church. Shadows were gathering in the valley, and in the clearing sky the full moon hung pale and ready. For a while she stood near the store, pretending interest in a seat on one of the pews being wiped dry by several women. Raising to tip-toe, she waved to an imaginary acquaintance and caught a breath of relief. Cottons were nowhere to be seen.

Price Loughrie came to the platform with his fiddle, and Ruth stumbled into a pew. Men twisted pegs, angled bows on strings and plunked with their ears close to the wood.

She detoured again around the campground, away from the music. At the tent, she folded the dead woman's coat into her saddlebags and picked up one of the bedrolls, gave Old Henry's Dog a goodbye scratch and saddled Ginger.

Still watchful, she led the mare to the old school building, but at least three families and one crying baby were sheltering there. Simpson Wainwright's new mill had part of a roof, a solid floor and a new-wood smell that was better than the old school, but she found campers there, too. Will's horse shed came to mind. Though it was near the music and crowd noise, she could sleep dry and slip away before dawn.

Behind the church, she unsaddled Ginger and put her in the fenced field, then crossed the alley to the shed behind the store. It had one boxy stall, a window facing the alley, hooks on the walls for tack, a bin for grain, and just enough floor space for her bedroll. The air smelled of leather and hay. Grateful for the privacy of walls, she spread the bedroll in the narrow space.

Outside, talk and music rose and fell in bursts, not a lot different from the Winkler she remembered, when young loggers had ridden down from their camps for Saturday night mischief. An ignorant girl, she'd feared nothing.

Wild fiddling and shrieks of laughter kept her awake and gave her an itch to watch, but the small window gave her no view. Restless, she crossed the alley to the shadowed wall of the church. Torches burned on tall stakes along the main street, and the full moon shone down. On the platform, two fiddles and a mandolin took turns at the melody line of "Turkey in the Straw," and a four-some clogged in the dirt. People in the pews slapped their knees. When the song ended, the dancers laughed and fanned their fire-lit faces. It seemed a pleasant send-off, something nice to remember about Will's town.

The fiddlers adjusted their pegs, then one tapped four beats and they swung into the opening strains of "Redwing," Homer's favorite. Alone against the side of the church, she sang the chorus. "Oh, the moon shines tonight on pretty Redwing…"

A new shadow came between her and the street, and she stiffened as a bulky shape slid near, smelling of whiskey. He sang the next line, "The breeze is sighing, the night birds crying…" Caught by his fine tone, she lifted her eyes. At that moment he glanced toward the fiddlers, giving her time to hide her shock.

Play-acting again, she sang louder, "For afar 'neath his star her brave is sleeping…" When he turned, her smile was ready. Even in the gloom she knew he was a Cotton, not the balding one and not Blanche's husband, but the youngest, the one Hargis said was crazy. Duck.

He grabbed her waist, lifted and set her down in the alley, and danced her toward the music in wide circles. Dizzy, she clutched his shoulders and matched his steps to keep from being dragged. The crowd clapped.

She tried to wrench away, but his hands were like clamps. In wild turns, she searched for help. Loughrie was not on the platform; Ruth was not in the pew. Piney was not in the crowd, nor Simpson Wainwright, Will or Virgie. She would have been happy to see Lucie, even Hargis, anyone who'd know the fright in her face.

Before the tune ended, Duck danced her into the alley and backed her against the church wall. "I've heard of you."

His chest was close to her nose. She folded her arm between them and wiped her face on her sleeve. "Not me. I'm new here."

He spread his hands against the building. "I've seen you around. The girl with hair like a bush. An outsider with a big bush of ginger hair. The girl who took my brother's kids."

She turned her head from the stench of his breath. "I didn't take his kids, I found them. I'd seen them with their grandpap, so I took them to the mill."

"Don't matter to me—they're my brother's hard luck. Hot, are you?" He bent closer and licked her neck. "Me too."

Her chest tightened. She dipped below his arms. "Let's dance another."

"I've had enough o'that. Let's do something else." He gripped her wrist and pulled her not where fiddles screeched and dancers stomped, but farther up the alley behind the church, in view of nothing but horses and a brushy hillside. He shoved, and she stumbled to damp ground on hands and knees.

When he dropped over her, she was ready, and with hands gripped together, flung herself up and batted the side of his head. Raucous laughter roared from the street. The blow sent waves of shock to her shoulders. Duck looked only surprised.

He grabbed her wrist, wrenched her to her back and straddled her legs. She knew what was coming, but instead of fear for herself, she had a sudden urge to hurt him. She bucked and knocked their heads together, a blow that made her sight waver and her head ring. He pushed her to the ground. *She was thirteen, on her back in the woods, two boys holding her down.*

Breathing rough, laughing in gasps, Duck pushed his elbow against her chest while he unbuttoned his trousers. His knee pinched the edge of her thigh. She pulled the knife from its sheath.

He threw the skirt over her head and palmed her mouth. Blindly she thrust the knife upward until the blade hit something tough—leather, bone or muscle—and stopped.

"Bitch!" He knocked her arm away, and she bucked again, loosening the skirt from her face. Her arm stung like it was cracked, yet she did not—could not—let go of the knife. His hand groped for it, but she circled her arm, swooped it back and pushed the knife into his belly.

For a moment her body hung suspended from his, joined by the knife. He sucked air in gasps and drooled spit onto her face. Her fingers locked around the knife and she couldn't remember how they were supposed to unclasp. When she pulled the knife out, wetness oozed over her hand.

Clutching his belly, Duck rolled off to his side. His moans and curses mixed with music from the street, the chorus of 'Dixie.'"

Her nose was thick with the scent of butchering. The sticky knife dropped from her fingers. On shaky legs, she backed against the church wall and stuck her fist in her mouth to plug a scream.

Duck's hand groped for the knife. She left the wall, kicked the knife away and picked it up. He fell to his back, face up.

They'd warned her—May Rose and Homer. If you carry that knife, one day you'll hurt somebody.

The music stopped, leaving a soft blur of street talk. Hunched in the shadow of the wall, she tore leaves of dock weed and rubbed them over the blade, her palms, her fingers. Crumpled the leaves in her fist and let them drop. Swished the knife and her hands in wet grass, lifted her skirt and swiped both hands on her bare legs. The knife was still sticky.

"Help," he said, a soft, weak sound that hurt her ears.

She ran from the shadows of the church, crossed the alley to the shed, pulled down her saddle and bridle and hurried out again. Then stopped. In the alley, entwined pairs strolled toward the field where Will's horse and her mare stood in moonlight bright as day. Not far from the shadows where she'd left Duck.

She backed into the shed and closed the door.

CHAPTER 21

Wanda hunched at the narrow window ledge in Will's shed, light-headed and chilled with sweat, listening for shouts of discovery, expecting that somehow Duck would burst in, barely alive or newly dead, a ghost from Hell. If he died, she too would fall into that pit. Maybe even if he lived.

The sky was bright with moonlight, but the alley was in shadow, and the window gave no view of the church's back wall where she'd left Duck.

Her eyes flicked over every dark surface in the shed for a better place to hide. A grain bin, too small. A horse stall. By day she'd seen hay raked in a corner of the stall, likely full of piss and shit, but a possible screen.

The next thing she knew she lay slumped on the floor with no memory of falling or how long she'd been there. The bedroll lay beside her, and on her other side, the knife. Groaning, she unkinked a knee, tightened her fingers around the knife and fumbled it into its sheath.

Muted talk drifted from the street. No music. Somewhere near, a mouse gnawed. Her mouth and throat felt like she'd been chewing wood. She rose to the window, took her canteen from a hook, and gulping water, watched the alley.

Fast, toe-tapping music started up again. Now if someone found Duck's body, or if he got to his feet and set men searching, she wouldn't hear shouts unless they stopped the music.

Will, Evie, May Rose, Piney—they must never know she'd pushed the knife into his belly. It was meant to be a tool, yet she'd carried it to feel safe. Did she smell like him? She sniffed her damp skirt. Was it bloody?

She unbuttoned and stepped out of her dress. The belt with the knife fell to the floor, and she peered in the dimness for a secure place to throw it away. Not the grain bin, not in the hay. Under the shed would be best, a low, dark space where snakes waited for rats. She wrapped her belt around the knife and sheath and shoved them deep in her pocket. When everyone slept, she'd stoop and toss them under the shed. Then somewhere along the road to Elkins, she'd burn the dress. She rolled it tight, pulled trousers and the traveling dress from her saddlebags and stuffed in the dirty one.

Whoops and hollers from the street meant dancing and drinking could last until dawn. In the middle hours of night, she might sneak the mare from the field. By daylight, her chance of escape would be less. She didn't fear justice, which might forgive a woman protecting herself. She feared the Cottons.

She waited. No worry about falling asleep; she might never sleep again. The passing of time seemed long as weeks. Finally she stopped listening for the music to end or for someone to throw open the door and drag her away. She sat facing the door with her back propped against the stall, dozing, waking, dozing. When finally the door opened, Will stood against a haze of dawn.

He eased the door shut. "They've been searching for you." The town was quiet, his voice a whisper.

She drew up her legs, squeezed her arms around her knees, and stared past his boots at the strip of light beneath the door.

"Seeing you holed up this way, I think maybe they're right. You killed Duck Cotton."

"He wasn't dead when I saw him."

Will stooped close. "He was dead when they found him. Coyne stopped the music, tried to get everyone to light a torch and search for his brother's killer."

Like a miracle, she'd slept through that, but now it was morning, late to be leaving. She stood and brushed down her dress. "I been here all the time, sleeping like a log."

Will hung a horse blanket over the window, shutting out the gray light of morning. "Everybody saw you dancing with Duck, but Coyne didn't get as much help as he wanted. Folks kind of drifted away. It's scary when someone like a Cotton looks for justice."

"He was looking for me? Because I danced?" A tone of panic slid into her voice.

"Shh, don't talk loud. It doesn't have to make sense. Coyne bothered everybody's sleep, asking about the girl with the bushy hair, trying to get your name. I don't think he got it, but a few hours ago someone pointed him to your tent."

"You were with him?"

"I was. I didn't want Coyne to hurt you or anyone. This is my town, and I'm all the law it's got. He was surprised when Loughrie came out of that tent, and I have to say I was too. Folks can't decide if Loughrie's the law or a bootlegger."

"He says he's been both."

"Coyne didn't want to mess with him. Loughrie said he knew you, but doubted you'd be able to kill anyone. Coyne kind of gave up after that. He may have gone home to get his brother. You'd best stay hid until I'm sure."

She gave silent thanks for Loughrie and Will. "I came here for a dry place to sleep."

"Whatever you say. Ruth came to me later, said your horse and tack were gone. After that I saw your horse in my field. I doubt many know it's yours." He touched the bridle she'd hung on the wall. "Did Duck hassle you for the gold?"

"Not that. Something else."

Will did not speak for a while. "I'm glad you're not the one dead."

"I'm glad you're the one found me." They stood inches apart. She wanted to fall against him.

"Coyne said he and Duck followed you yesterday. I got the idea that was about the gold."

A shaft of light fell beneath the window covering to the floor. If she confessed, would he turn her over to the sheriff? How long, then, before she got home?

"I got rid of the jacket so it would bring no trouble to anyone," she said.

"The sheriff should be here today."

They were silent for a few moments. Will leaned against the bin. He whispered, "Did you kill Duck?"

"How would I do that? I could hardly dance with him, he was that big. Was he shot?"

"Got a knife in the belly."

"Was the knife in him?"

"None found. They brought him to me. He's laid out on my bench. A few minutes ago, Ruth and Loughrie came say they're packing to go home. They want to be there in case Coyne follows you."

"I told Ruth I was leaving for Fargo. Maybe she was too drunk to take it in."

"She's sober now. They're worried, her and Loughrie. Me, too."

"Piney was with the miller's grandkids, Raz Cotton's kids. Is she going home with Ruth?"

"Don't know. Simpson's place might not be good for any of them if Raz comes back. He'll be riled as Coyne. I'll see if Piney's there, maybe ask Simpson to stay home a day or two." He touched the door handle.

"They can't prove it was me," she said.

"Doesn't matter. Coyne wants to hurt somebody, and since he's started a ruckus he'll not soon settle down. I'll bring your horse in here. There's almost nobody moving around yet—too much of a late night."

"Will, that bounty on Lucie's whiskey..."

"You said already. Give it to Piney."

"No. If something happens to me, take the bounty to May Rose. For Evie."

"You'll be fine," he said.

"I know."

The box stall had its own door to the outside, and Will brought Ginger in that way. Then he brought a bucket of water for the mare and an empty bucket for Wanda's use. He went away and came back with a small bread loaf.

"It's all that's left from yesterday," he said. "If you hear somebody scratching around outside, it'll be me. I'm gonna hang locks on the door latches."

"Thank you."

"Stay here one more day. After midnight, I'll come and let you out."

One more day. She needed him here, distracting her with talk. They couldn't prove it was her, but he'd said proof didn't matter to Coyne. Did it matter to Will, whether she'd done it or not? Shortly she heard the snap of a lock, then another.

Somewhere near, children chattered and squealed, but for most of the morning the valley was so quiet she could hear the distant tinkle of a goat bell.

Closed as it was, the shed grew hot, and she finished the water in her canteen. Heat lulled her to sleep, and she woke in the cool of evening to a buzz of talk and licks of practice music. She listened to changes beyond the shed, ordinary sounds of talk and trade. If Will's town grew, she hoped it was a good one. For her, living in Winkler now seemed impossible.

He came as promised, in the dead of night. Ginger stood

187

saddled and bridled, with her bedroll and long coat tied behind the saddle. He brought water for her canteen, helped her mount, and led the horse outside.

She ducked, riding under the door header, and closed her fist around the knife bundled in her pocket, but on horseback, she sat too high to toss it under the shed. The woods would hide it just as well.

Grass and mist muted the horse's steps as Will led her behind the store and on toward the road to Jennie Town.

"I hope we meet again," she said.

He squeezed her hand. "This will all be forgotten."

"You'll always be welcome in Fargo."

"I know. Stay safe."

She did not look back. He'd not offered to go with her. She'd like to tell May Rose how he'd helped, but that might bring her close to confessing about Duck. There would be other good things she could tell. How he'd cleaned up the town and brought people together to trade, how tenderly he'd treated the lost child.

The road led north, and after sunrise, turned shady and pleasant. A few travelers spoke and tipped their hats in passing. Ginger walked with no balking, and Wanda wondered if the mare would miss Old Henry, or be glad to reunite with horses and stable hands in Elkins. The farther they traveled from Winkler, the less she felt the need to throw away her knife. She buckled the belt at her waist and sheathed the knife in its old place in her pocket.

Mid-morning, she reached Jennie Town. She hadn't intended to stop, but Roy limped across the depot platform with a smile and a wave like she'd made him a special visit.

"Miss Bosell, get down and refresh yourself, you're welcome here." Roy held the bridle while she freed her feet from the stirrups and jumped to the ground.

"Virgie and Hargis has told me how you've got on at your granny's," he said. "You can catch me up on that, and I may have stories that's news to you."

"Thank you. I'll take refreshment, whatever you have." Something to strengthen her way. She felt recently wakened from a long illness.

He tied the reins to a post. "Just this morning I heard about Hargis and Lucie being jailed. I'm hoping you'll tell me there's no truth to it."

She steadied herself on the post. "Jailed! Where?"

"Over to Webster Springs, so they say."

"Who said?"

"I ain't seen or heard of him before, and I ain't good with new names. A Joe somebody, old guy. I'd have asked more about hisself, but he got me off track talking about Hargis and Lucie, and he didn't stay long."

Roy waited, like he was giving her leave to set him straight.

She did not doubt the story. Not many days ago she'd have laughed to hear of Lucie arrested. "Did he say why they're jailed?"

"I don't remember if he said it was due to moonshining or if I put that two and two together for myself. 'Course you know half of what's said ain't true. But he didn't scramble the names like folks do when they only partly know what they're talking about. 'Lucie Bosell and Hargis Boone.' That much was plain."

Wanda followed Roy into the public room. Ruth and Piney wouldn't stay at home and grieve—they'd try to get their ma released. Maybe Price Loughrie could do something. Maybe Lucie would bother the jailer so bad he'd turn her loose to get rid of her.

Wanda paced the dusty floor, sipping cider that had a hard bite. There was nothing she could do. "I have to get the train at Elkins. I'm needed at home."

"Well, sure. And it might not be them. But sit awhile, take the load off. He popped the cork on the cider jug. "Have another."

"This'll do me."

Heavy feet struck the platform. The depot door banged and a bulky shape paused in the opening. His face was shadowed, but light glinted on the tips of yellow hair, and she knew. Someone behind gave him a shove to the inside. Two of them, Coyne and Raz. She kept her hand in her pocket.

"G'day, g'day," Roy said.

Coyne shoved back his hat. "Who's your lady, Roy?"

There'd be no gain in playing dumb. Lucie would jump into the conversation to guide it as she wanted. Wanda tilted her head, studied Coyne, then Raz. "We saw each other a few times, back at Winkler. Was never introduced."

"This here's Miss Bosell," Roy said, like she was a famous somebody. "Lucie Bosell's grandgirl. These boys is Cottons." He pointed. "Coyne, Raz."

Coyne nodded toward a liquor jug on Roy's sideboard. "A Bosell. Ain't that interesting."

Raz stepped close. "I saw you at the grist mill."

Her fingers cramped. "I remember. Your wife was there. A real pretty girl."

Roy poured two shots of whiskey. "Raz, you got a wife? I thought you was a ladies' man."

"I got a wife. Better'n any whore I ever knew, plus she don't cost nothing."

Coyne raised his glass to Wanda and drank the liquor down. "Sorry, Miss Bosell, but Raz is a nasty talker. Him and his wife scandalizes Ma."

Raz smiled. "Blanche can't get enough of me. Nothing wrong about that."

Wanda sat in the nearest chair to hide the tremble of her knees and to put a table between them. "Was your brother the one killed the other night? He looked like you. I was sorry to hear it—we danced once—had a high old time."

Roy whirled to Wanda. "Duck was killed? That's news you could of told. Duck Cotton was killed, and you didn't say a word."

"I just got here. Anyway, you took it out of mind with news of Granny."

Roy pushed back his hat. "I'm sorry, boys, about your brother."

Coyne grunted. "We heard about that dancing. Maybe another time you'll tell us more. What's this about your granny?"

"She's in jail," Roy said.

The brothers raised their eyebrows and nodded like they appreciated Roy's news. "Done by our sheriff? We're out to fetch him."

"They're said to be jailed over to Webster Springs. So I'd say they was took by the law over there."

"Her and who else?"

"Hargis Boone," Roy said.

"Hargis Boone, there's a fool." Coyne slapped down his glass. "Roy, we need to buy or borrow a wagon to carry our little brother home to Ma. You got any such thing?"

"That I do. Let me show you."

Raz tipped his hat. "Goodbye, Miss Bosell. If you run across the sheriff, tell him to get up to Winkler and find Duck's murderer."

She nodded. "My sympathies to your family."

The door closed behind them. Wanda sat still. Nobody had fooled anybody, except maybe Roy.

CHAPTER 22

L ong after the Cottons hitched their horses to Roy's wagon and drove beyond sight, Wanda stood on the platform of the old depot and watched the road south. With Cottons on the move, no travel felt safe.

Roy sat on a bench in the shade of the eaves, counting paper money. He held up a bank note. "I never seen one of these before. D'you suppose it's good?" He answered himself. "Course it ain't. I knew when they paid they wasn't the type to have good money so handy."

Wanda glanced at the bills spread on the bench. "Might have been good not to mention about me being a Bosell."

He flipped the note over and smoothed it on his knee. "I'm sorry for that. I get flustered with some types of people. Don't you?"

"At times." Were Cottons ever flustered? Or Lucie? She lifted a bill. "This one's a greenback."

"One good dollar! They got my wagon and harnesses, plus a new piece of canvas tarp, all for one dollar. Why didn't I say I had no wagon?"

"Maybe you wanted them gone?"

"True enough, I did. A body needs to stay on the best side of bad folks."

The sun stood overhead. By riding steadily, she might reach the train station with only a few hours of moonlit travel. "Roy, if you had to go to Elkins by a different way, what would that be?"

"There's trails everywhere, some burned and blocked, some growed over, but they go off in all directions, so you gotta know your way. Smart folks stick to the road."

In the distance, a wagon appeared at the spot where she'd seen the last of Raz and Coyne. It had two people on the bench.

Roy shoved the bank notes into his pocket and came to her side. "Do you know those folks?"

She breathed easier when the wagon was close enough to show a woman beside the driver. He pulled the horses to a stop in front of the depot, and a fuss started between the woman and four small children trying to climb over the sides of the wagon bed.

The driver beckoned to Roy. "Might you know of a patch of mint nearby to here?"

"'Deed I don't," Roy said. "Got sassafras tea, cider and such. You're welcome to stop a while."

The children clamored. "Cider!" The woman pulled them back into the wagon.

Sour-faced, the man handed the reins to the woman and got down. "Keep them here or we'll never get started again." He belched, a sound long enough to have traveled from his toes, and followed Roy inside.

Liking the idea of traveling in company, Wanda stepped to the wagon's side. "Have you been to Trading Days?"

"We didn't get that far. My man got the stomach distress. He's been stopping every little bit to puke in the road." She motioned toward her children, now pushing each other for a favored seat. "They're disappointed, you see."

The man climbed back in the wagon and flicked the reins. The woman and children waved goodbye.

Wanda hesitated as the wagon moved on, then thanked Roy, mounted Ginger, and followed.

For a while the children peered at her over the tailgate. Later they wrestled and bickered. Every time the woman shouted at them to be quiet, the husband shouted at her for shouting.

Wanda let Ginger fall farther behind. The family's progress was slower than she liked, and she'd just decided to ride around and leave them when their wagon turned up a road angling down from the slope. The children waved and called, 'Goodbye, goodbye.'"

When Ginger followed of her own accord, Wanda flicked the reins and rode up beside the woman. "Does this road go to Elkins?"

"Not hardly," the woman shouted. "Just to our place."

"Good travel, then. I hope your husband gets to feeling better."

"Thank you." She did not look hopeful.

Back on the main road, Wanda pressed Ginger to a trot. Since she hadn't mastered the gait and the mare couldn't keep it up for long, they soon settled back to a walk.

The monotony was restful. She didn't remember anything along this road, but traveling the last time with Virgie, she'd paid less attention. Having Virgie along now would be all right. Or Will. A few weeks ago, he'd offered to ride with her to Elkins and have their photographs made. They might have sat for one together. She'd taken everything the wrong way.

Ginger snorted and picked up her ears, and Wanda twisted in her saddle. No one followed, though she couldn't see past the last curve. The mare did a sidestep and snorted again, maybe hearing a bear or a pack of dogs.

When the uphill brush crackled like wildfire, Wanda panicked and urged Ginger to go faster. Hooves pounded on the road behind, louder, closer, until she and Ginger were pinned between two riders, large men with yellow hair.

On both sides, Wanda's legs were jolted and pressed by their horses, their stirrups, their legs. Ginger stumbled, and Coyne tore the reins from her hands. She clamped and batted her hands at his face, but he leaned away, and her arms whipped the air. On the other side, Raz laughed and pulled her back by her hair.

Heat rose from her neck to her scalp, and her head filled with the screams of children: *Red Rover, Red Rover!* She rose in the stirrups and threw herself onto Coyne. His horse shied, and she fell into the space that opened between them, slamming her shoulder to the ground, and then her head.

~

"Miss Bosell."

She lay in the road with a man standing over her, blurry. Her face was damp and her breath shallow, like she'd had a restful sleep. Something scratched her neck, and she brought up her hand and touched thick, rough rope. Her vision cleared. Coyne stuffed a rag in her mouth, wrenched another between her jaws and tied it behind her head. The cloth dried her mouth. She struggled to swallow.

Raz held their horses. She could only hope they'd take her to the sheriff. They pulled her up and pushed her onto Ginger. She choked on the gag and tried to pull it off, but Coyne grabbed her wrists and squeezed them against the saddle horn. Raz tied them with a short rope.

Raz pinched her cheek. "We need help, Miss Bosell, and we've picked you to give it."

She sucked air through her nose until she was light-headed. They needed help, but not friendly help, or she wouldn't be tied.

Coyne took Ginger's reins and led up the slope. Raz trailed behind. Wanda leaned forward over the mare's neck to keep from being swatted by low-hanging branches. Sometimes she glimpsed the river. They were going upstream, back toward Winkler. Long ago there'd been a jail in Winkler, and a policeman, big Frank. At this moment jail and a big policeman sounded good. But they weren't taking her to any lawman, or they wouldn't have bothered with the gag. Would they make her steal, or something worse? Would she do anything to stay alive—anything so they'd take away the gag?

Coyne led them among the trees to a strip of rutted grass, a road, of sorts, with Roy's wagon at the side. Raz untied the rope from the saddle horn but left it hanging from her wrist.

She fought the urge to kick and elbow as they pulled her off the mare, tied her wrists behind her back, crossed and bound her ankles and rolled her into the wagon. Lying on her back with her knees up and her jaws stretched, she slowed the pounding in her chest by trying to understand their movements. Saw Raz take off Ginger's saddle, blanket, and bridle and throw them into the wagon. Wondered why he put his own tack on Ginger and harnessed his horse to the wagon with Coyne's. Watched till they covered the wagon bed with a white tarp.

Before Coyne tied down the last corner, he growled a warning. "Stay quiet or I'll gut you like a pig."

The wagon bumped through ruts, then made a turn onto a somewhat better road. By the time they stopped again, she felt bruised all over, but with shallow, even breaths, was managing not to choke.

Raz and Coyne untied the tarp and dragged her into the woods by the arms, face up. Her heels lifted scents of decay and left trails in the layer of dead leaves. She had a frantic thought that they were looking for a better spot to kill her.

They stopped and stood her upright, and Raz pushed her face against a tree while Coyne tied the end of her noose to a limb. She closed her eyes in relief when she saw the tree branch was not high enough for a hanging, just high enough to keep her from sitting or lying down.

Raz tied the mare nearby. She listened to fading footsteps and the last sounds of the wagon rolling away.

For a time, she was relieved to be upright in fresh air, an improvement that brought hope. But as daylight waned she felt desperate to sit. She flexed her bound ankles and feet, stretched her neck and shoulders, scratched her back and then her face against tree bark. Later, she worried that the Cottons would never return, that they'd left her and the horse to die of thirst. In a kind of delirium, she felt kindly toward the mare and nearly cried, wondering if horses and mules suffered from being hobbled and stabled in unfamiliar places, never understanding why.

It was dark when she heard the rumble of wheels. Coyne and Raz whispered as they lifted and dropped her into the wagon, raising a false hope that others might be near. Beside her lay something hard and moon-lit white. When they fastened down the tarp, trapping her with the air of the narrow space, she smelled rotting blood, and knew. It was Duck, wrapped in a sheet. She twisted to her side and put her nose close to the wagon boards with their chinks of fresh air. The knife pressed into her leg, a welcome discomfort.

Strains of music and a buzz of voices let her know when they reached Winkler. The wagon made a sharp turn. She imagined the wagon going uphill, traveling along a brushy track above the store, a detour around Will's blocked-off street. Then it turned down and rumbled onto flatter ground. The sounds of Trading Days faded, and with them, any hope that Piney or Will might recognize her horse.

Now over rattle of harnesses, wagon shudders, and the crank and bump of wheels, she heard snatches of the brothers' talk. She drew courage because they hadn't killed or beaten her. Yet.

"Ma's gonna take it… bury… "

"… them Bosells… "

"Get… "

"… jail."

Laughing.

In all the fragments, she heard nothing about revenge or their missing gold. They hadn't said anything since Roy's about looking for Duck's killer. Like Lucie, they might have another plan. And they wanted her help?

She'd been forming her own plan—think sharp as Lucie, act as obedient as Piney, and never stop watching for a chance to escape. But as the wheels bumped along, her head and shoulder throbbed and her throat burned, and she lost all sense of time and place. Faces appeared on the underside of the tarp, blending from one to the other, bearded men, distressed women in bonnets, no one she knew. One said, "How do I get to God's good earth?" A dark-haired man with a sharp chin answered. "This is it. Make the best."

A fresh breath jolted her awake. The wagon cover was pulled off and hard hands lifted and flung her, head down, over a broad back. The dark air was sweet with honeysuckle.

A man's voice whispered. "Open the door and get a light."

A lamp glowed to life. Head down, she saw a rag rug on plank flooring. Then she was dropped her to her feet and pushed onto a chair. The brothers stood before her.

"She won't go no place tied up," Raz whispered. "Leave her there or throw her in a corner. I'm going to bed."

"What if Ma wakes up?"

She grunted through her gag. She needed to pee.

"Then you find a place to stow her," Raz said. "Blanche is waiting."

"Boys?" The voice was high, like a child's, a call from somewhere in the house. A tiny woman appeared in a doorway. She wore a long white nightgown, and her pale hair was braided for sleep. "Did you bring your brother?"

Coyne put his arm around the old woman's shoulders. "He's in the wagon, wrapped and ready for the ground."

The woman's voice cracked. "I want a preacher."

"Next time the circuit rider comes, we'll take him to the grave and he can say some words."

"I want a preacher to pray over him before he goes into the ground."

Coyne sighed. "In the morning, we'll do what we can. I'm sorry we woke you. Let me help you back to bed."

His ma pointed with her cane. "Who's that in the chair?"

"Nothing to bother about," Raz said.

"It's a woman. Why's she bound up like that?"

"To keep her safe," Coyne said. "Pitiful, ain't she? We're helping a friend. This woman is crazy and dangerous, even to herself. Soon as we bury Duck, we'll take her to the asylum over at Weston."

Wanda bit down on her gag.

Mrs. Cotton came closer, tapping her cane. "You boys is good to help a friend, but does she need that rag in her mouth? Does she bite?"

Coyne yawned. "That's what our friend said. And she screams awful. We're doing the best we know how."

"I'm sure you are. Treat her gentle, poor creature."

Wanda pleaded with her eyes.

"You try to behave," Mrs. Cotton said. "My boys will take care of you."

"Ma, you go back to bed," Coyne said. "We'll get Blanche to tend to her."

"I've had a thought. I want you boys to sing at your brother's funeral."

"Ma, no, please," Raz said.

"'Safe in the Arms of Jesus.' For your brother. He'd do it for you."

"I get nervous, singing in front of folks."

"Think of him, not yourself."

"If I think of him, I won't be able to sing for blubbering."

"Never mind," Coyne said. "We'll sing, and we'll go for the preacher when we've slept an hour or two. Take the crazy woman to the shed."

"Blanche can do it. If I only got an hour to sleep, I ain't gonna waste it."

Coyne helped his ma out of sight and Raz clambered up steep steps at the side of the room. Hushed talk floated down, and soon Blanche appeared, wearing the long-sleeved dress.

"I didn't know it was you," Blanche said. She bent and loosened the ankle knot. "Are you really crazy?"

Wanda bowed her neck and slowly shook her head.

"I guess you are, or Raz wouldn't say so."

With her feet freed, she flexed her throbbing ankles. Blanche took her arm and helped her stand, but her feet were like clubs. Blanche pulled on her arm. "Come on, I gotta get back to bed."

Her feet tingled. Outside, she moaned through the gag, crossed her legs and wiggled.

"You gotta pee?"

She moaned louder.

"Blanche." A man's voice, Coyne in the doorway. "Lock the shed when you come out. I'm gonna stand right here till you do."

Blanche whispered. "Raz said not to untie your hands or that rope on your neck, but it'll be okay, honey. I'll help." At the side of a dark building, Blanche tied the rope to a post, hiked up Wanda's dress, drew down her trousers and pushed her to a squat. "Now go, I'll hold you."

She had no trouble obeying.

"This is what I do for my little girl," Blanche said, pulling up Wanda's trousers and letting her skirt drop. Then she stuck her arm through Wanda's and helped her into the shed. "Raz said I was to tie you to the anvil. You stand here while I strike a light."

Blanche kept her foot on the loose end of Wanda's neck rope while she lit a lamp on a shelf. Then she picked up the rope and tugged her toward an anvil on a low bench. Blanche looped the rope under the bench and tied it around the anvil, then pressed her hand on Wanda's shoulder. "Down you go."

There was just enough slack in the rope to kneel beside the bench, flop to her rear, and lie down.

Blanche stood back. "Now, ain't that nice?"

It was. Her arms and shoulders ached from being tied back, her wrists chafed against the rope and her throat was dried out, but her feet were free. Blanche left her in the dark.

When she flopped to her side, the ties at her wrist no longer dug into her back. This was what it meant to be helpless—grateful to piss and lie on a floor that did not move. Even so, her relief did not last long, for the floor was hard, and being grateful felt too much like giving in.

She flexed her legs, and her trousers ripped across something sticking up from the floor. Drawing up her knees, she touched her boot to a nail and probed to its top. It had no head. If she could get her face to it, the nail could rip her gag. It might even puncture the rope on her wrists.

With a mighty grunt she pushed her wrists against the floor, sat up, and scooted toward the nail. The neck rope tightened. Going farther would pull over the bench and anvil, which likely would fall on her if she couldn't see to dodge. By daylight, she'd have a better chance, because after passing the rope under the bench, Blanche had tied it from the horn of the anvil to the heel in a slip knot. If not for the gag that kept her jaws open, she could pull that knot loose with her lips. Tomorrow, as soon as there was light, she'd see how to do it.

Thoughts of escape briefly stirred her blood, but her eyelids drooped. She slept, an exhausting time of dreaming and waking, stretching, and watching for dawn.

CHAPTER 23

Daylight shone under the eaves, between boards in the siding, and onto the anvil, the bench, and the nail with no head. To ease the tension on her neck rope, Wanda wiggled closer to the bench. Next she crossed her ankles and pulled them toward her rear. Then with a heave and a push of knuckles on the floor, she flung herself upright.

Unbalanced, she pitched face-forward toward the floor, but righted herself and stepped over the bench. If she could pull or push the bench closer to the nail, she could bend and let the nail tear her gag.

The anvil was bolted down, and the bench was of stout, thick oak. For leverage, she backed against the wall and shoved with her foot. The bench rocked. She pushed harder, and bench and anvil toppled, pulling her with them. Her ribs hit the hard edge of the bench. Wheezing, she slid to her knees.

The shed door opened, and Blanche came in with a bowl and spoon. "Oh, Honey, what happened?"

Wanda's eyes watered.

Blanche helped her sit with her back against the overturned bench. "That old anvil, it's a wonder it didn't kill you." She pulled a stool close. "You won't bite if I untie this thing in your mouth? I didn't think so. You found my babies, and that was good. You won't scream, neither? You may be crazy but that don't mean I won't treat you kindly. My ma taught me that, be gentle with babies and them that's hindered in any way." Blanche loosened her gag.

Wanda spit out the cloth and croaked, "Water."

"I'm sorry, I didn't think." Blanche hurried out.

Wanda scooted a few inches closer to the nail.

Too soon, Blanche entered the shed with a pail and dipper. "I can't untie your hands, but I can help you eat. It's what I do for my babies."

Babies abandoned, yet present in Blanche's sorry, weakened mind. Wanda opened her parched mouth.

Blanche sat on the low stool and held the dipper while Wanda drank three scoops of water. Then she held out a spoonful of grits.

"I left my daughter," Wanda said.

The spoon wavered in Blanche's hand. "How old?"

"Eight."

Blanche stirred the grits. "Is she with her pa?"

"He's dead."

"I'm sorry. Was he a good pa?"

"Better'n anybody."

Blanche lifted the spoon again and Wanda opened her mouth like a baby bird. When the bowl was half-empty, she clamped her lips.

Blanche set the bowl in her lap. "Raz never wanted kids."

Wanda steadied her gaze on Blanche's shifty eyes.

Blanche ate a bite of grits. "Will you go back to your girl someday?"

"If I can get free. Raz and Coyne mean me to help them with something. They're not taking me to Weston. I think they said that just for you and their ma."

"They don't hide stuff from me," Blanche said, "but they never tell their ma what they do. She's religious and all, though she's got no charity for me."

"Life hardens some."

"Don't it?" Blanche dropped the spoon in the bowl. "I ain't sorry Duck's dead, he was always mean to me. Ma Cotton wanted them to go after his murderer but they got other interests now, I see the signs. Raz said your granny's rich."

"Not rich, no more'n you. Please, help me go home. My daughter's way out West and she's got nobody but me. Cut me loose and I'll run."

Blanche set the bowl on the floor and stood. "Your poor little girl. I'd help you in a minute if it didn't mean going against Raz. And what Coyne might do."

"Run with me. I'll take you back to your kids."

"That's sweet, but Raz is gonna get us all together soon as he does the next job."

"Then tell Mrs. Cotton I'm not crazy. I'm kidnapped."

"You just be good and you'll get home somehow. You ready to go pee?"

Blanche loosened the anvil rope and led her outside. Blinking in the bright light, Wanda saw a broad expanse of open ground, a small house in the center, and Coyne and Raz, saddling their horses.

Blanche tugged her rope. "This way."

Wanda glanced at the road. When the men left, she'd pull away from Blanche and run.

In the outhouse, she listened for sounds of men riding away. Blanche waited at the open door.

"Hurry," Blanche said.

"I'm hurrying."

Blanche tugged on the rope. "You're just like my kids. I ain't got all day. I think you're done."

Outside again, Wanda glanced toward the horses, Raz in the saddle, watching them, Coyne walking from the house. She judged the shed to be at least thirty paces away. Mrs. Cotton came outside and called, and Coyne went back to the porch.

Blanche tugged the neck rope and she stumbled over the

shed's threshold. Only after her mouth was stuffed and gagged and the neck rope wrapped around the anvil did she hear the horses galloping away.

"I may not get back for a while," Blanche said. "I gotta cook for when they come with the preacher. Ma Cotton wants a big spread after the funeral. I hope she won't be disappointed. Folks don't care for us much."

Blanche left her sitting against the bench, tied by a rope too short to let her lie down or stand up and too far from the headless nail.

Through the day she listened to distant voices, the arrival of horses and wagons and the bang of the outhouse door. When she thought anyone was near, she moaned and pounded her heels against the floor, but no one came. The rest of the time, she plotted. At present, the Cottons had all the advantages, maybe enough to make them over-confident. And because she'd given no resistance, they might think her as submissive and weak-minded as Blanche.

Long after dark, Blanche came in and lit the lamp. "He's buried, and more came to the service than I thought. But now, Coyne wants me to fix you up so nobody on the road will know you. I got an idea how to do that." She untied the gag and dipped water from the pail.

Wanda spit out the stuffing cloth and drank.

Blanche lifted a spoon of beans. "They didn't say nothing about feeding you, but I can't help being tender-hearted."

Wanda accepted a few bites, but was impatient to talk. "Did they say where we're going?"

"You're right, not to the crazy house. Home! To your Granny's!"

They thought Lucie was rich. Would they trade her for gold coins, for Lucie's recipe, or something more? It was a useless thought. They would never let her go.

Blanche put the bowl aside and fetched a pair of sheep shears from the wall. "I'm gonna make you a man." Giggling, she grabbed a hunk of Wanda's hair.

Wanda jerked away. "Blanche, if you cut my hair, Granny won't know me, and she'll shoot us all."

"Oh," Blanche said. "An old-lady bonnet, then. You can take it off when you get there." She scooped up the bowl and ran out.

The nail was still too far away and her neck rope too short, but Blanche had left the stuffing rag near Wanda's feet. She kicked it behind the water pail.

Blanche came back carrying a black bonnet and a long shawl. "Coyne says he knows Lucie's in jail and to tell you he wasn't born yesterday. But it'll be all right to hide you under these."

Again Blanche took her to the outhouse. A glance showed the dark blot of a man watching from the porch.

"They're gonna leave before it gets light," Blanche said. "I'll come and get your hair under that bonnet. It's got a black veil, so this thing in your mouth won't show. It's a lot of fuss for nothing, I think. You won't meet anybody traveling in the dark."

Back in the shed, Blanche retied the gag between her jaws. Without the stuffing, the gag wasn't bad.

She woke long before they came for her. Blanche stuffed the ends of her hair under the neck of her dress, pulled the bonnet over her springy curls, and tied it under her chin.

Blanche led her to the horses. She had a moment of relief when Raz untied her wrists and she was able to stretch her aching arms. He held Ginger's bridle and her neck rope while Blanche helped her into the saddle and re-tied her hands, not behind, but to the saddle horn. Blanche draped the shawl ends over the horn and reached up and pulled down the bonnet's veil. The blue night turned black.

"Don't do nothing foolish," Blanche whispered. "Go home to your girl."

"Oo-ooo," Wanda said through the gag, meaning "You too."

Blanche patted her arm. "You're welcome."

They traveled slowly, Wanda in deep darkness behind a veil

that grew wet with dew. Whatever the Cottons intended at Lucie's, she hoped no one was there, that Lucie had not wrangled her way out of jail, that Ruth and the marshal were on their way to Webster Springs to see her, and that Piney was safe with Blanche's children in Simpson Wainwright's house. And that the rifle stood in its corner.

Blanche had not tied her wrists securely, and Wanda soon pulled her hands loose and slipped one into her pocket. She thought of cutting the lead rope and racing away, but Ginger had no speed, the night was dark, and she didn't know where she was. The knife might help, should they meet anyone she could ask for help. The shawl was a blessing, for it hid her hands. When Coyne rode near, she wiggled them back into their ties.

"Your granny's place is around here somewhere. Where's the road to it?"

"Ah-o," she said.

Holding up her bonnet veil, he snapped open a pocket knife and cut the cloth gagging her mouth. The gag fell to her shoulders. He let the veil drop over her face. "Now where?"

"I can't see through this black stuff."

He pushed up the veil, giving her a view, when he stretched, of the revolver and holster at his belt. Misty light filtered through the trees, but nothing looked familiar. "Which side of the road should I look?"

He slapped her face.

She let out a slow breath. "I don't know because I don't know which way you've brought me. Up from Winkler, there's a trail on the left."

"So look to the right."

"Are you sure this is Granny's road?"

Coyne swatted at her again. She hated Raz for the bruises on Blanche and Ruby, but if she had to use the knife again, she hoped it was on Coyne.

She saw nothing familiar until they came to the fork and the sign that said "Bosell."

Coyne called a halt. "That there sign's a trick, and you know it."

She pointed the way they'd come. "Now I see where I am." Anger threaded her voice, and she struggled to be calm. At Lucie's, she'd know where to run and where to hide.

Coyne motioned them to turn around. "It's time to say what you know about the Bosell stash."

She felt a surge of relief. Lucie's stash, not their coins. She'd feared they'd beaten Will to make him say who'd bought the jacket. "Ma used to talk about a stash, but she's dead, and I ain't been around since I was a kid."

"We heard it's gold."

"Not likely. Granny's poor."

"She might live poor. It's what old folks do, no matter what they got. We know Lucie's in jail. Who will be to home?"

"Maybe nobody. Maybe my aunts."

"You better hope they want to keep you alive."

She pointed to a gap in the roadside trees. "There's the trail."

Coyne and Raz peered down over the bank. "Well, kiss my ass," Raz said. "Time and again I've passed and never saw it."

Coyne lengthened her horse's lead rope. "I'll go first, then her, then you. When we're down, stay into the trees till we know what's what."

The barking began before they were halfway down. At the bottom, dogs snarled and raced back and forth. Just two, no Old Henry's Dog.

Raz aimed to shoot.

"Save it for something better," Coyne said. "Stay while I see what's here." He handed her lead to Raz and disappeared from view, followed by the barking dogs. When he came back, he motioned Raz to follow.

They circled the cottage and stopped in front, while the dogs retreated to the pond. "Old lady bitches." Raz laughed. "Let's see if any other old bitches are about. He pointed his revolver at the door.

Coyne untied her wrists and pulled her out of the saddle. "I didn't see nobody, but let's make sure they're not still abed. Raz, open that door."

Raz entered first, and Coyne pushed her inside. There was no rifle in the corner.

They overturned everything in the cottage. Raz slit the straw mattresses and Coyne held a lantern and made her show him each jar and crock in the cellar house. With her hands free, she struggled against the urge to drive her knife into the closest belly.

"Here's what's gonna happen," Coyne said. "You direct us to Lucie's stash, or we'll leave you for a surprise. Won't matter if they come tomorrow or next month, you'll be dead and we'll be gone."

Goodbye, Evie. Goodbye Will, goodbye Piney and May Rose. Maybe justice for what she'd done, and escape from hurting anyone else.

She stalled, needing an advantage. "I don't know where the stash is, but there's two things here that Lucie prizes—her corn and her still."

"That right?" Coyne pulled her to the corn crib, a shed with breathing spaces in the siding. It was filled to the top with yellow ears. He stood with hands on hips, admiring it. "There's a little fortune in itself."

Raz picked up a rat-chewed cob. "Corn ain't as easy to carry as gold."

"Maybe the old woman has stashed her gold underneath. Why else would she keep all this? We'll check it out later." Coyne snapped Wanda's neck rope. "Show us the still, and no wild-goose chase." He farted, a long bubbly blast.

Raz gagged like he was going to puke. "You better go wipe."

She walked them past the pond. "This is a real nice place," Raz said. "What do you say we drive the Bosells out and bring Ma here? She could sit in the sun and fish."

"Ma likes her own place. Remember what we come for."

"There may be no stash a'tall," Raz said. "It's a snug house,

209

and the ground looks better'n ours. There's money in selling corn and making whiskey. Maybe they'd trade the girl for the deed to this here."

Coyne jerked Wanda's neck rope. "They're not that stupid, and me neither."

At the site, they cursed the size of the turnip still and the lack of good running water.

"The old woman's glory days is past," Raz said. "Let's shovel out that corn. I got a feeling something's hid under it."

Back at the corncrib, Coyne lengthened Wanda's rope and hooked it over his wrist so she could hold the burlap sacks while he and Raz shoveled. She looked at every stud and spider-webbed corner for a large implement, like Piney's long knife. Or a scythe. With a scythe, she might slice into both men before they could draw their guns. She wondered where it was, and if she could fool them into taking her to it.

Coyne's next shovel into the bottom of the mound started an avalanche of yellow ears that ended at their feet and uncovered a tail of a black snake. The tail wiggled into the corn. Blacks snakes ate rats and mice, and most folks said leave them be. But her pa had shown her how to grab the tail, pull a snake out of its hole and break its neck with a whip and a snap. She'd done that a time or two as a kid, showing off for boys, and when she felt hurt and mean.

She glanced outside. The dogs had long ago stopped barking, and now they sat alert, facing the far side of the meadow.

Coyne farted again and threw her rope at Raz. "Take charge of her, I gotta shit." He stomped out.

Raz slipped the loop of rope over his wrist, dug his shovel into the corn and let the ears slide into her sack. Behind him, a snake writhed in the corn, struck by the shovel.

Wanda waited one breath for the outhouse door to close and another for Coyne to drop his trousers and sit, then she seized the snake by the tail and whipped it at Raz's head. It coiled around his neck.

Raz dropped his shovel, yelped and grabbed at the snake with both hands. She pulled her knife and whacked through the rope.

Outside, she paused one moment, seeing the dogs race away, maybe to greet family, because they weren't barking. She longed to follow, but running across the meadow would leave her too long in view. From the crib came sounds of a shovel pounding the floor. With the outhouse on the far side of the cottage, she could not see Coyne.

The outhouse door slammed. She ducked behind the nearest tree and crept up into the woods.

CHAPTER 24

Horses' hooves had gouged slick slides in the steepest portions of the trail. Wanda crawled around them, grabbing tree roots to keep from falling, thinking only of putting space between herself and the Cotton brothers. They'd gone quiet after a few shouts, but not far off, brush crackled.

She ducked away from the trail and cut back through woods toward the still. When a rock outcrop blocked her way, she turned downhill and came out near the far side of the pond. From there she sprinted toward the hidden road, every hard footfall thumping in her head. The dogs were no longer in sight, but a distant clatter of harnesses and the bump of wagon wheels pulled her forward.

She found them in the tunnel of trees, Ruth and Loughrie on horseback, Hargis and Lucie in the mule wagon, and Old Henry's Dog on the bench between them. The other dogs bounded in circles, tails wagging.

Loughrie rose in his stirrups and waved. "Wanda!" The rifle lay across his saddle.

She held her side and breathed in gasps.

Ruth slid off Old Henry and fell on her in a hug. Old Henry's Dog leaped down and sniffed her boots and trousers. Ruth lifted the rope still hanging from her neck. "We been worried to death. Did Cottons do this?"

Now in the presence of help, Wanda trembled with fright. "They're here."

Lucie put a hand behind her ear. "What's that? Evalena's Girl, come here and account for yourself."

"Coyne and Raz Cotton are here. They've tore apart your house and corncrib, looking for your stash."

"My stash?" Lucie half rose from her seat. "You could of told them it's rotted to mush. Could of took them to the old home place and showed them instead of bringing them on us."

"Shut up, Ma," Ruth said.

Wanda laughed, teary-eyed. Old Henry's dog licked her hand, and she patted his head until she stopped shaking.

Loughrie motioned to Ruth. "Get your ma's gun."

Lucie sat down with a thump and clutched the shotgun. "I'll hold my own weapon, thank you."

Loughrie's horse pranced like it was starting a race. "Wanda, where are the Cottons?"

"Searching for me along the trail to the road, or back at the corncrib. Or riding this way across the meadow. They have revolvers."

"Good," he said. "I'll go through the woods and give them a surprise."

Ruth mounted Old Henry. "Then I'll circle along the other hillside and meet you at the trail."

Hargis stood in the wagon. "Wait just a minute. Let's go for the sheriff."

"He's right, get help," Wanda said. She didn't want Ruth riding into a shoot-out with Cottons.

"No law," Lucie said.

Ruth pulled the gun from Lucie's hands. "It's up to us to defend our place. Price, fire a shot if you need me. Someone get a hand on that dog and keep him here."

While Hargis worked the rope loose from Wanda's neck and

put it on the dog, Loughrie and Ruth rode side by side toward the meadow and parted, one going left, and one right.

"I don't feel natural without my gun," Lucie said.

"You don't want Ruth looking for them without it," Hargis said.

"I suppose. But I got nothing to protect us if they come here. Evalena's Girl, get up here beside me."

Hargis tied the dog to the side of the wagon, then poked through junk that had hidden their jars of whiskey. "I don't guess there's a weapon here somewhere?"

"Pull off one of them chair rungs if it makes you feel better," Lucie said.

Wanda climbed to the bench and drew her knife. "I've got this." It was less sticky, but had a tarnish that wouldn't wipe off.

Lucie peered at the knife, then into her face. "Did you kill Duck Cotton?"

Wanda flushed cold with the memory. "He made me dance with him. That's no reason to kill someone."

"But you got him."

She spit on the knife and rubbed it on her trouser leg. "I wouldn't be proud if I did."

"'Course not," Lucie said. "With that knife?"

Wanda pressed her lips together. Lucie sighed in a satisfied way.

Hargis slapped a chair leg against his palm. "You killed into a bad family."

"I didn't say I killed anybody. How did you two get out of jail?"

"Wasn't nothing," Hargis said. "Little bribe for the sheriff."

Lucie gave him the evil eye. "Hargis got us arrested, mouthing off to the wrong person. Then he offered the sheriff every bit of what we made off the whiskey. *Every bit!*"

A distant blast stopped their talk and held them in its echoes. Growling, Old Henry's Dog lurched at the end of his rope.

"Shotgun," Lucie whispered. "Ruth."

More gunshots—pops—not the shotgun or rifle. Wanda barely breathed. After a long silence, she slid the knife into its pocket sheath and covered it with her hand.

"Hargis," Lucie said, "peek out to the meadow and see if anyone's coming."

He ran toward the covered end of the road, swinging his chair rung.

Lucie leaned forward, hands behind her ears. "I don't like this not-knowing, and we've heard nothing out of the rifle. You don't suppose the marshal's in with the Cottons?"

"If he was, he could've sprung them on you before now."

"Maybe he's been waiting for something better. Did you tell Ruth about the cave?"

"I said I'd seen it."

"Likely she's told him. Tear me off one of them chair rungs."

Wanda reached into the wagon's junk and gave Lucie a leg from the Windsor chair. Lucie hid it under her skirt. Old Henry's Dog whined, and the other dogs raced into the woods, barking.

Hargis broke through the brush that blocked their view of the meadow. "Nothing out there." He stopped, eyes popping like a pig in a snare.

Wanda gripped the knife in her pocket and twisted in her seat. Coyne and Raz rode behind the wagon, revolvers out and pointed, Coyne leading a horse with an empty saddle. *Old Henry.* The horse had a smear of what looked like blood on its side. His dog howled.

Lucie howled too. "Where's Ruth? Where's my gun?"

Wanda's vision blurred. The other dogs snapped at the Cottons' legs. The men's horses snorted and shied.

"Old lady bitches." Raz aimed and shot at the nearest dog. Wanda screamed, and Hargis took off running toward the meadow. The dog, hit by no more than splattering dirt, fled yelping into the woods with Raz laughing and shooting after it. The other dog slunk under the wagon.

Coyne swore and shoved his gun against Wanda's back. "Raz! Forget dogs—Boone's getting away."

Wanda's chest tightened, and heat rushed up her neck. Lucie heaved the chair leg toward Raz, but it fell short.

Hargis dodged toward the woods. Shooting as he rode, Raz missed, but overtook him and knocked the gun butt against his head. Hargis crumbled to the ground. Lucie's nails dug into Wanda's arm.

Was Ruth dead? Where was Loughrie? He would follow the shots, but the way sound bounced, she might not be easy to find. Wanda laid a hand on Lucie's and found it ice-cold, calming.

Coyne moved his revolver to Lucie. "We'll take your stash, old woman, or shoot every last one of you. Starting with your young one here. I'm right tired of her."

Lucie locked a bony arm through Wanda's. "Well, I did have a stash at one time. It's at the other place, all ruined. She didn't tell you? Groundwater rotted it."

"Gold don't rot," Coyne said.

"Ha. I wish to heaven it was gold. It was greenbacks, buried in a graveyard. Now it's mush."

A sunbeam shone through the trees on Lucie's face, lighting her cracked lips and the fine white hairs of her chin. Decrepit as she might be, her arm felt like an iron bar.

Riding close, Raz smiled and lifted a hand to the sky. "Ladies, enjoy your last moment of life. Take a look at this good earth, smell the fine air, feel the sunshine."

Coyne clicked the hammer.

Any delay might help, like setting the wagon in motion. The reins lay at Wanda's feet, but the wagon brake was set, and only inches from Coyne.

"Speak now or say goodbye," he said.

Any delay. "I'm not ready to die. Granny's got gold in coins, hidden under her clothes."

Lucie shot her a hateful look.

Coyne nudged Lucie with the revolver. "Get it out."

Lucie fumbled at her waist, drew out a money pouch and tossed it to the ground. Raz got off his horse and shook the gold coins into his hand. "It's a start." He passed the coins to his brother.

Old Henry's dog strained at his rope. Did he hear someone coming?

Coyne passed the coins back to Raz. "You hold 'em, there's a hole in my pocket. And go ahead and shoot Miss Bosell. She deserves it, telling on Granny like that."

"Wait! Wait," Lucie said. "There's something better. Up at the old home place, barrels of whiskey. I'll tell you how to find it."

"Lies won't help now," Coyne said.

"It's real old whiskey, worth more than ever these days. I'll take you. If I'm lying, you can shoot me when we get there."

Raz bent to the wagon seat and spit in Wanda's face. "Miss Bosell, is there a stash of whiskey?"

She wiped his spit with her sleeve, seeing Evie with her arms stretched wide and her hands gripping the hands of her friends. *Red Rover.*

"Speak up," Raz said. "You know where it is?"

"I know the place."

"Then you can show us."

Again Lucie clawed her arm.

"I'll be all right," Wanda whispered. Then to Coyne: "It's a full day's ride. Through burned land."

Coyne led Old Henry to the wagon.

"There at the corncrib, she had a knife," Raz said. He jerked Wanda's hand from her pocket and pounded her fist. The knife clattered on the floorboards. Raz bent and swooped it up.

Children's voices drummed in her ears. *"Red Rover!"*

Lucie rose at her seat, fire in her cloudy eyes. "Where's my daughter?"

"That old gal with the shotgun? We thought she was you," Raz said. "She's out there with my bullet in her." He turned to Coyne. "Think we should go back and get her gun?"

CAROL ERVIN

"It's an old relic, not worth the trouble," Coyne said. "Shoot Boone and the old woman. Get close now and don't waste bullets."

Raz aimed at Lucie's head. Wanda tried to pull her away, but Lucie raised her chin and glared into his revolver.

His gun clicked. He cursed. "Empty. Coyne, you do it."

Coyne loosened a coil of rope on his saddle and tossed it to Raz. "If you're empty, I'll save my shot. Tie them. They'll starve before they're found."

Wanda squeezed Lucie's hand. Loughrie would come, and Lucie and Hargis would be all right. And Piney was safe. But Ruth? And herself?

Raz cut the rope and passed two pieces to his brother. Hargis lay in the weeds where he'd fallen, maybe killed from Raz's blow. Raz tied him while Coyne bound Lucie's wrists and ankles.

Coyne motioned to Wanda and she stepped from the wagon onto Old Henry's back. Beside the wagon, Old Henry's Dog chewed on his rope.

CHAPTER 25

Wanda doubted she and Lucie would meet again in this world. Likely in Hell, if the dead were allowed to meet. Coyne and Raz, too, and Duck, and all the rest who spent their days hurting other folks. Those that earned damnation would make Hell a fearful place, no need for fire and torture.

It was twilight when they came to Winkler. They hadn't gagged her again, but Coyne kept his revolver pointed her way. They rested the horses in the woods until darkness fell, then rode along the river. Will's dogs barked. She watched a small glow of light, higher than the town's other two, and thought of Piney, and prayed Loughrie would find Ruth, Hargis and Lucie.

"This way," she said, when they reached the creek that flowed into the river.

They followed the creek only a short distance before Coyne stopped. He pulled Wanda from her horse and tied her to a downed limb.

"We should of brought something to eat," Raz said.

Wanda heard fumbling in Old Henry's saddlebags.

"Hey, look what I found."

"I can't see what it is," Coyne said.

"A flask. Whiskey, by god."

"Give it here. It's been a hard day."

Ruth's flask. The creek rippled nearby, and Wanda's mouth was parched. "I need water." Coyne and Raz stomped around in the dark, settling themselves. She got nothing.

Wanda slept sitting against the tree limb with her arms tied at her back. When she woke at dawn, they were numb.

Coyne crouched at the creek, filling the flask. He motioned to his brother. "Let her relieve herself or she'll be stinking."

"Cut her loose?"

"Just her feet and hands, dummy. "Wrap that other rope around her neck and tie her to that branch if you don't want to watch."

"I don't mind seeing a little ass," Raz said.

"Just get going—we're close to town."

Raz tied the rope to a branch at the creek's edge, where she squatted, then scooted to the creek and dipped a drink with her hands. Every delay felt like another chance, but for what she couldn't imagine.

When she was finished, Coyne pushed her onto Old Henry and retied her wrists. "This is the way you come?"

"Granny and me, couple of weeks ago."

He nodded at the brush covering the road ahead. "You rode in the creek?"

"Mostly. Part of the road's not grown over so bad."

"Hey," Raz said. "Where'd that dog come from? Suppose somebody's coming?"

Old Henry's Dog nuzzled the horse.

It wasn't rescue, but the dog lifted her spirits. "The dog follows this horse, not people."

Coyne drew his revolver. "I'm gonna take a look." He rode away toward Winkler. Shortly he came back and waved them on. "Nobody coming."

Nobody. A whole night had passed, plenty of time for

Loughrie to find Ruth and Lucie, and plenty of time to come for her. She doubted, but hoped and watched.

All morning they trailed up the creek, Coyne ahead, Raz behind. Helping them find the whiskey cave wouldn't keep her alive unless it happened to be full of killer snakes. They'd kill her when they got what they wanted. Or tie and leave her somewhere to rot. That thought kept her alert.

Raz grumbled about going nowhere. Coyne rode alongside. "Who lives out here?"

She shrugged. "You should've brought Granny. I'm counting on this horse to know where to turn out of the creek."

Mid-afternoon, Old Henry stopped, and Wanda called to Coyne. "This is it." Their fire had left a black spot on the sandy road. He'd passed it by.

"Someone's been here," he said.

"It was us, Granny and me."

On the bank, Raz got out of his saddle, turned his horse and watched its legs. "Damn. I thought Buck was sliding a lot on rock. He's gone lame." Raz tied the horse to a slender tree at water's edge. "I'll double with her."

"Forget that," Coyne said. "Let her walk."

Raz pulled her off Old Henry. She scrambled uphill behind Coyne, her neck rope tied to his saddle horn, comforted because Old Henry's Dog walked at her side. The moment when Raz and Coyne found the whiskey would be her best chance to escape. She'd take their horses, too.

Coyne jerked the rope. "How far?"

Her neck burned. "Not far. That horse knows where to turn."

Sure enough, Old Henry led them through dead pines to the vine-covered chimney.

"This it?"

She nodded.

"Show us the whiskey."

Coyne and Raz rode behind as Wanda walked up the damp

ravine, wrists tied at her back, clay mud clumping on her boots. She stopped at the barrier of boulders.

"From here, you leave the horses and climb. If you want me to go, I need my hands free."

Raz peered up the ravine. "Don't untie them hands. I trust her about as far as I can throw her."

Wanda plopped down on a slab of rock. "Up a ways there's water drips off a ledge. The cave's below that. It's got brush over the opening—you'll have to hack it down."

"Fix it so she can't run," Coyne said.

Raz took the lead rope from her neck and bound her ankles, grumbling. "I'm getting tired of this."

Wanda forced a laugh. "You too?"

As the men struggled over the first boulders, their complaints made her hope for an accident. One of them might slip and get his leg caught. The other could fall and crack open his head. Lightning might strike, though the sky was clear. She tried to believe all would be well, Loughrie rescuing Lucie and Hargis, Ruth alive, only shaken from her horse's back, all of them riding to find her. Every passing minute told her to face the truth. Someday Piney would find all their bodies, and nobody would ever know what had happened.

Old Henry's Dog licked her face and lay down along her outstretched leg. She wanted Evie to have a dog like this. She had to get back.

Later she heard happy shouts. Raz and Coyne needed her no longer—they'd found the whiskey.

Time passed, and they did not return. They might now be rolling out the barrels, maybe lying about and sampling whiskey, for occasionally she heard bursts of laughter. She treasured every moment, a delay of something bad and a chance for something better.

Her ankles were tied, wrists crossed and knotted behind, but she was not completely helpless. No chance of slipping her wrists or ankles loose—Coyne had tied them tight. No sharp stone for cutting her ropes where she lay, but plenty of sharp tin down by the chimney.

The slab of rock beneath her was angled against the nearly vertical slope of the ravine. She might push to her feet, but her crossed, bound ankles made walking impossible. She stifled a scream. There was no good way, but surely there was some way to reach the chimney. By lifting and moving her ankles, then scooting her rear, she inched along the rock. It was small progress for a lot of effort.

From a hilltop she could have rolled, but to reach the chimney from the slope of the ravine she'd have to roll sideways, over and over. It felt like her only chance.

In her first turn, she fell from the slab of rock and landed face-down on the gritty slope. She flopped to her back in time to see Coyne and Raz leaping across boulders, hooting when they stumbled or fell. They jumped from the last rock and dropped to hands and knees.

If they noticed she'd moved, they didn't show it. Still laughing, they got to their feet and untied the horses. Raz swung into the saddle, took a swig from Ruth's flask and switched Old Henry with the reins. He held the flask in the air as the horse lurched forward. "Good night, sweetheart."

She clenched her teeth so she wouldn't sass or curse. Or beg.

They rode away past skeletons of pine. When Old Henry's Dog got up and followed, she cried.

CHAPTER 26

Night fell fast, with no moon. Rolling along a slope was harder than rolling downhill, but possible. Again and again Wanda dug in a boot heel or toe and flopped onto unseen, unknown ground. Thorns ripped her face and tore her lips, and sweat and blood replaced her tears, long dried. From elbows down, her arms were raw.

The Cottons were likely snoring beside the creek, but she couldn't worry about them now. Her thoughts of escape went no farther than reaching the chimney, finding a piece of tin and cutting her bindings. She tried scooting sideways, more work for less gain.

She rested, breathed, told herself to take it easy, she had all night. But at the end of a strong flop she lay dizzy and sick to her stomach. When she tried to go on, her knees smacked into a boulder too high to roll over.

At her present angle, she might push to her feet, lean against the boulder and somehow hop around it. With this in mind she thrust her shoulders forward and lifted herself into the air. Her victory lasted not even a moment, for her crossed feet didn't balance her, and she'd propelled too far. She dropped to the opposite slope, only a short distance, but her nose broke the fall. She licked and swallowed blood.

When she got her breath, she twisted again, growling like a dog in a death fight, heedless of everything but the need to go on, until finally she lay on flat ground. She looked up at a starry sky, then saw the chimney, a black column. Bats swooped through bare tree limbs.

With the chimney as a guide, she scooted one way and another to find a piece of tin. She might have all night, but now, no strength. She drew up her knees, stopped thinking, stopped seeing the sky. Slept, or fainted.

The bindings woke her when she tried to ease the stiffness in her limbs. The sky was no lighter, but she was ready to try again.

Finally her elbow scraped something sharp. A piece of tin. She fumbled it in her fingers and wiggled to get her wrists against it. The tin was a poor cutter, maybe rusting to crumbs, and the rope was thick. She grew dizzy again, rocking back and forth against the tin, and made herself rest, needing to be steady, not frantic. One image filled her mind: Evie, arms stretched.

The rope seemed less tight against her skin, or maybe her skin could no longer feel. The last strands snapped. She un-kinked an arm and brought it slowly forward, then the other with its bracelet of shredded rope. Rubbed feeling into her skin, pushed her hands against the ground and sat, felt for the tin and brought it to her ankles. Her hands shook as she sawed the rope and loosened her feet. Filthy but free, she let sensation return to her feet and legs. Fatigue held her to the ground as surely as fury had pushed her on.

She knew only one way out, the way they'd come in. Since Coyne and Raz had sampled whiskey at the cave and re-supplied Ruth's flask, they should be sleeping like dead men. She needed to go now, while she could sneak around them, or hide in a place they'd never find.

She crawled to the chimney and pulled herself upright. With a good stick, she might walk all the way home.

Her eyes had long ago adjusted to the dark, though everything was misty and gray. She kicked through debris, raising scents of ash, picking up and throwing down charred planks and stubby branches, nothing right for a walking stick.

Wind ruffled the brush, and insects trilled. Something large moved through the undergrowth. Clutching a shard of tin, she squatted against the chimney.

The silhouette of a horse passed near, head down, grazing, and a wet nose touched her cheek. She cried again. Old Henry's Dog licked her tears.

She touched Old Henry's back and ran her hands over his head. He had no saddle, but wore his bridle and dragged the reins, still tied to a thin branch. She broke off the branch and walked beside Old Henry until she fell over the stone step.

"Let's go home." She stood on the step and pulled herself onto his back.

Dark shapes of the Cotton brothers were sprawled in the place she expected, the sandy side of the road where she and Lucie had camped. Their horses stood nearby, tied to a bush. Eager to escape and afraid to step over the sleeping men, she left without cutting the horses loose.

The men didn't stir when Old Henry's hooves clicked on creek rocks. With luck, they'd waste time searching for him when they woke.

Once again, the dog led the way from the creek to stretches where the road was passable. She wrapped her hands in the reins and laid her head against Old Henry's mane, wanting to lie down and wishing she had a saddle and stirrups to keep her on his back.

Seconds at a time she dozed, waking abruptly with a sensation of falling or running from pursuit. Once, when Old Henry climbed up a steep bank to the road, she did fall off and woke with his hind legs lifting over her. Later, she thought she was arguing with Lucie, each accusing the other of hurting her daughter.

The sky lightened, and sunrise filtered into the valley with rays that glinted off the water and hurt her eyes. She closed them and tried to stay awake.

The dog's barks alerted her to horses coming toward her in the creek, first, her own, ridden by Simpson Wainwright, then Loughrie on his black high-stepper. Behind him, Lucie, her legs dangling on Hargis's pony. Behind Lucie, a stranger.

She swiped her tears and touched her torn lip, swollen and tender. The way it felt, her nose must be spread over her face. Everything she saw of herself was caked with dirt and blood.

"You've had a bad time," Simpson said.

Lucie rode forward, fire in her eyes. "I hope you killed them both."

"Couldn't. Ruth? Is she all right?"

"Bullet split her hand, if you can imagine. Lucky for us them Cottons is poor shots. And dumb. Doc's tending her." Lucie's voice quivered. "I'm glad we found you."

Wanda opened her mouth, but no sound came out. Simpson handed her a canteen, and she drank it dry. "Hargis," she said.

"He's got a big headache."

All alive. She needed to lie down.

Simpson capped the canteen and nodded toward the stranger, who'd stopped a few paces away. "This here's the sheriff. We're hoping to catch Raz and Coyne with the whiskey. It would suit me to have Raz put away for a long while."

The sheriff wore a straw hat and had a round, smiling face that didn't fit her idea of a tough lawman. But she was a poor judge of people. She supposed Will had told him about the cave.

"While ago, the Cottons were sleeping off a drunk," she said. "Right aside this creek. Could be there, still."

"Find them or not, we can empty the liquor," the sheriff said.

Loughrie shook his head. "Better if we catch them in the act of transporting. That may take a few days, for Lucie says they'll need mules to take the whiskey out."

Everything mattered less and less. She rested her head on Old

227

Henry's neck while the men spoke of places the Cottons might go for mules and kegs.

"Will has kegs," she mumbled.

"That he does," Simpson said. "And he's having a stock sale in Winkler on Saturday. Might be mules there."

"Let's wait for the Cottons in Winkler," Loughrie said.

The sheriff nodded. "If you fellers will help, I'll hang around."

"Someone give the girl a saddle," Lucie said.

Simpson dismounted, stood beside Old Henry, and caught Wanda when she slid down.

"I love this horse," she said, "but I'll be glad to ride my own. And I wouldn't mind stopping to rest and eat anything you might of brought along."

They had jerky. Old Henry's Dog stared at Wanda until she gave him half of hers.

On the return to Winkler, the men rode ahead, and Lucie and Wanda rode side by side. "The sheriff is going to dump out some of the finest whiskey made in this country," Lucie said. "I got nothing now."

"Your family's alive."

"I got no legacy."

"Better that way," Wanda said.

CHAPTER 27

When she opened her eyes, Will stood beside her in overlapping circles of light. She lay on his high leather bench with a wet cloth over her cheek and the side of her mouth.

"You're my favorite doctor," she said. He had a tender touch.

He lifted the cloth. Piney and Virgie had washed her in a tub of warm water and helped her into a clean dress. They'd walked her to this bench while daylight was still in the windows. She must have slept half the day. The dress was light brown with small red flowers, tight across the bosom. It might belong to Virgie, who was thin in every way. Womanly, Will called her. Because she curled her hair and dressed fancy?

He laid on a fresh, cool compress. "I need to get the swelling down so I can sew this. Tell me about your other doctors."

"There's only the one. He helped when my babies were born." She could not breathe through her nose, and her face hurt when she talked.

His fingers stroked hair from her forehead. "You had more than one baby?"

"Two more, stillborn."

"I don't remember May Rose writing about that. Was he a good doctor?"

"The midwife was better. The doctor didn't come in time for Evie."

He touched the swollen flesh of her nose. "I'd say this is broken. And you're going to have a scar at the side of your mouth and up here at your hairline."

"Don't matter. Will you ride with me to the train?"

"Take a sip." He held a dark vial to her lips. "I've got to stick here a couple more days, then I'll take you all the way to Fargo. We're hoping Coyne and Raz will come for kegs and mules, maybe today. The sheriff wants all of you to keep out of sight so they won't know we're on to them."

The medicine warmed all the way to her stomach. "Where's Ruth?"

"She's sleeping in the back room. Lucie's with her."

"I'm trying to remember how she's hurt."

"Hand and arm. The hand's the worst, fingers shattered. I did what I could, but she needs a real doctor."

"Is this today?"

A smile relaxed his eyes. "They found you today. Brought Ruth in yesterday."

"You can't fix her?"

"I can't save her fingers. Loughrie wanted to take her on to Elkins, yesterday. She wouldn't go."

Instead of taking Ruth to Elkins, Loughrie had led the search up the creek. "She sent him to find me."

"I don't know."

"Raz and Coyne thought Granny had gold. I worried they'd beat you…"

"You worried I'd told them." He lifted the cloth from her cheek and dipped it in water. "I thought about what I'd say if they accused you, but they didn't ask. I hope I wouldn't give you up about anything."

For her, he'd practiced a lie. He was nice now, but maybe

when she got well he'd be cold again. She touched his arm. "Is the sheriff here?"

"He's camped with Hargis at my coal mine. Cold food, no fire, no coming down here till Raz and Coyne leave with what they came for."

"Better not let them have kegs on credit or pay with paper money."

"I'd sacrifice a few kegs to put them in jail. Sheriff says they did odd jobs for an old man he found dead, tied and starved. There's no proof they did it, but he thinks my trunk was stolen from the old man."

"One of their horses was lame, and I got away on Old Henry. If they went back to where they tied me and found me gone ..."

"I know. They might not come here. The sheriff says he'll wait two days."

"They gave bad money for a wagon, down in Jennie Town."

"That's where they found you?"

She felt lighter, like floating on water. "Tell...sometime. Sheriff know...Duck?"

Will's face twitched. "He says he don't care who killed Duck, 'less it was one of his brothers."

Words melted on her tongue. What she'd done might never come out, but it hurt like a boil that needed to pop.

Ruth appeared in the circle of light. "How's our girl?" A sling held her right arm close to her body, and her fingers were thick with splints and bandages.

Will glanced at Ruth's fingers and back to Wanda. "Not quarrelsome, but she'll come back."

Wanda tugged on Ruth's skirt. "Sorry."

"Not your fault," Ruth said.

Will studied the unbound tips of Ruth's fingers. "I need to have a word with Simpson, and I'm going to put my horse in the shed. Come and lock the door after me."

Ruth slid the bolt in the lock and came to Wanda's side. When

Wanda clasped her good hand, Ruth clung like she was releasing pain.

"Hurts bad?"

"Like three rotten teeth." Ruth dragged a chair close to the bench. "The laudanum's wore off."

Wanda rolled to her side, facing Ruth. "I brought…trouble."

"I brought it on myself. Ma too. We've used up our luck." Ruth's cheeks sagged. "Price and me has got to get off the drink, though a jug of something strong would sure help now."

Wanda's lips and tongue felt thick. "Never good. Alone. Homer…kept me…straight."

"There's too much of Ma in both of us. Here I am, attached to Price, and the poor man wants to be a preacher. That's enough to keep me drinking. I don't know if I can stop, and if I can't, I fear he won't."

"Lean here."

Ruth rose and bent her ear close to Wanda's lips.

"I killed Duck."

Ruth laid her face on Wanda's shoulder. One of them was shaking, Wanda couldn't tell which. Maybe both.

Someone rapped on the door. Will called, "It's me. Open, quick." Ruth fumbled the bolt open, and he pushed inside and slid it closed. "Simpson says somebody's fording the river. Ruth, you and Wanda get in back."

"I can walk," Wanda said, but when he lifted her from the bench the room swirled. "Ruth needs—laudanum."

Will pulled the vial from his pocket and laid it in Ruth's hand. "This is all I got. Hurry." He nodded toward the door on the back wall, and Ruth hustled ahead and opened it. "Second door to the left," he said.

He laid Wanda on his bed, struck a match against the sole of his boot and lit the lamp. "Sound carries through here in strange ways, so don't talk. I'll tell Lucie to stay in her room."

The front bell rang and he closed the door and hurried down the hall. Wanda and Ruth leaned against each other on Will's bed.

Ruth held out the vial. Wanda shook her head, and Ruth tipped back and drank, then squeezed the vial in her fist.

It might be someone else fording the river, someone else at the door. Raz and Coyne might not know she'd escaped. They might pass through on their way to distant places and never stop in Winkler again.

Will's voice, the words not clear. Someone louder, maybe them. Tromp of boots, scrape of chairs. "Coffee?"

"Got some on the stove." Lighter steps, Will's.

"Anything to eat?"

"Canned stuff for sale. Deer jerky."

"Kegs?"

Cottons.

"A few. How many you need?"

"Let's see 'em."

The hall door creaked, then steps in the storeroom, a thin wall away from Will's bed. Wanda listened in a peaceful haze.

"These'll do," Coyne said.

"Carry what you want to the front."

Steps back and forth from storeroom to the front, more words, unclear. The bell jingled, someone coming or going. After a short time of silence, Will returned and spoke from the doorway. "They took their kegs. I said they could camp in the old school."

"You're mighty nice," Wanda said.

"We want them to stay awhile. I'll know where they are, at least for tonight. Loughrie will keep an eye on them at the stock sale. If there's no mules to buy, they'll move on. They said something about trading a horse."

"Don't let them see Old Henry."

"Your horses are at the coal mine with Hargis. Lucie's wagon is up there too."

"Old Henry's Dog. They'll know him."

"He'll stay with the horse," Ruth said.

Will came into the room and stopped at his locked cabinet. "They wanted credit to buy guns." He pulled on the lock, testing it. "I told them no guns on credit. I couldn't say I had none to sell. Folks know they're back here somewhere."

Ruth gripped her wrist. "They might try…"

"Yes," he said. "They might try to buy guns from someone tomorrow. Or steal. I took their worthless banknotes for the kegs, but a lot of folks won't. Not sure if anyone will trade mules for paper money, even greenbacks."

"They've got Lucie's gold pieces," Wanda said. "The ones from the jacket."

Their eyes met. He nodded. "I guess we both have a few regrets." He inspected the tips of Ruth's swollen fingers. "You better let Loughrie take you to Elkins tonight."

"I'm doing good," Ruth said.

"There was all kinds of dirt mixed with your bones and flesh, probably from where you fell off your horse. I couldn't clean it out good enough."

"Nobody could of done better," Ruth said. "If they're gonna rot, cut 'em off."

Will put his hand on Ruth's shoulder. "Say the word and I'll take you. Wanda can go along."

"It'd be a hard ride, night and day, and in the end, somebody will cut my fingers off. Don't you think?"

His smile was grim. "I'm sorry."

"Then save us the trip."

He squeezed Ruth's shoulder. "I need to sneak up to the mine and tell the sheriff that Raz and Coyne have come. I'll get Lucie to bolt the door and sit out front till I come back."

After he left, Lucie hobbled back and forth, bringing water and plates of cold beans. She mashed Wanda's beans so she didn't have to chew, and fed Ruth, who was awkward using her left hand and didn't care whether she ate or not.

Will returned with Loughrie and unwrapped Ruth's bandages.

"Let me keep them a little longer," Ruth said.

"Fingers tonight or hand tomorrow," Loughrie said.

Will opened his fist and showed a vial of dark liquid. "Look what Virgie had. Wanda, you go with Lucie to the back room."

"I can help," Lucie said.

Loughrie sat on the bed and put his arms around Ruth. "We'll do this."

Lucie touched Ruth's shoulder. "I'd take your place if I could."

Ruth nodded.

"We'll do it out front," Will said. "My bench."

He followed Wanda and Lucie to the back room, bringing water, clean strips of cloth, and orders for Lucie. "Wash your hands good and put wet pads on Wanda's lip. I'll sew it later." He hurried away.

Wanda lay flat and Lucie sat beside her with the basin in her lap. Again, there were distant footsteps and unclear words. Her eyelids were thick and heavy as her tongue. She wrenched upward at a scream. *Ruth.* Dogs barked. The basin rattled on the floor and Lucie fell on her in a faint. Wanda let her lie where she was.

Gray dawn spread enough light to show herself alone in the room, and Will standing in the open door. "Lucie's in my room with Ruth. How's your lip?"

He'd wakened her in the night to stitch it. She spoke from the side of her mouth. "Smaller. How's Ruth?"

He sat on the edge of her bed. "I took four fingers. She says it hurts no worse than yesterday."

"Smell coffee."

"I'll bring it. I need to shut you up in here today while I get out to the stock sale. The store has to be open, and my help will be cooking sausages out front. So I've put a bolt on the hall door. Don't open it for anyone but me."

"Today they get Raz and Coyne."

"Might take a day or two more." He left the room and came

back with Lucie, Ruth walking between them. Traces of blood had dried on her bandages.

"Doc did good," Ruth said.

"Bravest woman I ever saw," Will said.

Wanda kissed Ruth's good hand. Ruth blinked tears. They led her to Wanda's bed.

They couldn't go out, but they didn't have to be quiet. Outside, men shouted, animals bawled and bleated, wagons rattled. Inside, Lucie wondered aloud about Piney, why she hadn't come to see them, and how she was getting along with those kids. Finally she said, "I don't know what's got into her."

Wanda and Ruth smiled.

Midday, Will knocked on the hall door and brought in a plate with three fat sausages. "Whole families have come. This is the last of what we cooked. It's a good crowd." He looked worn out.

"Are there mules?"

"Six, brought in by one man. Simpson says if the Cottons don't buy them, the sheriff's willing to follow where they go next until he catches them with the whiskey."

The sausage was greasy and heartening. Wanda mashed hers and soaked each rich bite in her mouth before swallowing. Chewing pulled at her stitches.

"I can't say I like how this has worked out," Lucie said when Will left, "but I don't want no one else getting rich on my legacy, especially not them that are lazy and undeserving. We'll start over with a bigger still and a better source of water."

"I'm through with all that," Ruth said.

Lucie bit off a fingernail and spit it on the floor. "I guess you want to follow that marshal. I won't stand in your way, for there's plenty others I can bring in. Virgie, for one. She may be more useful than she looks. Now, Doc's an enterprising sort, and Piney's miller ain't bad for work, neither. But I did promise Hargis he'd have something good when I'm gone. I like to keep my promises."

Ruth turned so she faced the wall. "Give Hargis the old place."

"Did you say 'Hargis'? What would he do with it?"

"Sell it to a coal company. You said yourself they're stealing if they pay no more than taxes due. Let Hargis give you the money to redeem it."

Lucie shifted her eyes like the motion helped her think. "Does none of you girls care about our family's land?"

Burned pines against the midnight sky. A solitary chimney, tilted gravestones, a damp ravine. Her ma, risking everything to live somewhere else. "Let it go," Wanda said.

CHAPTER 28

She should have been grateful she wasn't tied, merely confined to the hot, windowless room, but she didn't know what to do with leisure. Ruth was restless in a different way, lying in bed, working her legs, her eyes squeezed shut. Calls of animals, sellers and buyers pierced the walls of their room.

Wanda put her fingers in her tangled hair and scratched her head, sending bits of leaves and grit to the floor. "I gotta get home."

Lucie paced the floor, watching Ruth. "We'll all get there."

"I mean my home."

"But you'll come back."

"Can't," Wanda said. "No money."

"We'll make some. We've lots of corn."

"I don't want that kind of money."

"Not liquor. I'll sell the corn."

Ruth's eyes popped open. "Sell the corn? Has the day of judgment come?"

"Ah, good to hear you talking," Lucie said.

Wanda poured water from a pitcher and crouched beside Ruth. "Will said you should drink as much as you'll hold."

"I'll just have to pee."

"Drink," Lucie said. "You haven't peed since yesterday, that we know of."

Ruth flopped her head side to side. "It's awful hot in here."

Wanda helped her rise enough to drink. "There's not a breath of air, and you're fevered." When Ruth lay back down, Lucie sat beside her and wiped her face with a wet cloth. Ruth's mouth relaxed in sleep.

Lucie got up and moved to the other bed. "She'll be all right, she always did heal good. Takes after her pa that way."

Ruth's pa. Wanda sat beside Lucie. "Was it an accident, how she shot him?"

Lucie gave one of her sideways looks. "How who shot who?"

"How Ruth shot Pap. Was it accidental?"

"Accidental, must of been. We was all drunk, and my memory ain't clear about all that passed, though I know for a fact Ruth wasn't the one shot him."

"She told me different. So you did it, or he shot himself?"

"No to both." Lucie wiped her own face with the cloth. "It was Evalena."

At first she thought Lucie was mixed up, answering a question she hadn't asked, telling some other thing her ma had done. Then the day rushed back, and she heard the screaming, and a sound that wasn't special at the time. A gunshot. Piney was showing her the kittens. When they heard the shot, Piney said, "Don't worry, it's just Pa shooting crows." Next, Evalena had come running and hurried her away to Winkler.

Wanda ran to the washroom, knelt in front of the toilet and threw up. Shaky, she stood and flushed, rinsed her mouth under the spigot and splashed water on her face. She wouldn't have believed Lucie's story had Ruth not tried to take the blame. Lucie might not recall every detail, but Ruth did, and she didn't want Wanda to know.

That day when they'd run off with no goodbyes, had she been

any comfort to her ma, or had she complained all the way? She recalled only anger at leaving the kittens.

Her family had been too careless about whiskey and guns, and look where it got them—shot, diseased, tied up, injured, and hiding in a hot room. She couldn't bring Evie here unless a lot changed. She also couldn't stay closed inside with nothing to do but think about her ma picking up a gun.

A dirty film floated on the water, grit from her hair. Virgie had promised to wash it after Will treated her cuts and bruises. Instead, the Cottons had come. She looked in the mirror and lifted a knotted mass, ignoring the reflection of her battered face, bothered by the sheriff's plan. Her hair would take hours to brush out, but she spied another way to fix it. Will's razor lay on a shelf under the mirror.

She let the water drain, then sawed a hunk with the razor and cut again until the washbasin was full of hair and her neck felt bare and cool.

Lucie pushed open the door. "You doing all right?"

She handed Lucie the razor, liking the shock on her face. "Trim it so it don't hang below a hat."

"Like a man's hair?"

"It'll grow back."

"Huh. I've always said so myself."

Lucie made her sit on the toilet, then yanked and chopped like she was cutting lilies from the pond. "This might not look good. It's been a while since I've cut hair."

"Doesn't matter." Wanda eyed the clothes hanging on the opposite wall. Will's mining outfit.

"I guess I'm done," Lucie said.

Wanda stepped out of Virgie's dress and into Will's overalls. She put her foot on the toilet and rolled up the cuffs.

Lucie gaped. "What are you thinking to do in that getup?"

"I'm gonna talk with the sheriff. His idea to capture the Cottons is too loose. He should jail them now and let us testify in court."

"I don't guess a court would take my testimony," Lucie said. "But if Ruth didn't need me, I'd go out and turn a gun on those Cottons myself."

"Yes, and shoot a few poor bystanders while you're at it. If you want to see my daughter, you'll have to give up your guns."

"Maybe I will. Maybe you'll stop carrying a knife."

"That too."

Wanda took Will's mining cap from its hook and set it on her wisps of curls. "Think anyone will know me?"

Lucie leaned back for a look. "Maybe the ones that's already seen your scratches and swelled-up nose. But if you're thinking to go as a man, you better do something about them tits."

Lucie found a dusty bolt of muslin in the storeroom, and they tore strips and wound them around her chest. She found a shirt in Will's room.

Lucie grinned as she unbolted the door to the store. "I'd sure like to watch this."

Outside, the sun beat down and the air smelled strong of manure. From the store steps, she saw men gathering at corrals of cattle and sheep. A few tables were set up, one with saddles and harnesses, one with the old woman's bottled fruit liquor, another surrounded by children playing with wooden toys. The sheriff was supposed to be at the mine, but before she went there she wanted to make sure Raz and Coyne were here.

She passed a tin-and-board pen of pigs, careful not to be particular, woman-like, of where she stepped. So far she'd passed no one who might give her away, such as Virgie or Piney. Likewise Will, Simpson, or Loughrie, who'd surely march her back to the store.

She spied the Cottons near the river where horses and mules were hitched to a long bar. Six mules, dark gray, side by side. The brothers stood a few paces behind the animals' rumps with other men in farmer hats. Loughrie was there too, seeming to listen to a man who pointed to one mule after another.

She stopped at a corral, leaned on the top rail and studied the bony cows. If the Cottons recognized her, she'd ruin the sheriff's plan as well as her own. Yet she couldn't stay away, like she'd not been able to stop watching the fire crackling through her ma's house, all those years ago. The first time she'd felt stronger than Evalena, who'd covered her eyes.

The Cottons left the horse traders and came to the corral, eyes to the ground, speaking together. Wanda stepped behind new onlookers at the rail and looked directly into Virgie's face. Virgie's mouth popped open. When Wanda frowned, Virgie nodded and hurried away. Again she gave her attention to the corral. A man ducked through the rails and stood among the jostling cattle, holding up his arm and shouting for attention.

Loughrie stepped beside Coyne, who tilted his head and appeared to listen. Why was he talking with them? She couldn't see their faces. In the other direction, Will stood at the sheep pen, holding a board while a man signed a paper on it. She expected Virgie to stop Will and point her out, but Virgie strolled on.

The auctioneer was chatting up onlookers and getting his spotters in place. Loughrie and the Cottons were no longer by the rail. Where now? Stepping back toward the sheep pen, she heard Loughrie's deep tones. He and the brothers faced each other with their heads pitched forward, the way people talked in noisy places. She rested her foot on an old foundation stone and pretended an interest in sheep while separating their words from talk of others.

"I know they're past their prime, but they'll do us." Coyne.

"Mine mules. I don't like 'em." Loughrie's voice.

This wasn't right. If Loughrie had to talk with the Cottons, he should encourage them to buy these mules.

"I offered to buy them outright, but he's signed them into the auction," Coyne said.

"We might do better at Staunton." Loughrie.

A group of running boys blocked their next words. She picked up again with Loughrie.

"... bids on the best mule, then he'll offer the others to the winner at the same price. Don't buy the lot unless the first one goes real cheap. Better to wait and bid on each mule as it comes up."

"Maybe," Raz said. "Maybe not."

"Have it your way. I'll see what that harness man can rig in the way of packing gear."

She flushed with disgust. Price Loughrie wasn't the man Ruth thought he was. He brushed past Wanda, and she lifted her eyes and watched his shoulders and fine hat mix with others. Bootlegger, deceiver.

"Hey, Buddy."

A man blocked her way: Raz, talking to her. She lifted her face.

"God-a-mighty," Raz said. "Were you kicked by a mule?"

She growled out the side of her mouth. "Woman done it."

Laughing, he nodded at her cap. "You been a miner?"

"Till I was bashed in a cave-in. That was the woman, the Martha Sue Mine."

He slapped her shoulder. "Lucky you made it out. Take a look at these here mules, tell us what you think."

Walking between Raz and Coyne was like standing too close to fire. They stood back while she copied what she'd seen her uncle do, placing one of her battered hands on a mule's rump, lifting its feet, sticking her thumb at the side of its mouth so it would show its teeth.

"Old, but sound and gentle." She itched to tell the sheriff about Loughrie.

"Thin and poor," Coyne said, loud enough for others to hear. "Won't haul a sack of flour."

"You don't want a barrel-belly mule." Something else she'd learned from her uncle. "Fat is a burden to their legs."

The mule trader looked hopeful, but the brothers strolled to the row of horses. Face on fire, she moved away through spaces in the crowd toward the store, where she could hide and think out what was true.

She passed the harness maker's table in time to see Loughrie lay down a wad of bills and walk away. Payment for something, possibly pack saddles, yet the mules had not yet been bought. Or had Loughrie made a secret deal? The crowd drifted toward sounds of the auctioneer offering the first cow. She sat on the top step and considered everything Loughrie had done and said. He'd grown up near the Bosells, probably heard rumors about the whiskey cave. A valuable stash of whiskey would be hard for a drinker and bootlegger to resist, even one who wanted to reform. She might forgive him for wanting the whiskey, but not if he'd fooled Ruth to get it. If he could prove himself innocent, she'd never have to confess her suspicions to Ruth. She'd give him that chance.

When the boy minding the store came out and watched the auction from the steps. Wanda slipped inside and knocked for Lucie to unbar the hall door.

In their room, she made Ruth and Lucie laugh, telling how she'd advised Raz and Coyne about mules.

She replaced the cap and overalls in the washroom and put on Virgie's dress. Lucie found a scarf she could wind over her hair.

It was dark when Will finally locked the store and invited them to sit out front for a supper of eggs and salted side pork.

"I'd like to talk with the sheriff," she said.

"We're supposed to meet later at Virgie's. I'll take your message."

"I said I'd like to talk with him. And the others. So if you're all getting together, I'll go too."

"You could ruin everything if Raz or Coyne sees you."

"I'm pretty well hid by my face."

That night Will led her through the damp basement and up a ramp to the freight door at the side of the building. The door had once opened onto a loading platform. Now it opened into air, with the ground darkly visible below.

"Wait and I'll help you down," he said.

She didn't wait, but jumped, twisting her ankle and scraping her hands in the dirt.

He clattered down a set of stone steps. "You should listen now and then, maybe think about taking help when it's offered."

"I'm okay." Her ankle felt broken. "You didn't say there were steps."

"I said I'd help."

"I'm sorry," she said.

"You're sorry? You're the one hurt."

"I'm not hurt."

He took her hand. "This way."

"Maybe I better lean on your arm."

She winced with every step.

Virgie welcomed them to a parlor made pretty with painted lamps, a loveseat, and two padded chairs with fancy legs. Only she and Virgie sat. Simpson and the sheriff stood on either side of the loveseat. Will and Loughrie stood near the door.

"They bought six mules," Loughrie said, "but still need pack saddles."

No mention of his payment to the harness maker, who might already be making what they needed. Wanda touched her neck where the rope had scratched. She followed the men's talk, but kept coming back to Loughrie.

The sheriff put a plug of tobacco in his jaw. "So we're talking days or weeks while they try to find pack saddles."

Her ankle throbbed. If Loughrie had his own plan, she'd best spoil it now. "Arrest them tonight," she said. "What they've done is plenty to put them in jail. I'll lead you to the cave tomorrow and you can bust up every barrel."

Loughrie frowned. "Catching them with the whiskey will add to their jail time."

His slow and reasonable tone made every one of her cuts and scratches sting. "Price, tell me this. I saw you today, helping them buy mules. So I wonder, are you with us or them?"

She didn't understand how he could stand there looking so pure.

The sheriff butted in. "You weren't supposed to be out."

"You about have to tie her to keep her down," Will said.

"I been tied too much these past days." She kept her gaze on Loughrie. "Them or us?"

"I'm doing what I can to help the sheriff. The Cotton brothers think I'll take them to a good buyer."

"And I think you're helping yourself, using the Cottons to fool us."

Loughrie tightened his lips like she was crazy. Will frowned.

The sheriff shifted his feet. "The marshal has helped us before."

"He's a drunk," Wanda said.

Virgie patted her hand. "Honey, we should let the men do it their way."

"I'll let the sheriff know where we go," Loughrie said. "Send a messenger, something like that."

The room quieted, waiting.

"Price."

"Yes, Wanda."

"Don't go. Ruth needs you. I have to go home, and Piney's got her hands full. Ruth's got no one but Lucie."

His eyes flickered. It was the only test she could think of, bound to embarrass him in the presence of men. But if he truly cared for Ruth, he wouldn't go. She hoped.

The sheriff ducked his head and pushed the tobacco plug to the other side of his mouth. "Ma'am, you women need to stay out of this."

She stared long enough for each to get a good look at her battered face. "I guess not. I spent two days and a couple of real bad nights with Cottons. I've the most reasons to want them locked away. Plus the whiskey is my family's loss. But for me, you wouldn't have a chance at it."

Loughrie cleared his throat. "I'll stay."

The other men shifted their feet. Finally, the sheriff spoke. "So is this the end of your marshaling days?"

"That's been over for a while. If we're done here, I'll tell Coyne the government has already raided the Bosell cave."

Again, Wanda doubted. "Someone should follow and hear what he says."

"I'll go," Will said.

Not Will, not with Loughrie knowing. Following the Cottons was the sheriff's job. She was about to say so when the walls shook with a gun blast. She had a lifetime of paying no heed to gunshots. Never again.

More gunshots. The sheriff grimaced and set his hat on his head. "They drink, shoot off their mouths and then their guns. Doc, we better check them traders' camps, just in case they ain't shooting at the sky."

Virgie touched the sheriff's arm and lifted her face. "Be careful. And come again for a visit."

Wanda tested her ankle. Maybe she could hop to the store.

Will and Loughrie stood aside and let the sheriff leave first. "Marshal, forget telling the Cottons anything for now," Will said. "Make sure Wanda gets back to the store."

She didn't look at Loughrie. Outside, she tried to hop on her own.

"Wanda, let me help."

She leaned on the arm he offered. It was hard to accuse a friend, and harder to get back to friendly feeling. "I won't say I'm sorry," she said.

"It's all right. We both care about Ruth."

Spots of light bobbed on the valley floor among the traders' camp fires. Dogs barked and voices rose.

Loughrie had a strong, steady arm, and going downhill, she had to let him bear most of her weight. It was easier to talk in the dark. "Was I right?"

They stopped so she could rest. "Partly. I want to put Raz and Coyne in jail, for what they did to you and Ruth. But I don't trust myself where liquor's involved. It's led me to trouble before."

"You got the Cottons up to this, kidnapping me to get Lucie's stash."

"I'd never do that. I never talked with them till yesterday. They invited me in, wanted me to help them sell the whiskey. I thought I'd get a share—for Ruth."

"Or a stash of your own."

"Wanda, this is hard for me."

"Hard for you? Lucie's lost a ton of money. Ruth's lost fingers. You see my face."

"I'm sorry. It's not easy to change."

She knew that well enough.

When they reached the street, they were stopped by the sight of a man sprawled on the store steps.

"Wait here," Loughrie said. He ran toward the store.

She hopped after him, afraid, because the door hung open.

Loughrie stooped beside the body. "It's Raz."

Raz lay on his back, head down, still as stone.

Wanda shouted as Lucie appeared in the doorway with her shotgun. "Granny, it's us, don't shoot!"

"Did I get him?"

Loughrie ran past her into the store.

Wanda hopped up the steps and wrenched the gun away, toppling Lucie into her arms. Loughrie came out in time to keep them from falling. He helped them inside to the table where Ruth sat cradling her bandaged hand. Their boots crunched on broken glass.

Lucie dropped into a chair. Wanda stood behind and braced herself with a hand on its curved back.

"They got in," Ruth said. "We heard the door glass break, then a racket in Doc's room, I think they was after guns."

Lucie pounded the table. "I scared the bejesus outa them cowards!"

"Ma shot up the place," Ruth said. "Things was popping all about."

Loughrie crouched and put his arm around her.

Will hurried in. "All right here?"

"I think we are," Wanda said.

One lamp glowed on their table and another burned at the cook stove. Will took a lantern from the wall and lit the wick. "Where's Coyne? Hurt or dead?"

"They both ran out when Ma started shooting," Ruth said.

Will carried the lantern outside. Wanda hopped to the doorway and watched men gather around Raz's body.

"No blood far as I can tell," the sheriff said. "Looks like he knocked the sense outa hisself."

Will set his lantern on a step and bent to Raz's chest, then felt his wrist. "He's gone."

The sheriff nudged the body with his boot. "Less trouble for us. Let's find the other one."

When Wanda came back inside, Ruth and Loughrie sat with their foreheads together and their arms on each other's shoulders.

He looked up. "I told her."

CHAPTER 29

Will said Wanda's ankle was sprained, said she should rest it a few days. Lucie said she'd take the sheriff to the whiskey cave herself.

"Wrap it tight," Wanda said. "And find me a cane and a bigger boot." This trip was for her ma.

She came out of the store at first light, just as the stock buyers and sellers were breaking camp, and found Hargis waiting with the sheriff.

Hargis lifted his hat. "If you don't mind, I'll just go along and help."

More likely to see the property before he gave Lucie cash to redeem it. He rode a new horse and carried a shiny hatchet. Out of habit, she'd buckled on her knife belt and let the empty sheath hang in her skirt pocket.

Because her hands weren't tied and she didn't have to manage Lucie, this trip seemed easy. She didn't even mind Hargis's chatter, largely a review of his service to her family that got grander and grander. "If Coyne has any sense, he's long gone," he said. "You can forget about him."

She'd never forget.

When they reached the Bosell place, she pointed the way to the cave and waited on the stone steps with her foot propped up. From here she could see gravestones peeking above the weeds. She didn't want to know if Lucie and her aunts had buried Pap in their graveyard or left him in the sinkhole. She didn't want to know how they felt about the way he'd died. She could manage only so many bad thoughts.

She prodded a stick through the weeds near the chimney, looking for the tin scrap that had cut her free. Scraps of tin lay everywhere, from the roof, she supposed, blown apart by the fire. One lay close to pieces of shredded rope. She put the tin scrap in her saddlebags and stuffed her knife sheath with strands from the rope. Not souvenirs, reminders.

Sounds of chopping echoed down the ravine, followed by a whiff of liquor in the wind. Then the fumes smothered the air, and she imagined Bosell whiskey splashing over the rocks, lifting its odors into the charred pines. For a moment she felt good, because her ma had often smelled like that. The next moment she felt bad, for the same reason.

They got back to Winkler a few hours after dark. The town still reeked like a barnyard, but the traders were gone and all was quiet. Hargis led her horse away, and she hobbled into the store.

Piney sat alone at the table. "They're all in bed. I waited up for you." She loosened Wanda's boot and propped her leg on a chair.

"I need to be more like you," Wanda said. "Sweet and helpful."

"Oh, my." Piney's face was weary. "I don't know what I should do."

"You don't know what you should do about...?"

"Simpson. He went to tell his daughter about Raz and bring her home, but she wouldn't come without Raz's ma. I guess they intend to live here now." Piney folded and unfolded the edge of the table's oilcloth cover. "Simpson wants me to stay. I don't mind the work, and I love the children. But the house..."

"Is small for all those people. And you'll be waiting on them hand and foot."

251

"The poor man needs somebody," Piney said. "He wants us to get married. But Blanche is like a child herself, and Mrs. Cotton…"

"I know."

"He's a good man. I can't leave him with such a burden."

"Aunt Piney, think of yourself. What do you want?"

Piney smoothed the folds she'd made in the oilcloth. "I'd like to be with him, just us and the children."

"Then marry him and make the best. Tell him you need a house of your own. You can stay with Virgie or go home with Ruth until he works things out."

"I think that's what I have to do. Of course Ma won't like it." Piney's eyes twinkled in the lamplight. "But she don't have the say."

Wanda sat with Ruth at Will's table. Loughrie was outside hitching the mules, preparing to take Ruth and Lucie home to their garden, geese, and dogs. Ruth and Loughrie had been extra polite to each other, like they were making up from a quarrel.

"Piney won't have time for us no more," Ruth said.

Simpson had started work on a three-room house for him and Piney beside the one with his grandkids, their ma and Granny Cotton.

"Even when something starts good, there's always trouble," Ruth said. "So maybe she'll have her trouble now, and later times will be better."

"She'll miss you, and Granny too. Come to see her, often as you can."

Ruth's smile was grim. "What I see will likely make me mad, her taking care of all of them."

"Come anyway."

"Sure. Maybe one day she'll hop in the wagon and go home with us."

"Or maybe your ma will butt heads with Mrs. Cotton and knock some sense into Blanche."

"I'll be sure to keep Ma away—Piney don't need more trouble. And if Ma don't sell that corn, I'll do it myself. Will can send the money to you. We all want you to come back. Him too."

Wanda didn't know what Will wanted, but she was pretty sure he didn't know either. She dug in her pocket and pulled out eight gold coins. "He gave me these outa Raz's pocket, so I have enough for the train. Get yourself well and stay off the liquor. I'd like my girl to grow up knowing both her aunts."

Ruth sniffed. "A good reason for me to walk the straight and narrow."

"Your man is another. You can help him stand or drag him down."

"He's gonna need a strong reason to quit."

"You can be that reason," Wanda said.

"I guess I'll find out. He admires Simpson and Doc. He's going to help Simpson build his mill and Piney's house."

Loughrie opened the door. "The wagon's ready to go."

Ruth waved him away. "Ma's in the washroom. We'll be out in a minute." She smiled. "Ma hates to part with the inside plumbing. Instead of digging out that spring for a bigger still, she talks of running a water line to flush a toilet."

"Well and good," Wanda said. They laughed until their eyes were wet.

When Lucie was ready, Loughrie helped her down the steps and into the wagon beside Ruth.

Lucie clutched Wanda's hand. "I'm glad you come. You and me could of done big things if I'd had a chance to bring you up."

"And I might of shot someone too."

Lucie's head wagged. "Your ma wasn't perfect."

"Too bad she didn't have a different kind of ma and pa."

Lucie lifted her chin. "That's unkind. She had you. I knew she couldn't raise you. When you was born I offered to pay her smartly to give you over to me. Ha, I see you didn't know that. Was it best she didn't take the money?"

Wanda had no answer. Without money, her ma had found a way to drink. With it, she might have drunk more. One thing was sure. "It was a mean bargain."

Lucie frowned. "Deed it was. I do regret some things. But you helped spill my whiskey on the ground. Ain't we even?"

"Not nearly."

"Well and good," Lucie said. "Come back. You can make me pay."

Ruth blew a kiss, and Loughrie tipped his hat and flicked the reins.

She watched their wagon out of sight.

This time she knew she'd get home. Will was going with her as far as Elkins.

They met Hargis and Virgie as they left the store. Hargis was shouldering a wooden crate and Virgie carried a wide-brimmed black hat.

"I'll bring our horses around," Will said.

Virgie held the hat for Wanda to see. "While Hargis and me minds the store, I'm putting some ladies' goods up for sale. But this hat is yours to keep." She turned the hat to show its plume of white feathers. "It's fancy for travel, but the only one I own with a dark veil." She tugged down the veil and wiggled a finger at her own face. "You know, to cover…"

"My busted-up face," Wanda said.

Virgie set the hat on Wanda's kinky curls. "Well, for travel, won't you want to stay private?"

In the heat, she doubted she'd care who saw her face.

Hargis pressed a bag of candy in her hand. "I won't say 'take care of yourself,' for you do that better'n most people. It's a good thing you and me didn't get together. By now, we would of killed each other."

"Take care of Granny," Wanda said.

"That I'll do."

Virgie held the door and Hargis carried her crate into the store. Will brought Ginger and his horse to the steps.

"I can go with you all the way," he said. "They'll look after things here."

She tied her long coat behind the saddle. "You're willing to leave Trading Day to Hargis and Virgie?"

"I don't have to manage everything."

"Sure you do." He was friendly again, but she missed the hugs and kisses. When she came back, she'd work on showing a better side of herself.

The hat was hot, and she took it off and fanned her face.

Will laughed.

"Now what's amusing?"

"With your hair cut short, your ears stick out like wings."

"Thank you so much for that encouragement."

"But it's good," he said. "The way you look now will keep away men who otherwise might be smitten by your sweet nature."

"I'm a Bosell. What we lack in sweetness is made up in other ways."

"You could be sweeter." He adjusted the girth on her saddle.

"The sweeter the woman, the more trouble she brings on herself."

"Wanda. You didn't get into trouble because of sweetness. It's time you let someone tame you a little."

She bristled. "That's not what I need."

"What, then?"

It hurt to say. "I need someone who'll make me think I'm good."

"All the time? No correction allowed?"

255

She was in no mood to be teased. "If I'm really bad. Sometimes I don't know what's right or what's true."

His face got the stark look she'd seen when he'd treated the lost child. "Pain is true. Love is right. When we love, we try to ease the other's pain."

Imagine that, Will talking of love. She took a happy breath.

They both looked back as they rode past Winkler's hand-lettered sign. The burned slopes looked greener. She patted Ginger's neck. She'd never wanted to leave the mountains.

MIDWINTER SUN

BOOK 3 IN THE MOUNTAIN WOMEN SERIES

A Second Chance for Love

Fifteen years have passed with only the exchange of letters among three families connected by love and misfortune. Now remnants of these families reunite when May Rose follows her reckless stepdaughter Wanda to a West Virginia ghost town.

The town has not been kind to either woman, but Wanda is determined to go back and capture the heart of a man who rejected her.

Barlow Townsend has come into May Rose's life again, yet like her, he is constrained by guilt and struggling to make a new life.

These are hard times for May Rose and her friends, because a town reduced to three households offers little to sustain them. To restore the town and remake their lives, all who return will have to break the chains of the past.

~

Look for *Midwinter Sun* on Amazon.

ABOUT THE AUTHOR

 I've been lucky. Years ago, I wanted to live on a farm, and my husband said "Let's do it." When personal computers were introduced, I wanted to know about them and own one, and lucky me, the school where I taught offered a course in Basic. When we bought our first computer, I discovered the writer's best friend--word processing. Before that, I could not write without crossing out most of a typewritten or handwritten page, and progress seemed impossible. When I wanted to shift from teaching to writing, the first Macintosh computers came out, and I was lucky enough to have, along with technical and business writing, the first "desktop publishing" service in my area. And when finally I had the leisure to give a lot of time to a novel, my husband didn't merely tolerate my commitment, he encouraged it.

Inspiration for the Mountain Women series came first from the mountain wilderness, both beautiful and challenging for those who live there. I appreciated accounts of early 20th century life and industry, the forerunners of today's technology and culture. When I read Roy B. Clarkson's non-fiction account of lumbering in West Virginia, (Tumult on the Mountain, 1964, McClain Printing Co., Parsons, WV), with more than 250 photos of giant trees, loggers, sawmills, trains, and towns, I found the setting for the first book in the series. Finally, I was inspired by men and women of previous generations who faced difficulties unknown today. Researching and writing these novels, I have felt closer to the lives of grandparents I never knew.

Learn more about author Carol Ervin at http://www.carolervin.com

facebook.com/carolervin.author
amazon.com/stores/Carol-Ervin/author/B0094IOERY
bookbub.com/authors/carol-ervin

ALSO BY CAROL ERVIN

The Mountain Women Series

The Girl on the Mountain

Cold Comfort

Midwinter Sun

The Women's War

The Boardinghouse

Kith and Kin

Fools for Love

The Meaning of Us

Hearts and Souls

The Promise of Mondays

Pressing On

Down in the Valley

Rona's House

A Novella, Prequel to the Mountain Women Series

For the Love of Jamie Long

A Christmas Novella

Christmas with Charlie

Other Novels

Ridgetop

Dell Zero

ACKNOWLEDGMENTS

One of the joys of writing *Cold Comfort* has been the generous and stimulating help from fellow authors on critiquecircle.com, principally Aimee Ay, Eamon Ó Cléirigh, Megan Carney, and Suja Sukumar. I love your good sense and your fine sensibilities.

I'm very grateful to family—Chuck Ervin, Diane Plotts and Jennifer Shaffer—for reading and offering suggestions and never once asking if I would please talk about something else.

This year I've been encouraged by the response of friends and strangers to continue the story of *The Girl on the Mountain*, published in 2012. Your good words kept me going. I promise to finish May Rose's story in the next book.

When I began *Cold Comfort*, I knew nothing about making moonshine, and what I read was confusing. I turned to the members of www.homedistillers.org. Several contributors to the history and folklore forum on that site tried to set me straight. Thanks, guys!

Finally, thanks to Michele Moore for being a super beta reader, and thank *you* for reading *Cold Comfort*.